TICKET TO DIE

By

Elaine Calloway

Copyright & License Notes

Acknowledgements

To my husband Dave: for the support, feedback, and mechanical expertise on wheel bolts and safety wires. You're the best!

To Carol – for your ongoing feedback, improvements, and support of my books. Thank you!

To Taryn Knight, Leafbreeze Creations, for another fantastic cover. You always surpass my best expectations.

To Dori Harrell, editor extraordinaire. You always take my disheveled mess and turn the manuscript into a workable story. Thanks for everything!

To the National Carousel Association group: Thanks for answering all my questions and putting me in touch with Bette Largent. The carousel community is a fantastic and generous one!

To Bette Largent: Your informative articles on carousel restoration, expertise and feedback were priceless in writing so many scenes of this book. Thank you for your generosity.

To Greg Mottola, writer/director/filmmaker: Thanks for allowing me to use your phrase 'giant-assed panda' from your coming-of-age film *Adventureland* (also set in an amusement park). Great movie with a fabulous 1980s soundtrack to boot!

To Family, Friends, and Readers –for all your ongoing support and belief in me. Y'all keep me going with the enthusiasm to keep writing more books. Thank you!

Additional Books by Elaine Calloway

NO GRITS NO GLORY, Southern Ghosts Series Book One

WATER'S BLOOD, Elemental Clan Series Book One
RAGING FIRE, Elemental Clan Series Book Two
EARTHBOUND, Elemental Clan Series Book Three
WINDSTORM, Elemental Clan Series Book Four

Connect with Elaine Calloway online at **www.elainecalloway.com**.

CHAPTER ONE

Amanda Moss clutched the red amulet dangling around her neck as the Welcome to Alabama sign ushered her and her boyfriend, Jake, into the Heart of Dixie state. Notwithstanding the South's humid reputation, an icy chill shot down her spine.

She shut her eyes tight. Breathed deep. This eerie, cold feeling had happened before. Fate never changed despite her wishes. *Our family has always been different, dear. Why do you insist on hiding who you are?* Her aunt's age-old words echoed in her mind, taunted her with the truth.

"You okay?" Jake asked.

Amanda opened her eyes. No need to let Jake see her odd behavior. Not again.

"I'm fine. How much further?"

They'd left Athens, Georgia, at 8:00 a.m. and had taken back roads to enter Alabama on Interstate 10 near the Gulf Coast. Now the clock said 3:00 p.m. Her calves twitched and cramped from being in the car so long. If only she could snap her fingers and they'd magically be transported to Abandon, Alabama, in the blink of an eye.

Sadly, that desirable talent had been gifted to her aunt Anzhela, even though Amanda would gladly trade in an instant. Her own gift—if anyone could call seeing and hearing the dead a gift—kept her up nights, haunted her dreams, prevented a normal life.

Jake, the ultimate engineer, scanned every gauge on his Honda Civic dash with an analytical eye. "About an hour. Do you need to stop? There may not be much at the park."

"We aren't going to the inn first?"

She coughed, trying to swallow the growing knot at the back of her throat. Of course he wanted to see Zephyr Land first. The man wasn't the type to waste daylight.

The old amusement park—now abandoned—had some kind of roller coaster enigma that he needed to research for his upcoming publication, one that would push him ahead of his colleagues for a department promotion at the University of Georgia. While he studied the coaster, she planned to log and photograph the wear and tear of the Victorian carousel for her apprenticeship entry. The ideal trip for both of them to get to know each other better while furthering their careers. She longed for a career that allowed her artistic development, an outlet for the vivid colors her mind painted. Carousels told stories…she could help restore their designs and preserve their tales.

Jack adjusted the air-conditioning vents. "The park is the turnoff before the Abandon Inn. Seems a logical choice to go there first."

"Right."

Logical. Of course.

"Do you need anything?" he asked. "We'll be near Mobile soon. I can stop."

"Something cold to drink would be great. I doubt the park will have a vending machine."

He arched his eyebrows. "Even if they did, you don't want to get something out of a machine that's been rotting for years."

"Good point."

Reaching for her hand, he lifted her palm and kissed it. Dimples formed on his tanned cheeks as his blue eyes lit up.

"Look in the backseat," he said, offering a charming wink. "I got us a couple of bottled waters at the last stop."

The man thought of everything. A nice trait after her previous relationships. His ability to plan ahead could definitely outweigh his logical engineer side. Jake was ahead of the curve on so many things. He listened—*really* listened—to her thoughts and feelings. They could talk for hours about every subject under the sun—except the supernatural. Most of her ex-boyfriends ignored her while feigning love. Same as her parents had.

She grabbed a bottle and drank. "You're the best." The cold water sent a wave of relief down her parched throat.

"You're welcome." He scratched his chin, where the stubby light-brown hair began to show. "You have everything you need for your project?"

"Yep."

"What are you logging again?"

She offered a tolerant smile. He tended to forget things that didn't revolve around equations, facts, and figures. Anything artistic wasn't in his skillset, but like the old saying went—opposites attract.

"The carousel's condition. The weatherworn paint, any metal breaks or chips in the horses or other pieces. And my suggestions for the best methods to restore them."

"If they like your report the best, you'll get the apprenticeship?"

Her stomach fluttered at the mere mention of a new career. "Yes. I have my best camera lenses and a log book to document my findings."

Keeping his gaze on the road, Jake said, "You're a great photographer. I'm sure that skill will come in handy."

She couldn't help but smile wide. Given his practical nature, his compliments were always sincere. He might not offer flowery speeches, but he meant what he said. After years spent deciphering her parents' verbal motives, what was said because it was expected versus what they had truly meant, she appreciated Jake's sincerity more every day.

"Thanks." She took another sip of water. "I'm glad we have this chance to get away. And thanks to your project, no one else will have the opportunity to access this particular carousel, since the park is locked."

He gave her a wink. "I've got connections. Besides, I've been looking forward to us taking a road trip."

"Me too."

Though admittedly, she had hints of nervousness. They'd only dated a month and hadn't spent the night together yet. This getaway would test how well they managed together twenty-four seven, and sharing a room.

In Mobile, they stopped briefly at the attorney's office to get the access key for the abandoned theme park. Then, as they headed south along Mobile Bay, the scenery changed. Tall pine trees lining the interstate faded away into a thick fog. Scraggly live oaks draped in Spanish moss and knobby-kneed cypress trees flanked the road for miles, interrupted only by the occasional patch of saw grass.

Jack turned off the highway onto an old state road when he saw the navigation sign Town of Abandon, Five Miles.

Amanda shifted her sitting position, hoping to ease her tight muscles. The serpentine path in front of them left behind any semblance of civilization. With every curve, they seemed to travel deeper into an unknown world—one long ago forgotten. On the right, a decrepit brown sign with chipped white paint said Welcome to Zephyr Land.

"You weren't kidding," she said.

"About what?" Jake kept a steady grip on the wheel, navigating slowly in the dense fog. They drove under a wrought-iron archway entrance, pulled into an empty lot, and parked.

"The town and the park. This place looks haunted, like something out of an old movie."

His eyes gleamed with mischief, and he cackled in a loud voice. "Bwaa ha-ha. Welcome to the haunted amusements."

Giving him a playful slug in the arm, she said, "Don't start with the scary stuff. This place is creepy enough already."

As jovial as she felt when he did something fun, she couldn't ignore that tingly feeling on the nape of her neck. *No. Forget about all things ghostlike. Stretch your legs and relax.*

Jake turned off the ignition and stepped out of the crimson Honda Civic. He opened her door, extending a hand to help her up. A warm feeling bubbled inside her. Despite his engi-nerd personality, he'd always been the ultimate Southern gentleman.

"Thanks." Her knees wobbled as she walked around the car. Eight hours was too long for one day, even with meal breaks. On the trip back, maybe they could stop in Pensacola to enjoy the beach, if time allowed.

Amanda arched her arms above her head. "Feels great to get out of the car."

"I hear ya." He twisted his back left and right and cracked his neck a few times. "Walking around will help."

"Okay, but remember, we need to check into the inn before dark—"

"There's the roller coaster," Jake said, the admiration evident in his voice. Right now he wasn't thinking of getting settled in, relaxing. Like an ecstatic kid in a toy store, he wanted to explore everything.

All the larger rides—the roller coaster, the Ferris wheel, the big swings—looked to be in the rear of the park, providing a skyline effect in the wispy fog. Haunting.

They approached the entry gate, where he searched for the key they'd obtained from the lawyer's office.

She watched him with a grin. "I know you don't need a key to open that lock, but let's not access your superpower on this old gate. Okay?"

He shot her a wink. "Aw c'mon. Just this once?"

The man loved figuring out how locks and bolts worked. There wasn't a lock he couldn't finesse to his wishes. And he'd been known to perform a magic trick or two.

"Use the real key. Otherwise, we're trespassing."

"Oh, all right." With a playful pout, he unlocked the gate using the key.

They strolled through the entryway and along the boardwalk. Rotted pine boards and debris lined the only walkable path through Zephyr Land. Nature had taken back what she wanted.

Halfway to the rides, a decaying ticket booth barely remained vertical. Amanda stopped short at the sight. The kudzu's ropelike vines coiled around the structure like a boa constrictor squeezing its prey. But that wasn't the creepiest part. The main insignia Ticket to Ride had been crossed out. In red graffiti, the scrawled words Ticket to Die made her skin crawl.

"Maybe we should wait until tomorrow to examine the park," she said.

Jake turned, his eyes narrowing. "Why?"

"It's...creepy."

He sighed. "What you're feeling is in your head. Your imagination. We're alone in an abandoned place, so it seems haunted."

"Seems? What if it is? Isn't the reason you're here to investigate the roller coaster derailment that killed all those people?"

Jake's lips pressed into a thin line while impatience flickered in his eyes. "Yes, but I have permission to be here as an engineer. It's going to help my work."

She ignored the rising guilt inside her. The last thing she wanted was to interfere with his career.

"I know. It's just that—"

"Don't be fooled by superstition." He stepped closer and kissed her forehead. "The supernatural isn't real. It's a means for charlatans to rob foolish people blind."

Amanda swallowed hard. She knew damn well the supernatural was much more than that, but she wasn't about to debate her knowledge in the middle of an eerie park. The paranormal was the one taboo subject between them.

"Come on," Jake said. "Let's go take a peek, just for a few minutes. Then we'll go to the inn."

Amanda glanced up at the Ferris wheel. Unkempt weeds and bushy vines had gobbled up every passenger seat. In this misty fog, clumps of overrun greenery disappeared halfway to the top, giving the impression those souls on the ride had disappeared into another world.

"Only for a few minutes," Amanda said. "We've had a long drive. I need to relax at the inn."

"Fair enough."

Jake's feet practically sprinted to the roller coaster. She stayed close by his side, not wanting to get lost in a place like this. The fog prevented the option to take photos. That task could wait until tomorrow.

The roller coaster towered overhead with a corkscrew design that pushed its way through the mist. To the left stood one of those giant swing rides where people were suspended midair at forty-five degrees. The tarnished chains swayed in the wind, sending another wave of goose bumps down her arms. The breeze wasn't strong, but the swings moved as if invisible children continued to ride them, even now.

To the right, she saw a red-and-white tent with a carousel sign. She half expected to hear calliope music emerging from the tent, but silence loomed.

"See?" Jake said. "Isn't this place fantastic? This park will help both our careers."

She ran her fingers through her hair, trying to calm the adrenaline surging through her every pore. He had a good point. Focusing on her apprenticeship entry would keep her mind off everything else. Like the cold prickly feel from the hairs on the back of her neck, which grew more intense with every step. Or how she knew without a doubt that she and Jake were not alone in Zephyr Land. Based on a lifetime of unwanted experiences, she sensed the presence of other beings—beings she could never let on that she could see or hear.

Not if she wanted a normal life.

CHAPTER TWO

Jake ran his fingers across the cold steel rails of the roller coaster track—nicknamed Death Trap ever since the accident—with a sense of awe. Despite the inevitable rusted surface, every curve, banked turn, and weld had been perfectly engineered. A work of art.

How had such a creation killed all those people?

"If I didn't know better, I'd say you were infatuated with an amusement park ride," Amanda said with the mischievous smile he'd loved the minute he met her.

"Just impressed how the men who designed this coaster were ahead of their time," he said.

"Yeah? How so?"

That's one of the things he enjoyed about Amanda. She paid attention, revealing genuine interest in him and his work. Not only did she ask relevant questions, she had the brains to understand. Most women's eyes would glaze over, but not Amanda's. Her insight and natural curiosity prompted him to dig deeper. The old saying was cliché but true. She made him a better man.

Jake gripped the running rails, tried to shake them. No movement. Even after being left to rot, the structure remained intact.

"They incorporated everything. Velocity, wind patterns, centrifugal force, and even gravity for every loop, twist, and turn."

"What about safety?" she asked.

He walked under and around one of the elevated curves, admiring every angle. "That's the strange part. A coaster designed this well shouldn't have had any problems."

Amanda reached out, placed a perfectly manicured hand on the steel tracks. "Seems strong, but didn't you tell me this coaster flew off the tracks one day? Literally?"

He smiled at the long-haired beauty who asked the million-dollar question. "Yep, but it makes no sense. Everything was top notch. To this day, I don't understand it. That's the point of publishing my article."

"Did the lawyers or insurance people ever find out what happened?" she asked.

"No. They deemed it a freak accident. The park eventually opened as planned, but no one came, especially after people nicknamed the ride Death Trap."

"Sad. That's why the place became abandoned," she whispered.

"Yep." He stared upward at the coaster silhouetted against the sky. "The company shut it down. Place has been abandoned for over a decade."

She put her hand to her forehead, attempting to block the early evening sun threatening to burn off the fog. "I'll bet you loved erector sets when you were a kid."

He turned and winked at her. "How'd you guess?"

The color rose in her pale cheeks, which matched her red lips. "You're an open book."

"Is that a good thing?"

Women in his past never thought so. They complained he didn't have enough mystery, enough imagination to surprise them with unique dates. What was so wrong with dinner and a movie? A week in an amusement park? Amanda actually seemed to enjoy his presence, and she blushed sweetly whenever he paid her a compliment.

Amanda smiled. "For me, yes. I like being able to read your moods."

"Glad it works for you," he said, slowly turning his attention back to the coaster so she wouldn't see him blush. She paid him compliments too, often without realizing it.

Things had been good with Amanda in the last month. Though admittedly, he woke up every morning wondering how he'd managed to land someone so beautiful. Her curly locks framed her angular face, and she had the biggest hazel eyes he'd ever seen. On occasion, they turned the brightest shade of green, changing with her moods.

They'd met by sheer chance. She'd attended a music documentary showing at The Cine—the indie cinema in Athens, Georgia—and he'd been there with his boss. They'd both stayed for the Q&A sessions after, and she'd made it a point to say hello. And he hoped they never said good-bye…

"Jake?" she said, knocking him from his reverie.

"Sorry. What?"

Her eyes were rounder than normal, her pupils enlarged. "I asked if you heard that."

"Heard what?"

Slowly, she turned her head to the right, toward the House of Mirrors. "That."

His gaze followed where she looked, but he didn't hear anything except the chirping cicadas and frogs calling out their mating sounds.

"What is it?" he asked.

"I thought I heard a scream."

He darted his gaze left and right, using his military training to look and listen for any semblance of an intruder. Nothing.

Taking her hand, he said, "C'mon. It's probably just the eerie atmosphere that has you spooked."

"There it is again! Please, can we go to the inn now?"

He bit his lip. "No one else is here, Amanda. We're fine, and we have permission to be here. We aren't trespassing."

She crossed her arms. "It's getting late in the day. Can't we come back tomorrow?"

"You really want to go, now?"

Clutching the amulet around her neck, she nodded over and over. "Yes. Now."

He opened his mouth, fully ready with a slew of arguments. How abandoned places like this park often played with the imagination, how her urgent need to leave made no sense, how there were no such things as ghosts. She was a grown woman and should know that.

And yet, her trembling voice silenced every ounce of logic in his arsenal. Instead, a wave of empathy flowed through his veins.

"Okay, hon." He leaned in, clasped her hand. "We'll go."

"I appreciate it," she said. The gleam reappeared in her eyes, the corners of her lips curled into a smile. "Besides, after today's long car ride, I'm ready to chill."

He nodded. "We'll get set up at the Abandon Inn, relax, then come back here tomorrow when we're both fully rested."

"Thanks."

As he drove away from the park, he wondered if she would be better tomorrow. Maybe with a good night's sleep, she'd be less prone to superstition and ridiculous ideas. After all, what rational person believed in ghosts?

She reached over, touched his hand, and sent a tingly sensation through him. He'd dated his share of women over the years. No one affected him like Amanda. So how could he criticize her, when he hadn't told her about his childhood or why he dismissed anything supernatural as hokum?

CHAPTER THREE

Amanda breathed a sigh of relief when Jake pulled into the Abandon Inn parking lot and shut off the engine. He had listened to what she needed. Good thing, because the screams and shouts from other beings at Zephyr Land had almost pushed her to the point of telling him the truth.

And that wouldn't be a good thing.

"I'll get the luggage," Jake said. He made a quick jaunt out of the car and opened the trunk.

Amanda glanced around the property. The Abandon Inn, the only structure on this massive plot of land, resembled every haunted-house painting she'd seen. White clapboard, black shutters, turrets, and gingerbread trim. Yellow lights glowed from tiny windows on the second floor, like the house had eyes that watched them.

Hmm. Maybe Zephyr Land would feel safer than this place.

Jake shut the trunk and hoisted the luggage up the three steps onto the inn's front porch. Amanda remained next to the car, studying the house. The front entrance seemed normal with a variety of white wicker chairs and porch swings. As she stepped forward, the swings moved and creaked—but there wasn't any wind.

She swallowed hard. "You're sure this is the place?"

Jake turned to her. "Don't tell me you're having doubts again. There's no such thing as ghosts, Amanda."

His tone, though he likely didn't mean to, sounded almost condescending. Like he was talking to a young child, claiming there were no monsters in the closet. She wasn't a child.

Then again, with all the eeriness of the day, had she been acting like one?

"Let's get checked in," she said, then sprinted up the steps and passed by him as if nothing were wrong. "The sooner we can relax, the better."

He sidestepped her and opened the front door. "Give me the chance to be a gentleman."

She smiled, his words calming her anxiety for the moment. "Thanks."

Once in the lobby, Amanda wriggled her nose. The room smelled like a mix of old carpet and mothballs. Probably from one too many Gulf Coast hurricanes that crawled inland and dampened the carpet. A hat rack stood in the corner, but instead of hats on each perch, there was an assortment of colorful umbrellas.

A long marble desk surrounded the check-in area, though no one was around. She glanced up. "Look at the ceiling."

He did. "Wow."

Across the ceiling, someone had painted a mural of Mobile Bay and the town layout of Abandon. A winding staircase with black iron railings led the way upstairs.

"It's not what I expected," Amanda said. *In more ways than one.*

Jake set down their bags, spotted a bell on the counter, and rang it. A sharp ding echoed in her ears.

"One moment!" a woman's thick Southern voice called out from the back room. "Clive, the underwear does not go on your head, you old fool!"

Amanda and Jake exchanged glances. What kind of place had they stumbled upon?

"We, um, had reservations?" Jake said.

"Be right there!"

After several seconds of boxes shuffling and drawers slamming, a woman in her late forties with the biggest beehive hairdo Amanda had ever seen strutted into the lobby. She looked like someone out of the 1950's beach movies.

"I'm so sorry," the lady said. "My name's Pearl. You said you had reservations?"

Jake nodded, handing her his confirmation e-mail. "For six nights."

Pearl squinted her eyes at the printed sheet of paper. "Sorry, hon. I can't see squat without my glasses."

Amanda wondered how the woman could tell the man's underwear was on his head, but she didn't say anything.

"Now where are those damn bifocals?" Pearl asked. She began shuffling things around on the desk.

Jake cleared his throat. "Ma'am..."

"Don't worry. I'll find 'em. They always go missing, those silly things—"

"Ma'am, they're on your head."

Pearl glanced up, eyes shining as if Jake had just solved her every problem. Then she ran her fingers through the mysterious brown beehive. "Goodness to mercy, they are! Thank you, young man."

"Jake Mercer," he said with a smile. "And this is Amanda."

"Pleased to have y'all at our little inn. You're in room 202, upstairs on the right. We serve free breakfast from six until ten, so just wander into the dining room if you want something. Any questions?"

Jake filled out the credit card information while Amanda scanned the lobby. In the far corner, near the hat-turned-umbrella rack, a small girl about five years old stood watching her. She had big blue eyes and midnight-black hair. Jake and Pearl didn't appear to notice.

"Hi," Amanda said.

The little girl's eyes grew wider. "You can see me?"

Crap. Amanda's heart thundered in her chest. Those spirits she could typically see were semitransparent, easy to detect. This little girl looked as human as anyone.

Amanda shook her head and turned her attention back to Jake.

"I'm Sarah. Tell my mom you see me." Sarah pointed to Pearl.

"Your mom?" Amanda said. Out loud. Crap.

"Whose mom?" Jake asked.

She bit her lip. How could she explain this? Maybe play dumb? "Hmm?"

"You said something about someone's mom," Jake said.

"Did I?"

With narrowed eyes, Jake turned to Pearl. "Did you hear her talking to herself?"

"I did, but my husband, Clive, does that so much, I honestly didn't pay attention."

"Let's go upstairs," Amanda said.

The way to get out of this situation was to get away from it. No ghosts, no beings. Just a rational week ahead with her boyfriend.

"Tell her!" Sarah screamed. Tears started to fall down the little girl's face. "You're the first guest in years who can see me. Please."

Sarah's high-pitched voice reverberated in Amanda's ears. Perhaps Amanda could mention something?

"Pearl, I'm sorry, but I wanted to ask you a question—"

"Sure thing, honey. What is it?"

"Do you have children?"

Pearl's eyes glistened, and a tear pooled at the corner of her eye. She grabbed herself a glass of water before answering, "A long time ago."

"Amanda, let's leave Pearl alone and get to our room," Jake said.

Sarah let out a long shrill shriek, the kind that could split eardrums. Amanda's hands flew to her ears, and she shut her eyes.

"What is wrong?" Jake asked, his eyes narrowing. He suspected something. Again. Not good.

"I'm sorry. My ears hurt—"

"Why don't you go upstairs and rest, hon?" Pearl said. "That'll make everything feel better."

With a firm hold, Jake held Amanda's hand. "Yes. Come on."

Nodding, Amanda followed. When she reached the staircase,

she let Jake go ahead of her so she could turn her attention back to Pearl.

"Sarah says hi," Amanda whispered.

Water spewed from Pearl's lips as she dropped the glass onto the floor. "Excuse me?"

"Sarah."

Pearl froze, her pupils enlarging so much that her eyes appeared black. "I think you need to go to your room and rest now."

Amanda nodded and then hurried up the stairs.

"What's going on? I heard a glass break," he said.

"Pearl dropped her water. Everything's fine. C'mon, let's go to our room and relax."

Jake arched an eyebrow—his usual expression when he didn't believe her—but he said nothing, just put the key into the door lock for room 202.

Once inside, Amanda began to unpack. Jake's scrutinizing gaze followed her every move, but she tried to ignore it.

"Aren't you going to put your things away?" she asked.

Jake rubbed his chin, sat on the edge of the king-sized bed. "What happened downstairs? Why'd you upset Pearl by asking a personal question about whether she had kids?"

Amanda paused while hanging a blouse in the closet. She racked her mind for what to say. They hadn't been dating long enough for her to tell him about her gift. What's more, she never wanted to. She deserved a normal life. To achieve that, she needed a normal relationship.

"I don't know. I didn't mean to upset anyone." She cleared her throat.

Jake studied her for a long minute. "I need to be honest here. I know I've never told you about my background…"

That makes two of us.

"My mom had delusions. Saw things that weren't there," he said. "She always said random things, things that hurt others."

Amanda sat beside him on the bed, surprised. "I didn't know."

"Dad and I watched her go from educated English professor to a woman who had no idea what she was saying."

Amanda's stomach clenched. His mom had a mental illness? Or had his mom perhaps had a gift she denied as well? This could get far more complicated than she thought.

"I'm just tired," she said, trying to keep her breathing steady. Fortunately, she already knew she wasn't mentally ill. Been there. Done that. Got the T-shirt from the shrinks.

Convincing Jake she was fine might be an issue, however.

"After a good night's sleep, I'm sure tomorrow will be better."

He traced his finger along her cheek, played with one of the curls in her hair. "I hope so."

Every cell in her body wanted to move, to get up out of this intense stance where Jake might be able to see the truth, to see who she truly was. Change the subject. Move around.

"Things will be okay," she said. "Now, let's see what kind of view we have from our room."

He reached for her hand, but she slipped away from his grasp.

Pulling open the red-and-blue checkered curtains, she took in the panoramic view. "Wow. Come look."

With an audible sigh, he stood behind her. "Whoa. Nice."

"Isn't it?" Amanda pointed to the left. "We can see Zephyr Land from here. Look at those old lights surrounding the park. Why would an abandoned place keep the electricity going on the perimeter?"

He shrugged. "Probably to keep trespassers away."

"Makes sense." Amanda looked to the right where a scattered grouping of Victorian homes and front porches lit up the black night. "We should check out the old homes while we're here. I could get some camera shots of them too. Maybe make a calendar featuring them for our friends."

"Good idea." Jake put his hands on her shoulder, began kissing her neck. "I knew this trip would be great for us."

His touch sent pleasurable jolts down to her toes. She put her arms around his neck, staring up into his blue eyes that twinkled by moonlight. He leaned in, kissed her lips. Put his arm around her waist and pulled her toward him.

Don't get in over your head. He doesn't even know the real you yet.

Her aunt Anzhela's words echoed in her brain, almost like her aunt used some form of psychic energy without having to be in the room.

I don't want him to ever find out about the real me, Aunt Anzhela. Leave me alone.

But you're not being fair to him or yourself, dear.

Amanda sighed and withdrew from Jake's intense kisses. "Listen, today's been a really long day. Can we just sleep for now? No intimacy until tomorrow night?"

Suspicion flickered in his glance, but he nodded. "Yeah. I'm tired too—I just love being near you."

She kissed him again. "I know, but I want our first time together to be right."

"Tomorrow night then," he whispered. "Can't wait."

Amanda smiled. Maybe by tomorrow night, she could get her aunt's voice out of her head, and everything could move forward. Maybe.

CHAPTER FOUR

At quarter till midnight, Declan meandered across the old Alabama plantation grounds. Scheduled to meet up with his boss and mentor, Connell, he thought it best to arrive early. One rule remained the same in life and death—never piss off the boss.

He kept his steps light, careful not to disturb the velvety-green grass. Even though he'd crossed over and now held only a semitransparent appearance, he continued to offer respect for historic places. One never knew the power of sacred Earth.

The historic plantation seemed eerily quiet this time of night, even for a ghost. Live oaks stretched for a quarter of a mile up to the main house. Their thick branches draped with Spanish moss formed silhouettes against the full moon, and hundreds of stars twinkled against the dark sky.

There were worse places to meet. Besides, given the locale, maybe his next assignment could get him back to Savannah—a good thing. He'd spent one too many winters in Idaho hell.

Pounding hooves broke the silence and shook the ground. Two majestic horses, one black and one white, pulled an old carriage up the lane and stopped at Declan's feet.

"Connell? That you?"

The horses snorted loudly and kicked the ground with their feet.

"Easy, boys," Connell said. He stepped out of the carriage, wearing a long black coat and a top hat. "Meet Thunder and Lightning."

"Nice." Declan petted Lightning's nose. "But you look like you stepped out of 1880's London. What's with the whole getup?"

Connell smiled. "Camouflage."

"For what?"

"Humans. This plantation has a haunted history. Supposedly, an old carriage roams the grounds. Figured I'd do my best to fit in. Damn ghost hunter types are becoming more of a problem for our kind," Connell said.

Declan wondered if he should've come in disguise too. "Tell me about the new assignment."

Connell patted both horses' heads, which bobbed up and down, nuzzling his hand. "Stay, boys. I need to discuss business." He pointed to the seashell-pink plantation house down the alleyway. "Walk with me, Declan."

They walked the long stretch toward the house. "I don't mean to get ahead of myself," Declan said as his voice cracked, "but any chance this assignment will get me back to Savannah so I can see Brianna?"

The blond hair framing Connell's face shook in a resounding no. Not a surprise. Family visits were few and far between—if allowed at all—and he'd had more closure than most. The best he could hope for was finishing the next assignment early. Maybe then Connell would see his way clear to allow a side trip to Savannah so Declan could see his little sister again.

"I need you to remain in Alabama," Connell said. "This job is near the Gulf Coast, close to Fairhope. Beautiful campgrounds. I'll even give you two days off when it's over. You can go anywhere you want, even Bourbon Street in Louisiana."

"I didn't like how Bourbon Street smelled when I was alive," Declan said. "What's this assignment?"

"It's complicated."

Declan arched an eyebrow. "Sounds dubious. Is it one individual or a group of people who need to cross over?" He, and other afterdeath consultants, had helped the dead cross over into the next realm for more than ten years.

Connell turned and resumed his walk back to the horses, stopping to trace the intricate bark of one of the trees. "This job is…well, it doesn't look good for us."

Connell, like Declan, had proud Irish roots from when they were both alive. Admitting a mistake didn't come easily.

"What do you mean, doesn't look good for us? What's the job?" Declan asked.

"A group of people at Zephyr Land. Probably thirty or so."

"The abandoned amusement park? When did they die?"

Connell bit his lip. Glanced up at Declan. "That's the issue. They died over ten years ago."

Declan's throat tightened. "Wait a second. You're saying these people have been dead for ten years and no one has been sent to help them cross over? Talk to them?"

"Sadly, yes," Connell said. "Somehow, they were overlooked."

Declan leaned his back against an oak, sank to the ground, and held his knees. "Those people are either going to welcome me with open arms or try to kill me as an intruder."

Connell flashed a knowing smile. "Then it's a good thing we're already dead, now isn't it? Come on. Let's walk back."

They returned to the carriage. Connell reached out and smoothed Thunder's black mane. "I like animals. Magnificent creatures."

"Why one black and one white?"

With a narrowed glance, Connell said, "You should know that. Good and evil in everything, the balance of power."

"Ah." Apparently boss man had become more Zen since entering the South. "So, I'll go to Zephyr Land tonight."

"Good. This one is time sensitive. Get the people crossed over. Let's hope we can keep this mistake contained in my region. If my manager finds out, we'll all be shipped to Montana in winter."

Declan nodded. Too much like Idaho, and he'd do anything to avoid both. "I'm on it."

With a shrill whistle, Connell snapped the reins. Thunder and Lightning charged forward, their magnificent feet thumping the ground, eager to reach their next destination.

Once Declan was alone, he looked up at the moon. Shut his eyes and envisioned the amusement park where he needed to be, where he would instantly be transported. He took a deep breath, prepping his mental body armor to face the thirty angry souls who'd been long forgotten.

Showtime.

* * *

Declan walked the debris-filled path inside the amusement park.

At least he didn't need keys anymore, for the park was padlocked.

A soft wind blew a few dying pine needles across the boardwalk. He stopped short. Where was everyone? He'd been helping the newly dead transfer to the next realm for years now. And one thing that all dead spirits had in common? They made noise when they thought someone was nearby to help.

Then again, these poor folks had been abandoned just like the amusement park. No one looked for them for over a decade. Perhaps caution was the best approach.

"Hello?"

The night air remained still. Only the cicadas broke the quiet with their evening symphony of rattling chirps.

"I'm Declan. I'm here to help you cross over. I know you were forgotten about…"

Silence. A sudden gust of air made one of the Tilt-A-Whirl chairs creak on its axis. Declan jumped, glaring at the squeaking wheels. He knew there was nothing to be afraid of—after all, he was a ghost—but sharp noises unsettled him.

"Hello?" he repeated.

"Hi."

The voice was small, a tiny female whimper that echoed in the air. He glanced around, trying to find the source.

"Where are you?"

"Are you here to hurt us?" the voice said.

A child? The soft tones reminded him of his kid sister when she'd been afraid of closet monsters.

"I'm here to protect you. Bring you all to your orientation so you can move on." He tiptoed across the pavement, scanning every nook and cranny where a child could hide.

"But grown-ups lie."

He pivoted around, noting the voice came from the kids' playground. "Sometimes they do, but I'm telling the truth. Will you come out and talk to me?"

Stepping closer to the little-kid swings, merry-go-round, and yellow plastic slide, he tried to imagine where a child would hide. When Brianna was little, she'd always hide in the platform at the top of the slide to avoid being seen.

Slowly, he walked closer and stood at the foot of the slide to glance up at the landing. Bingo. A little girl, no more than five, sat clutching her knees to her chest. Her hair fell across her shoulders in black ringlets, and her gray-blue eyes were wide with fear.

He knelt down, looking up at her on the slide platform. Using his big-brother, caring voice, he asked, "What's your name?"

"Becca."

"Hi, Becca. I'm Declan." He smiled, hoping to gain her trust. "Will you come down so I can talk to you? I'm looking for a group of people who died here. I'm here to make everything better, get everyone to the other side."

Her large blue eyes stared at him with such intensity, he shifted the weight in his feet to avoid squirming.

"What took you so long?" she asked.

He bit his lip. How could he explain such a thing?

"Long story, but nobody realized you were here until now. My boss sent me to get you." He opened his arms, ready to catch her. "Will you come down so I can help you and the others?"

Her eyes narrowed, like she wasn't sure whether to trust him or not. So much like Brianna. Stop. He couldn't think about his sister now. Get the job done, and maybe Connell would see his way clear to grant a favor.

"I'm not going to hurt you," Declan said.

"I know."

He gave her a big reassuring smile. "I'm ready to catch you."

She scooched herself forward, then let a playful giggle escape as she slid down and into his arms. "That was fun!"

"You did great," he said. "Can you tell me where the others are? My boss said there were thirty people or so?"

Her chin quivered. "Over there."

Declan looked where her tiny hand pointed. A graying woman in her fifties, hair tight in a bun with the stern face to match, saw them and approached. "Who might you be?"

"His name's Declan," Becca said. "That's Aunt Opal."

He extended his hand. "Pleased to meet you, ma'am. I'm so sorry it's taken this long to collect you, but I'm here to bring you to the next realm."

Opal looked him up and down, suspicion radiating from those discerning eyes. "We can't leave this place. Believe me, we've tried."

"Not without someone like myself," he said. "But now that I'm here, we should be able to cross. Can you gather everyone?"

Opal rolled her eyes. Odd gesture from an elderly woman, but he overlooked it, considering she'd been stuck here for so long.

"If you can magically get us out of here, then fine. I say we can't leave."

"You'll see, ma'am. I just need everyone together."

Nodding, Opal let out a hoarse yell. "Everyone, get over here now!"

Declan rubbed his aching ear. Her attention-getting method wasn't quite what he'd expected. Slowly, the young and old, women and men, moseyed out of nothingness and formed a large group where they stood.

"I've got everyone," Opal said. "Now what?"

"Leave it to me."

Declan smiled. He hadn't anticipated things moving this quickly. At this rate, he'd be able to get the job done today and visit Brianna in Savannah. Perfect.

"Hello, everyone," he said. "I'm Declan. Sorry for the delay, but now it's time I take you to the other side. First thing's first. Remove any piercings or jewelry you may have on. The portal tends to yank metal out of your skin."

A few raised eyebrows and startled whispers later, everyone followed him to the entrance gate. "I'm going to lead you to your orientation, where you'll receive instructions on your next locale, assignments, and how things will go from here on out."

"About damn time," one man said, his crooked mouth turning

into a malicious smile.

Declan cleared his throat. He wasn't surprised at the negative attitude, not after what these souls had been through. At least they weren't becoming violent.

"Ready? Let's go." He started walking. Ten paces later, the hairs on his arms prickled. Was someone watching him?

He turned around. None of the souls had followed. They remained inside the park's gate.

Opal put her hands on her hips, leaning forward like a lecturing school teacher. "I told you, Mr. Genius. We can't leave."

Staring at their inability to cross, he cussed under his breath. Why hadn't Connell told him about the possibility there was more to their deaths than coincidence?

"Tell me what you remember about the day you died," Declan said.

"How many ways can you say splat?" Opal balked. "We rode the coaster…it threw us off the tracks. End of story."

Declan looked at Becca's tiny face, frozen with fear. "Perhaps you might consider rewording your answers, for your niece's sake?"

Opal crossed her arms in a huff. "No sense shielding the kid, when she was with us that day."

Declan thought otherwise, but he had no parental rights over the child. One thing was for certain—dealing with this woman would be a challenge. He needed to keep everyone calm until he knew the best plan of action.

"Did the insurance investigators find any reason for foul play?"

"No, smart guy. You can Google the obituaries if you want," said the sneering man from earlier.

"Sir, there's no need for sarcasm. I have the paperwork. I need to know what y'all remember," Declan said, keeping his tone as flat and nonthreatening as possible, despite the irritation rising in his soul.

"Why does it matter?" the man asked. "Does it have anything to do with us being forgotten about for a decade?"

Other souls looked to this man and nodded in approval. Declan needed to keep things smooth, or he'd have an attack mob on his hands. Connell definitely wouldn't approve of that.

"I'm sorry. I didn't catch your name?" Declan asked.

"Chester."

"Chester," he began, making every effort to keep his voice even toned. "Yes, it does. I'd been told your deaths were accidental, so I was sent here to help everyone cross over. If your deaths were intentional…"

Opal uncrossed her arms and stepped forward, apparently assigning herself the speaker of the group. "What are you saying?"

"I'm saying the only reason souls can't leave a particular area or dwelling is because they've been murdered."

Opal's eyes narrowed. "You mean, the derailing wasn't an accident?"

"Yes. Maybe someone sabotaged the coaster as a prank, not knowing what would happen? Unless…"

Chester stepped forward, puffing out his chest like he was in charge. "Unless what?"

"Someone knew exactly what they were doing. That person wanted to kill every one of you on the ride."

"What?" Chester said. "The women and children weren't even supposed to be on the ride to begin with."

Declan glanced at the faces of men, women, and children who had become forgotten souls that day ten years ago. Could someone have wanted to kill someone specific, and killing everyone made the whole thing seem like an accident?

"Tell me why," Declan said. "Who was supposed to be on the ride?"

Chester's already-brown eyes turned almost black. "Me."

Another exec-looking sort appeared from the crowd, looking as preppy as Chester. "And me. I'm Andrew."

"Why just the two of you?" Declan asked.

"The park wasn't open to the public yet. Our firm designed all the rides in here. Andrew and I were going to do the pilot run of the coaster with us both seated in the front car. There were photographers, press, others here to make it a big celebration before the public could use it."

Declan glanced at Becca's tiny face. "Then how did she die? How come it wasn't just you and Andrew?"

Opal cleared her throat. "We insisted. I've always played second fiddle to my sister, and I didn't want to wait until the second ride of the coaster. I wanted on. So did the other wives and kids."

"And we let them," Andrew murmured. "It's a decision we've

regretted for ten years."

"I see," Declan said. "Did anyone know about the women and children going on the ride ahead of time? Or was it spur of the moment to let the others ride?"

"Spur of the moment," Chester said. "But the premier ride with Andrew and myself had been publicized for weeks in the local papers."

Things were beginning to make sense. Declan motioned to Opal to keep Becca busy, keep small ears away.

Walking straight up to Andrew and Chester, he asked, "So, gentleman. I need to ask who would want you both dead."

"No one. People love us. We build amusement parks," Chester said.

"Do some thinking. Come up with a list of names," Declan said.

"What can the rest of us do?" Opal asked. "How do we get out of here?"

Declan rubbed his temples to ward off the impending headache. He hated telling the dead they were trapped. It was bad enough being dead.

"I'm going to help you." Declan took a deep breath. "Your killer is still alive and well, otherwise my presence would've been able to negate your ties to the park. We'll find a gifted human who can learn the killer's identity and bring the murderer to justice."

"So we're going to be stuck here forever," one of the souls scoffed.

Declan took a deep breath to calm his frustration. Connell would have his head on a platter if he messed up this assignment.

"Everything will work out." He wouldn't end up in Timbuktu again—he'd make sure it worked out.

Andrew, Opal, and the other adults circled around and began to complain. Only Becca stepped toward him.

"You said we could go. When can we leave? I never got to say good-bye to my sister," she asked, her voice quivering.

Declan knelt down, touched her forearm. "I'm sorry, sweetheart. I don't know, but I'm going to do my best to help everyone here."

"You promise?"

Lordy, those blue eyes reminded him so much of Brianna when she was little. Just as scared and knowing.

"Yes," Declan said, chuckling to himself. "You don't realize this, but I know firsthand what happens when someone breaks a promise to the dead. I will keep my word, Becca. That's a promise."

She threw her arms around his neck. He held her in a safe embrace, determined to be the protector she needed. There was no way he could fail now.

CHAPTER FIVE

Morning sunlight streamed across Amanda's face, teasing her just enough so she couldn't return to the restful sleep she'd enjoyed only moments earlier. She tossed off the covers, glanced at her cell—8:00 a.m. Jake remained asleep, so she crept out of bed and headed to the shower.

Not that a shower or clothes would ever prepare her for what today would bring. Yesterday, she'd had the weary-and-tired excuse to leave Zephyr Land. Today? She'd need another reason if she heard more screams. Or saw Sarah in the lobby again.

When she stepped out of the bathroom, all dressed and ready, Jake let out a long yawn and stretched his arms above his head.

"Hey," he said. "You couldn't sleep?"

She smiled at him. "The sun's too bright."

He blinked his eyes, rubbed the sleep off. "I'll get up."

"No," she said, uncertain if her tone could be construed as sharp. "I mean, why don't you relax until you're ready? I'm craving coffee, so I'll just meet you downstairs when you're up and around." There. That sounded better.

"You sure?"

"Absolutely." She walked over and kissed him on the forehead. "See you downstairs when you're ready."

With that, she crept out and took care not to let the door slam. All hotel doors, but particularly older properties like the Abandon Inn, tended to slam by default.

She walked down the inn's staircase just in time to hear Pearl yelling at her husband again.

"Clive, stop watering the plastic plants! You've got puddles all over the office!"

Amanda caught Pearl's exasperated eyes and smiled. "Tough morning?"

"That man is gonna drive me into an early grave, I swear." Pearl shook her head. "Never mind him, though. Breakfast is in our dining room. There's coffee on."

"Thanks." Amanda walked closer so no one else around might hear. "I'd hoped to talk with you for a few minutes. Join me for a cup?"

A wild laugh echoed from the back office. "Zip-a-dee-doo-dah! Zip-a-dee-ay!"

"Clive! Be quiet!" Pearl returned her attention to Amanda. "Sure, give me a few minutes."

"See you in there," Amanda said as she made a beeline to the coffee machine. She didn't know Pearl or Clive, and she sure as hell didn't want to get in between them.

Moments later, she took her first sip of hot coffee. And immediately reached for more sweetener.

Pearl entered the room and chuckled. "I got that coffee when we took a trip to Louisiana. It can be shock to the system if you're not accustomed to the chicory."

"It is stronger than I'm used to, but it's a great flavor."

"Well, everything in the South has its own flavor, its own set of ingredients."

The extra sweetener made the coffee more palatable. Pearl grabbed herself a cup and sat down in a club chair across from Amanda, an old-fashioned early-American coffee table between them. "So, you wanted to talk with me?"

"Yes. Um, and I'd like you to keep this confidential."

Pearl's lips curled upward in a half grin, and her eyes gleamed. "Intrigue. You got it, sugar."

Amanda took a deep breath. "Last night, when I asked if you had kids, I mentioned the name Sarah."

Pearl nodded. "You startled me, no doubt about that."

"I don't mean to pry, but who...I mean, how..."

Could she trust Pearl with her secret? The woman probably already knew, but one thing life had taught her—people may pretend to be open minded, but sometimes they weren't.

"She was my daughter. I had two girls, Sarah and Becca. Twins."

Amanda took a sip of hot coffee, allowing for a pause before asking the next question.

"Had? Past tense?"

Pearl looked down, intently focused on her coffee cup. "They died ten years ago."

A pang shot through Amanda's heart. "I'm so sorry. I didn't mean to upset you or stick my nose in where it doesn't belong—"

"You're gifted, aren't you?"

"Gifted? Um..."

Pearl's eyes gleamed. "You can! You can communicate with

those who have passed!"

She opened her mouth to speak. That's when Jake arrived.

"Morning," he said. "I see you've got coffee."

"All the fixings are over there," Amanda said, pointing. "You'll want extra sweetener to compensate for the chicory."

Jake nodded. "I heard that rumor somewhere." He turned to fix himself a cup.

She let out a deep breath. "You can't let anyone know," she whispered. "Especially him. We can talk later if you want."

Pearl stared at her for a long moment, shaking her head. "I've waited a long time for someone like you. We had a man at the inn about five years ago, like you, but he got spooked. Left in the middle of the night. I always wanted to finish that conversation."

Jake joined them, sitting on the edge of Amanda's chair. "Coffee smells good."

Amanda nodded, and she exchanged knowing glances with Pearl. Maybe Pearl could be someone she could help, someone to confide in...

Until the time came to tell Jake the truth.

* * *

An hour later, Amanda stepped out of Jake's car and onto the boardwalk of Zephyr Land.

"This is going to be great," he said. "You did bring your camera, right? If you get a break from your carousel log, can you take a few photos for my position paper? Some close-ups of the guide wheels and the circuit will help."

"I have everything in my backpack," she said. "Don't worry. I'll get a few photos for you first. Then I'll work on my photos while you examine the coaster."

"Sounds great."

The spring in his step reminded her of a kid in a candy shop, needing to move fast and examine every candy bar and rope of licorice. She breathed deep, then followed him. *Just get me through today.*

A sudden gust of wind knocked over a clown statue. Amanda jumped, her adrenaline in full surge.

"You're not going to start that haunted talk again, are you?" Jake asked.

She bit her lip. "I hate clowns. It's a normal reaction."

He grinned. "Fair enough. C'mon."

They passed the carousel. It sat inside a large red-and-white tent with side panels that had been ripped and torn away. Tattered horses with large mouths and unruly manes moved in small increments on the slightest breeze. The once-shiny gold poles now looked textured with rust. Creepy, to say the least, but at least she had enough material to write about for her apprenticeship opportunity. Oh, what she could imagine for this carousel…

"Hello?" a male voice said.

She turned to Jake, presuming he had spoken. Yet Jake continued full speed ahead toward the coaster. He hadn't even stopped to glance at the carousel.

"Can you hear me?" the voice said again, incredulous.

Ignoring the words, she sprinted to get away.

"Hey! You *can* hear me!"

No, I can't. I won't.

She ran toward the coaster, but Jake wasn't there. Oh no. Hearing ghosts, and now Jake had disappeared. What now?

"Jake! Where are you?" she screamed as loud as she could.

"In here."

The voice came from an aluminum structure resembling a shed near the roller coaster. She bolted inside, out of breath when she reached him.

"You okay?" he asked.

Nodding, she clasped his hand. "Fine now."

"Can you take some close-up photos of these?" He pointed to the crushed metal fragments of what used to be roller coaster cars. "I need macro shots, as close to the bolts and steel as you can get."

"Sure."

She took tiny, quick breaths to resume her normal breathing. Quietly enough to not alarm Jake so he wouldn't ask what startled her. She couldn't say a word about the voice she'd recently heard in Zephyr Land. Not after last night.

Jake ran his hand along the warped and crumpled steel. "Some of these are too damaged to get decent shots of the wheels, but try to get all three wheel types in your photos. If you can."

"Three wheel types?"

She stared at the mangled metal. Most of the roller coaster cars looked like an eighteen-wheeler had run over them. She didn't even know roller coasters had three sets of wheels. How was she supposed to get photos of them in this heap?

"See this?" Jake asked, pulling out a sheet of paper from his back pocket with a diagram of a normal-looking roller coaster car. "Each car has three sets of wheels. The road wheels, which run along the track. The guide wheels on the side of each car keep the car from shaking side to side."

"And the third?"

"The upstop wheels."

The silence after he spoke made her smile. This was a dance they did since they started dating. He loved her to ask questions about things so he could give answers and impress her.

"What do the upstop wheels do?"

The sparkle in his eyes proved she'd made the right choice by asking.

"These are essential," he began. "They're the wheels that make contact with the brake system. They also prevent the train from falling off the tracks."

"But didn't you say this coaster fell off the tracks in midair? Stands to reason the upstop wheels didn't work."

"Exactly." He pointed to the worn paint of the few remaining bolts. "That's what I'm going to find out."

"Gotcha." She adjusted the aperture of her camera and looked through the viewfinder. As she did, her finger touched her red amulet necklace.

"I know you can hear me," the male voice said again.

Pulse racing, she backed up. Almost fell over her own feet.

"Whoa," Jake said. "You okay? What's wrong?"

The same thing that's been wrong all my life.

"Just dizzy, I guess," she said, scrambling to her feet. *Don't let Jake see you talking to spirits again. Keep him occupied.*

With a firm arm on her camera, she ignored the soul speaking to her. She concentrated on the upstop wheels, the flaking paint of the cars, and the remainder of the scrap heap. Anything to stay busy.

"Fantastic," Jake said. "Each of these can go in my paper as appendices."

"You're welcome." She backed up, figuring she would get a few more wide-angle shots of the stretch of metal.

That's when he appeared in her viewfinder. A man in his twenties, shaggy-like brown hair but not unattractive. His green eyes held the most determined look she'd ever seen.

"I know you are gifted," he said. He stood with his arms crossed, legs apart.

She screamed, more from his sudden appearance than from fear.

Jake spun around, eyes puzzled, at her shriek. "What the hell?"

Stumbling back a few steps, she yelled "I need some air!" and ran out into the open space.

Jake followed. "What's wrong?" he asked, gripping her shoulders. Tension radiated from his fingers.

"Air. Need air."

He gestured in all directions. "Out here, you have all the air you want. What's up with you, Amanda? You're acting strange."

Great. His curiosity had shifted into impatience. She had to put a stop to this, make him believe things were okay.

"I'm fine. Forget about it." She shook her head, trying to appease him and shrug off the experience.

"No." He looked around. "There is no one here besides us. We have permission to be here. I don't know why you're so freaked out. All the supernatural creepy stuff? It's poppycock for the masses. It's not real."

Maybe he would believe her if she told him she had seen an intruder? No way would he believe anything supernatural.

"I thought I saw someone—"

"Stop." He reached out and grasped her forearms like she'd been a petulant child. "Just stop."

She stared at her feet, unable to meet what would inevitably be a stern glare. Things had been so much easier in the city. She'd been able to hide her gift, blend into the loud noises of everyday life. But here? In Abandon, Alabama, at a decrepit amusement park? The voices and visions were overpowering.

"I'm sorry," she said, looking down.

Off to her right, the shaggy-headed man said, "You know, it's none of my business, but you shouldn't have to apologize for who you are."

She glared at him. A lot this ghost knew about the real world.

"Amanda," Jake said, lifting her chin up to gain her attention.

Steeling herself, she met his gaze. His blue eyes were dark with concern, but he no longer seemed angry. But how could that be?

"I don't know why you're behaving this way," Jake said. "We are safe. You believe me, don't you?"

She swallowed hard. "Y...yes."

With a charming wink, he said, "Then there's no reason to be scared."

"Okay."

"So," he began, his voice turning authoritative. "No more being spooked. You're a grown woman. Smart, logical. Don't be like the masses, being fooled by charlatans and haunted stories."

"Okay."

One day she needed to find out exactly why he had such a hatred for charlatans. It wasn't the first time he'd used that word, and the term was an old-fashioned one compared to con artist or scam.

She caught a quick glance at the shaggy-haired soul standing nearby. He didn't act like a threat. If she was forced to speak with him, she could do it—without Jake knowing.

"I'm fine now," she said. "Thanks."

Jake smiled and leaned in for a quick kiss. "Why don't you go do your carousel research? I'll be right here if you need me."

"All right."

The male spirit said, "Meet you near the carousel. We need to talk."

"Okay," she whispered.

"Who are you talking to?" Jake asked.

Crap. Jake. Keep calm.

"Nothing. I'm going to examine the carousel now."

With a dubious expression, Jake nodded. "Good."

She turned, forcing her feet to walk as quickly as they could toward the carousel. One day, Jake would find out about her gift. It was inevitable.

Until then, she would keep her secrets.

CHAPTER SIX

Declan stepped inside the red-and-white tent. He eyed the variety of carousel horses and selected a large palomino with a wavy white mane. Lighter colors in fairy tales and myths tended to be associated with good rather than evil. His choice might put the woman more at ease. Right now, he needed every bit of help he could get.

A minute later, the gifted woman approached.

"Hello," he said. "Thanks for meeting me."

She stopped, rubbing her fingers over the American flag colors of one of the WWII flag horses before hopping onto it.

"They buried me in a coffin cloaked in the American flag," he said. "I've always liked the war horses."

"So you were military." She gripped her horse's gold pole, and paint chipped in her hands. "Who are you? What do you want with me?"

"My name's Declan. Yes, I was in the air force, before a training exercise cut my time short."

"I'm Amanda. How long have you been dead?"

He shrugged. "I lose track. Twenty years at least. I'm one of those souls who help others cross over."

Her hazel eyes flickered with bits of green. "Cross over?"

Offering her a knowing smile, he said, "You're quite good at pretending, you know."

Color rushed to her cheeks, and she looked away. "I don't think you—"

"No, forgive me. I'm not one to judge." He offered her the most charming smile in his arsenal. "But I know who you are. You know what crossing over means. You're even familiar with what my kind does, helping newly dead souls on to their next realm."

She bit her lip. "Why do you say that?"

He slid off the horse and walked over to her. Looked directly into those lovely eyes. "I know your aunt."

"Shit!"

He laughed. "Guess that's not good news?"

She brushed a clearly annoying flock of curls away from her face. "My aunt keeps insisting what I have is a gift—"

"It is."

"No. It's anything but. I can't walk down the street without seeing dead souls everywhere. They never leave me alone. When I'm in the city, I can hide it from most people. But here—"

"It's harder to keep secrets. I know."

"What do you want? If you know my aunt, there's no way I can outrun you." She gave a slight chuckle. At least the girl had a sense of humor. Her hand released the pole, and she leaned her head against it lightly.

"I'm in a—situation."

"Meaning?"

"My boss, Connell, sent me to this park to help the departed move on. There was a misunderstanding, and these poor dead folks have been waiting for me to show up for ten years."

Her right eyebrow shot up. "So things remain disorganized, even in the afterlife?"

"You have no idea. Connell will kick my ass to some godforsaken place on my next assignment if I don't get this one done."

"What exactly do you need?" She sat straighter and seemed genuinely interested. Maybe she'd help...

He leaned back on the horse adjacent to hers. "I didn't know these people were murdered. I thought the roller coaster accident was just that—an accident."

Her jaw tightened, and the pupils seemed to push all the green in her irises away until her eyes were almost black. "You're saying someone killed them. On purpose?"

"Yes." Now came the tough part. "I need you to find out who."

"WHAT?"

Or maybe not... "I'm a ghost," he said. "There's not much I can do in terms of research and questioning humans. Most humans can't see me."

She glared at him. "Because I can, you're telling me I need to find out who killed these people?"

"Yes." He sighed. "I know it's a lot to ask—"

"Damn straight!" She crossed her arms in front of her almost as if she was protecting herself.

"Isn't your boyfriend researching the roller coaster already? All you need to do is continue that research. Question locals. Call the insurance company or the lawyers. I can give you some information from the other souls—"

"Wait a second." She hopped off her horse, stepped off the carousel, and walked to the exit of the tent. Peeking through the slit, with Declan peering over her shoulder, she saw Jake remained occupied near the coaster.

"Amanda, you can help these people. Until their killer is brought to justice, these souls can't cross. It's eternal limbo in a creepy abandoned park."

"Stop." She shut her eyes and rubbed her temples before opening them again. She turned to face him. "You're not just talking research. You're saying I need to catch the killer?"

"Well, the cops can catch the guy, but I do need you to help—"

"Risk my life? Jake's life? To help the dead move on to their next home? Isn't that your job, not mine?"

Declan stared at the floor for a minute before resuming eye contact. He knew he was asking the world of her. She didn't deserve this, but she was the only one who could help.

"Yes," he whispered.

Amanda cleared her throat. "Then let me be completely clear in my answer. Hell no!"

"But—"

"No! No buts. No nothing. Stay away from me and Jake."

She stormed toward the exit. Before she left the tent, she turned around once more. Perhaps she'd changed her mind?

No. Her last look was one of utter defiance. She would need a great deal more convincing.

Or he would be screwed. Forever.

* * *

Declan paced the canopied walkway in front of the plantation. Twenty or so humans meandered the grounds, waiting for the daily tour to begin. He sighed, hoping they'd be inside the mansion when Connell arrived.

If only he could have a cigarette. A shot of Jameson. Something to calm his nerves. One of the many problems of being dead—no more vices.

How could he tell his boss that he'd had no luck whatsoever with Amanda? Connell wasn't the hard-ass that some authority figures were, but he wasn't exactly a pushover. Not even close.

Moments later, a pretty brunette came out and gathered the public together. "Ladies and gentlemen, we're about to start our tour. If you'll follow me, we'll begin with the parlor."

The humans slowly followed her into the house. Good. The last thing he needed was a superstitious human eavesdropping on his conversation. One problem alleviated, in the nick of time.

Pounding hooves shook the ground. Declan could feel the vibrations in his toes, even though the two horses were in ghost form. They charged forward, manes blowing with fury. Then they drew closer. No hesitation in their steps, no slowing down.

He glanced around for an exit strategy. Why hadn't Connell slowed them down? The carriage swayed back and forth, ready to topple any second.

"Connell?"

Clop, thunder, clop. Noisy snorts from the horses exhaling.

"Connell!"

Was the boss trying to run him over? Declan sidestepped to the right. "Stop the horses!"

A shrill "Halt!" echoed from the carriage with no driver. With the quickest obedience he'd ever seen, Thunder and Lightning plowed their front hooves into the ground and stopped short. Maybe the occasional horse footprint was what kept the legend of a haunted carriage alive.

Declan caught his breath. "You in there?"

What seemed an eternal moment of silence followed.

"Hello?"

The carriage door flew open. Connell leapt out and stormed up to Declan's face. For a split second, Declan expected his boss to throw a punch.

"This had better be good," Connell said, impatience seething from his cold glare. "Because if you interrupted me to ask if you can see your sister again, I swear—"

"No." Okay, maybe Connell could be a hard-ass. Declan swallowed hard. Whatever had the boss upset, now was the time to play the respectful card. "Sir."

Connell's tight jaw appeared to loosen at the gesture. "Then why did you call me here? I'm trying to stop a war. What's so urgent?"

"Sorry," Declan whispered. He searched his mind to formulate the right words. Complaining about the complications of the amusement park job wouldn't go over well. Not with Connell's current mood.

"Talk."

"The people at Zephyr Land can't leave. They were murdered."

"What?"

"They're bound to the property. I can't escort them over or finish the job until—"

"Till you find a gifted human." Connell shook his head, his blondish hair falling back behind his ears. "Damn it, I'm forbidden to bring in other gifted humans. That includes your sister."

Forbidden? By whom?

"There's a gifted young woman staying near Zephyr Land already."

Connell's eyes widened. "Then why did you call me here? Convince her to help get the villain, and bring the souls to the next realm. You don't need me to tell you that."

Declan stared at the ground. "It's not...quite that easy."

Thunder, the black steed, pawed the grass with his foot. Connell petted his long nose. "I agree, boy. These things aren't ever easy."

"Sir?" Declan asked with all the reverence he had. "What do you suggest I do? You know we can't force the gifted ones to help us. Brianna was different. She didn't want to embrace her gift either, but she had the reward of seeing me in the end."

Connell didn't make eye contact. Instead, he moved on to pet Lightning, the alabaster horse who nuzzled under his commanding hand.

"Do you know the best part about horses, Declan?"

Better to let the boss answer than try to guess and appear stupid.

"No, sir."

Connell's piercing blue eyes seemed to stare right into him. "They go where they're supposed to. They do the task at hand, directed by where they're led with the reins. They don't complain, make excuses, or otherwise cause trouble."

"I'm not trying to cause an issue, sir." Declan shuffled his feet. "I know this assignment is important for our entire network."

"Then figure it out!"

Excuse me? Declan stepped back at the harsh voice. Even Lightning bobbed his head up and down at Connell's loud tone.

"I will," Declan said. "I only wanted to keep you abreast of the situation."

Connell's audible sigh could likely be heard as far away as Birmingham.

"I appreciate the update," he said. "But I need you to handle this. Find out something you can give the girl if she cooperates. Something that won't upset the balance of dead and living."

"That's a good idea."

Connell patted both horses and stepped into the carriage. After sitting down, he turned his attention back to Declan.

"If I need an update, I'll summon you. Do not contact me. This war is getting worse."

"What war?"

"None of your concern. Liam will have my soul on a platter if I leave again. Understand?"

Liam? Declan hadn't heard that name mentioned in over five years. Most of the time, Connell managed his own troops and didn't talk about the higher-ups. After their very first boss, Aiden, had transferred back to Ireland, Declan had assumed Connell had been promoted. Guess Liam was the one giving orders now.

"What happens if I need to talk to you again?" Declan asked.

"Do not interrupt me again. Not until you resolve this case."

"But—"

"Go. You have a lot of work to do."

"That's an understatement," Declan muttered.

"Handle it!" Connell shouted a quick command to the pair of horses. "Remember to get it done. Or else."

The horses kicked up pieces of rock and dirt onto Declan's legs when they sped away. He shook off the debris and took a deep breath. That meeting had not gone as planned—not at all.

There was only one thing he could do now. Return to Zephyr Land. Convince Amanda to speak with him again. Then somehow get her to agree to help. Otherwise, there would be hell to pay.

CHAPTER SEVEN

Amanda snuck behind the tent and toward the other rides to avoid being seen by Jake. If he knew she'd left the carousel and wasn't concentrating on her work, he'd become more suspicious. *I don't want to talk to the ghost near the carousel* wasn't a good answer. Not for Jake, not for anyone.

If she had to be cursed with this ability, she would deal with it on her own terms. Explore the park. Learn more about these other ghosts for herself.

Her small steps on the paved boardwalk cut the silence with a series of eerie clacks. On the left, the abandoned log flume looked like a topiary experiment gone bad. Kudzu had coiled its way around the ride, and mosquitoes flittered over random pools of water left from a recent rain.

Thick humidity draped Zephyr Land, almost like a large blanket over this haunted park. When a slight breeze blew, the warm air on her cheek felt like she'd been kissed by something. Someone.

She swallowed hard. Reached into her purse and found the pepper spray. Just in case.

Something moved in her line of sight. Spinning around, keeping an eye in all directions, she noticed the fortune-teller machine off to the left. Wait a second. Was it—moving?

Gripping the pepper spray tighter, she approached the dilapidated box. Inside, the brunette mannequin's head moved. Moved? Amanda swallowed hard. Darted a glare around the machine with no electrical cord to be found. Was her mind playing tricks, or was someone messing with her? Old-timey carny amusements didn't just start working on their own. Not in an abandoned park.

Yet the mannequin bobbed her head up and down. Her long fingernails clutched a white crystal ball. Suddenly, a tiny white card flew out of the machine's mouth.

Amanda walked around the fortune-teller box. Kudzu and overgrown weeds covered the ground. So how could the machine function like it did when Zephyr Land was open and functional?

Tinkling chimes resounded in the air. Amanda stared at the tiny white card now blowing across the pavement. As much as she didn't want to know—she had to find out. She picked it up and read the inscribed text: *We know you are here.*

Amanda shuddered. Turned and started to run back to the carousel.

"Help us," a chorus of voices whispered.

"Leave me alone, whoever you are!"

Frigid air seeped across every pore on her skin. Every cell went clammy. Then almost immediately, the feeling vanished. Silence.

With trepidation, Amanda continued her trek toward the carousel tent.

A woman's curt voice rang in the air. "Most folk with the sight say 'excuse me' when they walk through one of us."

Amanda spun around. How could she have missed seeing this latest soul? A woman in her fifties, neatly dressed with a navy jacket. She could've been an FBI agent in her human life. She had the official-looking appearance coupled with perfectly coiffed hair pulled into a tight golden-blonde bun.

"I...I'm sorry?"

The woman frowned. "I said you should excuse yourself if you're going to walk through one of us."

Now this ghost was lecturing her on manners? Amanda did a quick glance back toward the coaster. No sign of Jake nearby. The fortune teller had ceased operating too.

Good. She would be free to talk.

"I didn't see you." Amanda cleared her throat. "What's your name?"

"Opal." She eyed Amanda up and down, like inspecting a piece of fruit at the market. "And you are Amanda?"

"Yes. How'd you know my name?"

Opal rolled her eyes. "We all know there's a human with the sight here, trust me. We've waited long enough. Been trying to get your attention."

Amanda glanced back at the fortune booth. Maybe ghosts had been operating the box?

"Besides," Opal added, "Declan told us about you."

"Right." Amanda bit her lip, unsure how to continue the conversation. What exactly had Declan told them?

The scowl on Opal's brow grew more intense. "So why don't you want to help us?"

Oh. Guess Declan pretty much told them everything.

"I didn't say I didn't *want* to," she said.

"No?"

"I said I *couldn't.*"

Opal put her hands on her hips. "Same thing. Now stop all this dillydallying and help us."

Dillydallying? I'm practicing self-preservation. If she helped these poor souls, who'd help her when Jake walked away?

"Even if I could help, how am I supposed to find the person who murdered you ten years ago? We're only here for a week."

"You're human. Be resourceful." Even in her semitransparent state, the ghost could glare.

Opal's argument seemed much too simplistic, yet Amanda couldn't argue.

"I can't tell the man I'm dating that I see ghosts. Surely you can get someone else to help? This is the South. Aren't there a higher number of gifted people here?"

With a stern glance, Opal said, "We don't have anyone else. You're it. Some people would be honored to be selected."

"Not me."

Amanda turned to storm off but tripped over a bucket of tools and fell. Sharp scrapes and cuts sliced her right leg as blood oozed.

"What the hell? That wasn't there a minute ago."

Opal towered over her. "Correct."

"You put it in harm's way so I'd fall? What kind of ghost are you?"

"What kind of human are you?"

Amanda bit her lip. Hard. Telling this ghost exactly where to go and where to stick certain things wouldn't accomplish much.

"Help me up at least?"

A sweet, sickly smile crossed Opal's face. "I'm sorry. It's not that I *won't*. It's that I *can't*."

"Seriously?" Amanda sighed. Forced herself to stand up. A thin line of blood trickled down to her ankle.

"We can help each other," Opal said. "You find our killer—I'll leave you alone."

"Ultimatums don't work on me," Amanda said, digging in her jeans pocket for that fortune-teller card, which she used to wipe off some of the blood.

Opal circled Amanda, showing in every angle of her peripheral vision. The formal-looking woman looked like something in a House of Mirrors, appearing one second, disappearing the next, and then materializing behind her.

"Let me put this plainly," Opal said. "I know you turned Declan down, but he's only been here for a few days. I've been here for ten years. Trust me. There's nothing I won't try to get out of here."

"Like trip someone," Amanda muttered, then wondered what else Opal might do.

"Exactly."

"Manipulative bit—"

"No cussing, please. There are children present."

Amanda glanced around, seeing no one. "You're lying."

"She's not," a tiny girl whispered.

The little girl with curly black hair in ponytails appeared out of nowhere. This was different. Amanda wasn't accustomed to ghosts fading in and out so quickly. In the cities she knew, they often hid behind things and showed themselves slowly. Here in Zephyr Land, they appeared in an instant.

"Sorry," Amanda said. "What's your name?"

"Her name's Becca. She's my niece."

"Hi, I'm Amanda." She knelt down and studied Becca's young face. "You look familiar."

Becca shrugged. "I haven't left here since we died. And there's nobody to play with. Sarah couldn't come to the park."

Sarah? Amanda choked. Fought to breathe. Cold air flooded her veins.

She suddenly knew why this little girl looked familiar. She looked identical to the ghost child she'd seen at the Abandon Inn. But how could one be dead at the inn and one at the park?

Stop. Breathe. The situation is too unlikely. Just learn what you can and get out of here.

"Are you okay?" Becca asked.

Amanda sat on the pavement, her head between her knees. "I will be, as soon as I can get back to the Abandon Inn."

Opal's eyes widened. "You're staying there?"

The knot in Amanda's throat plummeted to her stomach. "Yes."

"My sister Pearl runs the place. My other niece Sarah should be there too."

"I've met them."

"You could bring them here, to the park—"

"Wait just a minute," Amanda said. She stood up, regaining her footing.

"What, you have better things to do than help us?" Opal said. "You're in an abandoned amusement park, for crying out loud. A lot of tasks on your plate besides hanging with some guy?" Becca scooted, nearly floating, to slightly behind Opal.

Amanda bit the inside of her lip. She'd been raised to respect those older than herself, but Opal was making the situation challenging.

"I'm supposed to be studying the carousel. I have to write a thirty-page paper on its restoration—"

"I'm sure that's all good for you." Opal smoothed one rebellious hair back into her bun. "But let's be serious. You need to take care of this first."

Opal's presumption only sent irritation coursing through Amanda's veins.

"Why? Why do my plans always come last? Since when did I get elected as your local translator between the living and dead?"

Opal's lips flattened into one sharp line. Her jaw twitched as the anger radiated from her eyes. She said nothing, just let the icy glare do all the talking.

Amanda wanted to retract the words the minute she'd said them, especially since Opal's expression was an exact replica of Amanda's aunt Anzhela when she became angry. Amanda stared at the ground, knowing full well what her aunt would say if she were here now.

The same things she'd told Amanda all her life.

A gift is also a responsibility. You must nurture it, not deny it. To refuse to use your gift is to spit in Universe's face. Our family is different. You must embrace it. Always use your talent to help others.

Amanda took a deep breath. "I didn't mean to imply that your situation wasn't important—"

"Clearly, you did." Opal studied her with stern eyes. "You try living in limbo, stuck in this humid hellhole for ten years. See how patient you are when you find someone who can help you leave."

Opal had a good point. Amanda had only been in town since yesterday.

Becca walk-glided forward and tugged on Amanda's shirt. "Yes?"

"Why won't you bring my sister here?"

Amanda glanced into those innocent young eyes. How could she explain that she couldn't move ghosts from one place to another, even if she wanted to?

"Things don't work that way," she said, her words sounding as lame as she feared.

Becca stuck out her bottom lip, the way only a five-year-old could. "Why can't you try?"

A sharp pang hit Amanda's heart. She couldn't say no to such a young child. But how could she get a ghost at the inn to come with her to the park?

"Tell you what. I'll talk to Pearl and Sarah. Maybe I can figure out something?"

Becca's frown did a quick one-eighty. That wide grin on such a young face tugged at every heartstring Amanda had.

Opal nodded in approval. "My sister might know more about the accident—or rather, murder—than we do."

With a resolved breath, Amanda nodded. "I'll talk to Pearl and Sarah. I can't promise anything else."

"It's a start," Opal said. "I appreciate you being willing to try. Guess it can't be easy having the sight."

Opal's phrasing was old school. Most people called the ability to see the dead a gift, a responsibility, a calling, or talent. She called it the sight.

Amanda shrugged. "The worst part is not being able to tell anyone, especially Jake."

Opal shook a crooked finger at her. "You've got the sight. One day, that boy is gonna find out. May as well come clean now."

"No, it's better to wait."

Opal shot her a knowing glance. "Your choice, but I predict this will backfire in your face."

"Don't worry about me."

Amanda wasn't about to let Jake find out about her ability. All she had to do was get Pearl and Sarah's help, do some chatting with ghosts without Jake noticing, and then these departed folks could cross over. Then she could spend the rest of their trip researching the carousel.

Things would work, despite her awkward ability. They had to—one way or another.

CHAPTER EIGHT

Jake blinked twice and then returned a critical gaze to the track's left side rails. Before any coaster opened, technicians and inspectors walked the track. First to check the left side of the rails, ensuring no loose hardware. Then another trek to check the right side. Since this was a steel coaster, he could only walk along the level areas, not the loops. Good plan, since he didn't like heights to begin with.

He reached into his backpack to get his binoculars. Crap. They must be back at the hotel. The best way for him to inspect the tip-top of each loop, and he'd forgotten the key tool he needed.

Leaning back, he jotted some notes in his notebook. He found himself doodling Amanda's name. What? He couldn't help but smile at how often she crossed his mind, even when he should be focused on work.

That's when Amanda approached. From the other direction? Why? Not that he wasn't glad she'd joined him. He always felt more alive in her presence, and he missed her...even when she was in the carousel tent.

"Hey. Where have you been?"

She shrugged. "The tent for the carousel grew too humid, so I took a walk."

"By yourself? You should have asked me to come with you."

He walked closer to her, glancing around to make sure no one else was nearby. "Even though we have a key to the park, vandals can hop the gate at any time—"

"Relax," she said, her voice giving off hints of irritation. "I kept the pepper spray with me."

"Good." He leaned in and kissed her. "You sure you're okay?"

"I'm fine." She swallowed, the look in her eyes like a guilty kid who'd been caught with her hand in the cookie jar. What was she up to?

"If you say so." He reached for her hand. "C'mon. I want to show you something."

She wrapped her hand in his and followed. He took her along the flattened part of the track and shone a flashlight where the first incline swept upward into a series of turns.

"I've walked most of this track, inspected the left side."

"Find anything?" she asked.

"No, but I need my binoculars to further examine the loops."

She grinned. "Good thing. For a minute, I thought you were going to tell me we were going to scale tall roller coasters."

"In a single bound," he added with a wink.

"Ha-ha." She stepped carefully along the track, balancing with the grace of a gymnast. "I saw your binoculars next to your books at the hotel."

Jake sighed. "Figures. I'll get them later. Come back here."

"We should do more research on the derailment," she said. "What events led up to the coaster flying off the tracks? Maybe there were witnesses that live nearby?"

He gazed at her. No other woman had seemed interested in his work before. Quite the turn-on. He touched her cheek, brought her face close to his. Kissed her lips and tasted strawberry lip gloss. She trembled under his touch. Damn, he wanted to take her right there in the middle of the park.

"You're doing things to me," he whispered.

Her cheeks flushed red. "Tonight, lover boy. Not here."

Kissing her on the nose, he said, "You sure? I hear the Tilt-A-Whirl can be fun."

She glanced toward the rusted pods on wheels. "Um, I don't think so."

"I knew a few college buddies who used to brag—"

"Let's just keep things simple." She kissed him on the cheek. "First, we go to the library. Get some background info on the coaster accident."

"And second?" he asked, winking at her.

Those ivory cheeks filled up with crimson again. He loved watching her blush.

"C'mon, lover boy," she said. "Let's go."

* * *

Amanda sensed her flushed cheeks returning to normal when they entered the Abandon Library. Thank heavens. She hated blushing, being put on the spot. Being noticed, period. Those things made her supernatural abilities even more difficult to embrace.

The historic library, like most buildings in the area, had once been a Victorian home. As such, the interior had perfect nooks and crannies for reading.

"Where should we start?" she asked. "Internet searches?"

Jake shook his head. "I've already done what I could on the Internet. Figured maybe the librarian might know more about the history of the town. Maybe they have copies of old papers that covered the derailment?"

"Good point," she said, glad for his enthusiasm and proactive nature. At this rate, he could solve the case, and those ghosts in Zephyr Land would leave her alone.

The old hardwood floors creaked as they walked to the librarian's desk. Scattered papers, office supplies, and a lukewarm cup of coffee sat on the desktop, but no librarian.

"Is there a bell?" Amanda asked. "Something to get their attention?"

Jake glanced around. "Looks like no one has stepped inside this place in years. I can't imagine we'd be bothering anyone if we just call out for assistance."

"Hello?" Amanda said in a medium tone. No response.

"Anyone here?" Jake asked, his voice louder. "We need some help."

The rustling of boxes and files came from the back room. "Is someone there?" a voice asked.

"Yes," Jake said. "We need to talk to the librarian."

More rustling. Teacups clanking against each other. A woman's whispers that clanged in Amanda's ears. Familiar whispers.

No. It couldn't be—

"Hello." The woman wore a flowing skirt, peasant blouse, and a teal scarf with amethyst stones intertwined with her long hair. "The librarian isn't in today, but I'm filling in. I'm Anzhela."

Amanda's throat tightened. *Aunt Anzhela, do not let on that you know me. Do not.*

Anzhela met Amanda's stern glance with one of her own, then quickly turned to make pleasantries with Jake.

"How can I help you?"

"Yes, thanks," Jake said with a wide smile. "We need to ask you about Zephyr Land. Are there any old newspapers that covered the accident, any correspondence we might find?"

"Let's see, shall we?" Anzhela clicked a few keys on the computer keyboard to run a search. "Ah, here we are. Not much, but a few local reporters wrote articles speculating what happened. We have articles in the *Abandon Journal* you can view for yourself. And there are some national articles and videos too. An incident like this always gets nationwide attention."

"I've already found what I can on the Internet. I'm interested in the local angle." Jake beamed at Amanda. She made a feeble effort to return the gesture. She did not need this. Not right now.

Anzhela pointed to a series of drawers against the back wall. "Local folks say the derailment was deemed an accident. The fire burned most of the evidence, I'm afraid."

"The fire?" Amanda asked.

Her aunt made brief eye contact. "Yes. There was an electrical fire after the accident. Burned down the original garage where the coaster cars were kept. I'm sure you and your"—she made a glance at Jake—"*friend* will want to research that too."

"Great. This is exactly what we need," Jake said. His face shone like a boy with a new bike as he sprinted to the back wall.

"Let me know if you need anything," Anzhela called out before turning her attention to Amanda.

"What are you doing, dear?" Anzhela whispered.

"Me?" Amanda said. "Why are you here? You're supposed to be in Savannah."

"I have the gift of going place to place. To do what's needed." Her aunt's jade-green eyes held such intensity in that long stare. "I don't ignore my gift—like some."

Amanda bit her lip and leaned against the desk. She wanted to scream, but that would only make Jake suspicious.

"I can't talk about this now. Jake's over there."

Anzhela looked to where Jake opened files and scanned through folders. "What have I told you all your life? You must entrust the people in your inner circle with who you truly are. This is not something you can hide. Not from those you want close to you."

"I'm going to do my damn best to try." Amanda pretended to fiddle with some pencils on the desk in case Jake looked their way. "I never wanted this gift. I just want to get rid of the ghosts at the park so I can work on the carousel analysis."

"One leads to the other." Anzhela reached out and touched Amanda's hand. "Deep down, you know I'm right. You must tell him the truth. Then both of you can resolve the situation."

"No." Amanda glared at the aunt she knew and loved but who could not possibly understand. "Jake doesn't like anything supernatural. I tried dating guys who seemed to embrace the paranormal. At least, they said they did, but when I told them…they freaked. This time, Jake cares about me. What if he…"

Anzhela's sad eyes lowered. "You can't have a real relationship without truth."

"I'm truthful about everything else." Amanda remembered back, scanning the high points in her dating time with Jake. "This one…thing…can wait."

"Your choice. Be prepared for the consequences."

Amanda opened her mouth to ask what could possibly be worse than ghosts talking to her, when Jake strolled back over.

"Hey. Look what I found." He pointed to a page in an article that listed witnesses from that day. "Maybe we could find these people. Talk to some of them."

Amanda nodded. "Sure."

Jake glanced between Anzhela and Amanda like a tennis match. "Everything okay here?"

"Fine," Amanda said. She glared at her aunt. *Smile and act casual.*

"Yes, fine, dear," Anzhela said. "You two be careful if you go talking to witnesses. Folks round here are secretive."

At the word *secretive*, Amanda winced. That was a tiny jab directed at her, but no matter. She knew what she was doing.

"We should go," Amanda said. She reached for Jake's arm. "Maybe grab lunch back at the inn, then talk to the locals."

"Sounds good." He turned to Anzhela. "Thanks for all the info, ma'am."

"You're quite welcome. Feel free to visit me anytime."

Amanda did a double-take glance at her aunt. "Maybe."

If Jake decided to return to this library, Amanda would need to be right by his side. Who knew what kind of mayhem her aunt would cause if she got Jake alone to tell him about her family?

CHAPTER NINE

In the old shed behind his house, Randall Kern yanked the blue tarp off the gasoline cans. Dust leapt off the reddish-yellow metal containers and swirled in the afternoon sunlight before landing back on any surface it could find.

He preferred the old-style gas cans rather than modern red plastic. Yet these old-timey things were getting more difficult to find. Stepping carefully between the table saw and shelves cluttered with knickknacks, he added two more gas cans to his collection, which made forty.

Sharp dog barks came from the front of the house. Damn it. In the ten years since the disaster at Zephyr Land, no one had knocked on his door. No one even gave him the time of day anymore. After those bastards at Bello and Toale ruined his reputation, every ounce of Southern neighborly goodwill wilted up and died. No one came knocking unless they didn't know better.

Meaning whoever stood at the door must be from one of those Bible-toting religions. Seemed new crops of 'em appeared every week.

"I'm coming, Catfish."

When Randall returned inside the house from the backyard, his German shepherd hadn't left the front door. Catfish stood tall, fur erect down the slope of his back. He barked loud, baring large white teeth.

"Who we going to scare away today?" Randall chuckled. He approached the front door, reaching for the dog collar to hold Catfish back. Then he opened the door.

Three little old ladies instantly widened their eyes at the dog. Their mouths formed three simultaneous *O*s as they turned their gaze on Randall.

"Sign says no soliciting," Randall said. "What are you doing here?"

The middle woman with the round face spoke. "I'm sorry, sir. We didn't see any sign."

Just like most people. Damn, he hated strangers knocking on his door. What right did they have? Push their agenda on him? Only person who better had come knocking was Ed McMahon. And he was dead.

Randall turned his head to the left and pointed. "The sign is right there…" But it wasn't. "What the hell?"

"Like we said, there wasn't a sign. We're sorry to bother you. Perhaps we should go."

Catfish inched forward. Randall kept a tight grip on the collar. "What did you do with my sign?"

The color washed away from their faces. "Nothing," they said in unison.

"Crap." He shut the door and ordered Catfish to go to his crate. Now to investigate what the hell happened to his sign. Stepping outside, he saw his No Soliciting sign broken into three large wood pieces on the lawn. "Damn neighborhood kids always messing with me."

"We'll mark your house as no soliciting," the round woman said as they walked backward to get away.

"Tell all them other religions the same!"

Their waddling forms eventually faded from sight. Randall picked up his debris, glaring up and down the street. "Damn this place. Never was any good to me. Not then, not now."

* * *

Randall marched through the aisles of Home Improvement Warehouse. An array of signs including Beware of Dog and No Soliciting were for sale in different colors.

Why couldn't they have the one he really wanted? "Stay the hell away from my home."

"Can I help you, sir?" a young kid asked with a plastic smile. Damn overachieving idiot.

"No. Got what I need." Randall reached for the brightest red sign he could find, then went to the tools department.

Tracing his fingers along a hammer's edge, his imagination returned to Chester and Andrew. Every time someone knocked on his door in this small Alabama town, it was a reminder of how many people no longer came to his door. A curt reminder of how those bastards had ruined everything.

Voices in the next aisle knocked him from his thoughts.

"The library finally had some visitors this morning."

"That's amazing. They ask for directions, or did they actually come to get a book?"

"Nah, they wanted to see old newspapers about Zephyr Land."

Randall froze. His muscles clenched, he held his breath. It had been ten years since the accident. Who the hell would be asking questions now?

"The whole county knows the police and insurance inspectors deemed the derailment an accident. Those kids aren't going to find anything new."

"One of them got permission to be in the park. He's working on some paper. Apparently the guy is an engineer."

The lump in Randall's throat boomed into his stomach. Not only were there tourists sneaking around and looking for info, but one was an engineer?

Not good. He tried finding out who had been talking on the next aisle, but when he casually walked past, whoever it was had left.

He looked up at the aisle pointers for different supplies. Maybe forty cans of gasoline weren't quite enough. He'd get a few more. Just to be safe.

CHAPTER TEN

At a local lunch place after the library, Amanda bit into her corn bread and moaned. "This is amazing."

Jake dipped a fry into a wad of ketchup. "You've never been to LA?"

"Los Angeles?"

Jake grinned. "Lower Alabama."

"Ha-ha." Even living in Georgia, she hadn't had down-home vegetables like these before. Green beans with actual flavor. Catfish with a light dusting of corn meal. Fresh biscuits hot from the oven. Fried okra. Corn bread that melted in your mouth.

After a few minutes enjoying her meal, she reached for the papers he'd copied at the library. "This says there are four witnesses to the accident. All of them still live here, according to the phone book. We should speak with them this afternoon."

"What about your carousel research?"

"I can start fresh tomorrow." *Once the ghosts are gone.*

"Let's not dismiss what you need," he said. "This trip is about both of us."

A warm feeling bubbled inside her. She'd picked a considerate guy, but right now, she didn't want him to be.

"Let me help you today. Besides," she said, "the sky is cloudy. The last thing I want to do is spend a day at Zephyr Land in the rain."

He looked up at the graying feather-like clouds in the sky. "Good point."

"Great, then it's settled."

Relief washed over her. No more dealing with Zephyr Land ghosts. At least not for the rest of today.

"Anything in those papers about the fire the librarian mentioned?" Jake asked.

Amanda coughed. The food burned the back of her throat, and she reached for the glass of ice water.

"You okay?"

She nodded. "Was the part about the fire true? I mean, the lady said herself she wasn't the official librarian—"

"Didn't you like her?" Jake asked, his brows narrowing.

Like her? A complicated question indeed. She was family. Everyone had wacky relatives in the South, but hers raised the bar.

"She's fine," Amanda said. "But no one's mentioned a fire until now. Maybe the woman was mistaken."

"Why would the substitute librarian lie about a fire? It doesn't make sense."

She chewed her sandwich, worry going down her throat with every bite. "Let's not bother the librarian again."

Jake washed down a taste of icy Coke. "Why?"

Stall him. Pivot the conversation. Turn it back to focus on the tasks at hand.

"I'm only saying we should focus on interviewing the witnesses. I'll do analysis on the carousel tomorrow."

He shrugged. "You seemed distant at the library. You and the woman looked like two Chatty Cathy's whispering. What did you say to her?"

Don't tell anyone about who I really am?

Amanda's mouth went dry. She grabbed her drink. "Nothing."

Jake cocked an eyebrow. "You don't chat that much with a stranger over nothing."

She searched her mind for an excuse. A way to get off this topic and dismiss the strange secrecy that had become her existence. There had been too many moments like this one, her needing a quick escape from his scrutiny.

"I...I mean..."

In her peripheral vision, she noted a name jotted down on the papers they'd copied.

"Look," she said. "Randall Kern. Why does that name sound familiar?"

Jake's eyes widened. "Seriously? He was only one of the top roller coaster designers in the country."

"This says he was one of the witnesses."

Jake gave a decisive nod. "Let's interview him. It would be an honor just to meet the man."

Amanda smiled to herself. Men were game to go along with anything as long as they thought the idea was theirs to begin with.

"Sure, let's go."

When they arrived at Randall's house, Amanda's mouth fell open. The Colonial style house looked like it had once been a quaint Southern home. Not anymore. Termites had chewed through every corner and beam, and a few side boards were missing. The front lawn appeared worse. Like a garage sale had vomited everywhere.

"Is this guy some kind of recluse?" she asked.

Jake appeared surprised too, learning his hero was a slob. "I don't know. The world hasn't seen much from him lately. His great stuff was twenty, thirty years ago."

She reached for the car door handle and let herself out. "Maybe this is what happens when a genius doesn't have anything else to work on?"

He joined her beside the car, gazing at the junk-strewn lawn. "I guess so."

They dodged the many rusted metal scraps covering the front lawn and reached the door. With a firm hand, Jake rammed the door knocker three times.

No answer.

Jake walked the length of the porch and tried to peer in the old windows. "I don't see anything."

She glanced around. "Looks like he isn't home. Let's go to the other witnesses' houses and then come back."

"May as well."

They trod carefully back to the car. Jake started the engine, then squealed the tires as he raced to get away.

"Whoa, what's the rush?" Amanda asked. "The next witness, a Mary Galden, is only around the block."

Jake put on his main poker face. Flat lips, unclenched jaw, gaze straight ahead on the road. Making it impossible to figure out what he might be thinking.

After a silent quick ride, he finally spoke. "Randall Kern was one of the greats. Books were written about him. Television how-to shows interviewed him all the time. So what the hell happened that he's now living like some wild woodsman gone insane?"

Amanda shrugged. "I don't know. Some people can bend with the times, like a tree in a storm. I guess others can't."

"I don't want to end up like him."

"What? Why would you end up like that?"

He didn't answer, just glanced at the paper with the witness addresses.

They pulled up to a sage-green shotgun house. He shut off the engine.

"Jake?"

Turning to face her, he said, "I often wondered why Randall Kern didn't continue to design roller coasters. He's not retirement age yet, and the man was a genius."

"And?"

"Whatever happened had to be enough to halt his career and turn him into someone with a junkyard lawn."

"You can ask when we find him."

Jake fiddled with the keys before removing them from the ignition. "If I don't get this department promotion, my career will stall out. It will be five to six years before another one opens up, and I'm too young for tenure. Maybe that's what happened to Randall. Maybe the newest technologies came along and drove him out. I don't want to wind up some recluse—"

"You won't." She put her hand on his right leg. "Trust me."

He smiled but didn't seem convinced. In that moment, she knew how important this promotion was to him. She knew he'd wanted that as the next step, but until now, she didn't realize just how powerful the consequences would be if he failed.

"C'mon, let's go talk to Mary," Amanda said.

Nodding, he slipped the keys in his pocket and stepped out of the car.

Mary's door was a lovely shade of taupe that offset the sage-green paint. In the center was a collection of dried flowers with colorful ribbons. Below it, a gold knocker.

He knocked twice. Seconds later, an athletic-looking tan woman answered the door.

"Yes?"

"Mrs. Galden?" Jake asked.

The woman took a few gulps of water from the monogrammed bottle she held. "Who's asking?"

"Jake Mercer, ma'am. I'm an engineering professor at University of Georgia, and I'm trying to determine what happened to the coaster at Zephyr Land ten years ago."

Her eyes widened, and she licked her lips. "Call me Mary. Come in."

They entered, and Amanda immediately noticed the décor. Most adult women had pictures of family, maybe a colorful design of some sort on their walls. Mary's walls were covered with posters of Olympic runners. The den resembled a sports shop more than a woman's home.

"Have a seat," Mary said. She went into the kitchen and brought back three bottled waters. "Hydrate while we chat."

"Thanks," Amanda said as Jake studied one of the posters on the wall.

"We hope we aren't disturbing you," Amanda said. "Your name was on a list of witnesses at the Abandon Library. This is important to Jake."

Mary's chapped lips turned into a frown, making her face appear tight. Like she'd had too many cosmetic surgeries.

"Are you okay?" Amanda asked.

"Fine." Mary's gaze met Amanda's, yet the woman seemed to stare far off into space. "Your boyfriend is lucky to have someone so supportive of his career."

"I tell her that all the time," Jake said with a wink. "So, what can you tell us about that day?"

Amanda cleared her throat, hoping Jake would get the hint to take things slow. Mary appeared saddened all of a sudden. Rushing the topic of the deadly accident wasn't the best way to get information out of her.

"This must be difficult," Amanda said, hoping to put some empathy into the conversation. "But we need to know more about what happened."

Mary nodded. "I was the office manager at Bello and Toale. They were in charge of the coaster's design, along with all the other rides in Zephyr Land."

"So you kept the place running," Amanda said.

Laughing, Mary said, "How'd you know? Are you an office manager for a place too?"

"Right now I'm a receptionist for a finance company, but I hope to get an apprenticeship at a carousel restoration company soon."

Mary nodded. "The carousel. I remember telling Bob we should go on the carousel."

"Bob?" Jake asked, his scrutinizing gaze seeming to hang on the name.

Tears spilled down Mary's face. "My husband."

Amanda and Jake exchanged glances. There was nothing in the file about her having lost a husband at Zephyr Land.

"Forgive me, but I want to clarify by asking. He was one of the passengers on the coaster?"

"Yes. He wanted to be the first to ride it, just like everyone else at the firm."

Amanda rested a hand on Mary's. "Tell us what happened."

With a heavy sigh, Mary said, "Everything had been put in place. All the rides, all safety checks. It all passed with flying colors, so we had a company promo the day before officially opening the park."

Amanda thought of Opal and the other ghosts, who must have worked at the company too. Well, not Becca, of course.

"Were relatives of the employees encouraged to come?" Amanda asked.

Jake shot her a questioning look, which she shrugged off.

"Yes," Mary said. "There were children, teens, and all the execs." She motioned to her sofa, and Jake and Amanda sat side by side. An agitated Mary sat in the recliner opposite them, her legs crossed, her toe jiggling.

Jake leaned forward and clasped his hands together while resting his elbows on his knees. "What do you think happened? You said it yourself—the rides had passed all safety checks."

Mary sat silently for a moment. "I wish I knew," she whispered.

Amanda jotted down some notes. "Do you think someone could have sabotaged the ride, wanted revenge against your firm for any reason?"

"You think someone rigged the coaster?" Mary's voice cracked, and she wiped away the surging tears.

"Amanda," Jake said with a stern tone. "No, ma'am, we are just doing our research at this point. I don't know what caused the derailment. Not yet."

Amanda bit her lip. She hadn't meant to upset Mary, but she knew damn well someone had murdered those people deliberately. The ghosts had told her so.

A lot of good that answer is.

"We were in the amusement park business," Mary said. "Why would anyone want to hurt those innocent people?"

"That's just a theory," Jake said. "From an engineering perspective, your firm did everything right. We're just looking for any alternative reason as to how this happened."

Amanda rustled her notebook pages, glanced at the other

witness names. "Do you know any of these people? Malcolm Smith, Terry Bako, Randall Kern—"

"Randall, yes. I know him."

"Where are you going with this?" Jake mouthed.

Obviously, he didn't want to hear that his hero and engineering mogul would have murdered those people. But Amanda needed to get to the truth, and fast. Get the ghosts released so she could have some peace.

She furrowed her brows, hoping he would keep quiet and let her ask the needed questions.

"Tell us about Randall. We tried going by his house, but he wasn't home."

Mary shrugged. "He used to work for the firm. Decent guy. Volunteer firefighter, that sort of thing."

"He worked for your firm?" Jake asked. "That's not in any of the newspapers or articles."

"You must not have found the lawsuit papers," Mary said.

Jake arched an eyebrow. "Lawsuit?"

Mary waved a dismissive hand. "It was all bollocks. Randall wanted more credit for the design than he was given. He's some engineering hot shot, you know—"

"Yes ma'am, he is," Jake said. "He was one of the pioneers in the industry."

"Well, the way I heard it, he wanted more recognition and more money. The partners—Andrew and Chester—wanted to get rid of Randall because he was being the squeaky wheel. Always complaining. Always saying they were doing things wrong."

"Like what?" Amanda asked. Maybe this Randall guy had motive.

Mary brushed through her hair with her fingers. "The partners ended his contract, claiming no more work was needed. Randall sued, claiming they used cheap equipment on the coaster. Something about shoddy bolts. The whole thing was one big mess."

"Aren't roller coasters required to have Grade Eight or Grade Nine bolts?" Jake asked. "I started to inspect the circuit this morning, but I haven't been able to access all the parts to the cars yet."

"Yes, we used Grade Eight premium," Mary said. "Accusations went back and forth for weeks. Once we won the lawsuit, we replaced everything to ensure all bolts were premium and accounted for. The firm took every precaution. That's why the derailment is such a mystery."

"How long ago was the lawsuit?" Jake asked.

Mary stared out into the backyard, thinking. "I guess about twelve years ago?"

Only two years before the accident? Might be coincidence, might not.

"Do you think Randall or anyone else could have wanted to hurt the people at your firm?" Amanda asked.

"Bite your tongue," Jake said. "Look, I'll admit the guy has turned into a recluse, but he is an engineer at heart. He would never design anything dangerous."

Mary adjusted her sitting position and nodded toward Amanda. "He's right. Randall was ultra-safety conscious. Even though things didn't work out with his employment, I can't see him killing anyone deliberately."

"You don't think he's dangerous?" Amanda asked, continuing to ignore Jake's questioning glare.

"Randall helps at the VA hospital, volunteers in the community. Why would a killer do that?"

"Agreed," Jake said. "Why would a killer do that?"

"I don't know," Amanda said. *But I know someone killed those people. They're still in Zephyr Land.*

"Is there anything else you can remember about the day?" Jake said.

Mary talked about how perfect the day had seemed—bright sunshine, giggling children by the picnic tables, how happy everyone had been.

Amanda listened, made mental notes, but let Jake do the remainder of the interview. Her suspicions were now directed at this Randall Kern. The sooner she could gather enough information, the better off things were going to be.

CHAPTER ELEVEN

Jake clenched his fists all the way to the car. He pressed unlock on the key signal and pushed a random tree branch out of the way. Then he parked himself in the driver seat and started the engine. Waited for Amanda to get in the car herself. He wasn't in any mood to open the door for her. Not right now. And yet, his Southern upbringing rang in his ears even as he sat there, angry. He should've opened the door for her, no matter what.

With a slow but steady hand, Amanda unhooked the passenger door and got in. "Are you okay?"

He turned and glared at her. "What the hell was that about? The woman lost her husband, and you go around making accusations, when you don't know anything about what happened that day?" This was a completely different side of Amanda.

"Neither do you," Amanda whispered. "I think there's foul play involved. Seeing her natural reaction, getting her side of things, is how we figure this out."

"This isn't a cop show. We aren't Starsky and Hutch!"

Once the words escaped his tongue, the guilt seeped in. He hadn't meant to yell, but she behaved like this was a game. It wasn't. Didn't she understand he needed to keep her safe? Why didn't she understand how much she meant to him and he couldn't afford to lose her?

She looked away from him, staring out the window. "I didn't say we were. But you have to admit, if there wasn't any reason for the coaster to fail during safety inspections, the foul play must have happened postconstruction."

"Maybe, but we stick to the facts. There's no evidence of foul play. And I, for one, don't believe the father of modern roller coaster design would suddenly go insane and decide to kill dozens of people. That's crazy talk." Most of the time, Amanda kept him on his toes. This was different. How could she not see that? Then again, she'd always been on point before…

She turned to meet his gaze. "You're the one who was so shocked at your hero becoming a recluse. We don't know this man's life or motivations. Under the right circumstances, anyone can hurt anyone—"

"Would you ever do something like that?"

Redness crept from her neck upward and across her cheeks. "I'm only saying, people have reasons for what they do."

"Maybe, but I would never do anything like that. People should be honest with each other, not accuse others of wrongdoing without facts."

"Why don't we try talking to Randall again?"

Jake cleared his throat. "Good idea, but let me do the talking. Please don't insult the man."

"Fine."

He continued to drive. Anytime a woman said the word *fine*, things were anything but. He wondered how to make things up to Amanda later, apologize for his outburst. Meanwhile, he'd take his chances with Randall. Maybe the man could shed some light on the whole situation. Give some insight into what happened that fateful day at Zephyr Land.

* * *

A minute later, Jake stepped out of the car and walked around to get Amanda's door. Even though she'd ticked him off with her approach at Mary's house, he still had guilt weighing on him for not being a gentleman. His mother had bred Southern manners into him, often with no mercy.

"C'mon," he said, taking her hand. "Looks like he's home now. That 1978 Dodge pickup truck wasn't here earlier."

"Sure."

He put his hand on the small of her back to lead her across the minefield yard of junk. At the door, he released her and knocked.

Loud dog barks from inside echoed through the door.

"Guess he had his dog with him earlier," Amanda said. "There wasn't any barking before."

Jake nodded. "Remember, let me interview him."

"Okay."

The sound of multiple deadbolts was followed by the door opening. "Can I help you?"

"Mr. Kern?" Jake asked. "Are you Randall Kern?"

"Who wants to know?"

Jake glanced down, noticed the dog's panting mouth—with lots of white sharp teeth—trying to escape.

"Catfish, back!" the guy yelled.

"Great name for a dog," Jake said, smiling.

"Who are you?"

"Jake Mercer. I teach engineering at University of Georgia. I've wanted to meet you for a long time, sir."

"You're a fan trying to find me?"

"Yes," Jake answered. He gave Amanda a knowing glance. They needed to pretend like this was a hero-worship visit, then bring up Zephyr Land. Otherwise, any talk might scare him off.

The door unlatched and opened wide. "I'm Randall Kern, yes."

Jake extended a hand to shake. "A thrill to meet you, sir. This is my girlfriend, Amanda Moss."

"Hi," she said as she shook his freckled hand. Sign of a redhead, and Randall's red wiry hair fell unkempt to his shoulders. The kind of haircut that looked better under a baseball cap.

"Forgive me. Folks round this way don't often come by. Why don't you kids come on in?" Randall said. He motioned to the rear door. "Catfish, go on. Outside, boy."

The black-and-tan German shepherd made a snuffling sound before turning and trotting away.

"Have a seat."

"Thanks." Jake chose the couch, and Amanda sat on the opposite cushion. Across from them, Randall leaned back in a rocker.

"You two on your way to New Orleans? Lots of fun in that city."

"No, Abandon is as far west as we're going this trip." Jake cleared his throat. "Your roller coaster designs are amazing, sir. You were so ahead of your time—"

"A lot of good it did me," Randall quipped. "I got arthritis so bad, I can't even draw a straight line to plot or design anything anymore."

"Sorry to hear that. We studied your methods in college. I use them as examples of perfection in my lectures."

Randall gave a half smile, which matched his lopsided reddish mustache. "Nice to hear my work helped someone."

Jake leaned forward. "I don't mean to pry, but I'm trying to do a position paper on the derailment at Zephyr Land."

Randall frowned. "A shame, all those people."

Out of the corner of his eye, Jake noticed Amanda studying Randall's every move. She'd already assumed he was guilty. Now she sought evidence to make her case. Let her assume all she wanted. As long as she kept quiet and let him do the interview—

"Mr. Kern," Amanda began.

Crap. Why couldn't she have listened? Jake cleared his throat, took the lead.

"What do you think happened ten years ago?" Jake said, shooting Amanda a scowl.

Randall scratched his head and reached for a nearby baseball cap to cover his wiry hair. "Bello and Toale was notorious for going cheap on the essentials. That's why they ended my contract."

"What do you mean, going cheap?" Jake asked.

"Telling the public they use Grade Eight premium bolts when they're using cheap metal scrap from foreigners."

"You're saying they cut corners in safety to make a buck?"

Randall gawked at Jake like he had three heads. "Wake up, sonny. Bello and Toale is in the profit business, not the artistic passion business. If Chester Adding the Third could save ten cents on a screw, he did. And the cost of his egotistical greedy crap? Those people's lives."

Jake ran his fingers through his hair. "Bello and Toale had a great reputation. Why would they ruin it with faulty equipment? Wouldn't the insurance adjusters have determined the cause and held them responsible?"

"Of course."

Jake pieced together all the data. "I don't understand. How is it they didn't get caught?"

Randall shook his head. Then he reached into his wallet, pulled out a crisp fifty-dollar bill, and snapped it between his fingers.

"Because this is always the most powerful form of government. It outranks safety officials. Customs clerks. Everyone."

"You're saying the firm bribed the safety inspector?"

"You bet," Randall said. "It ain't the first time either."

Amanda patted Jake's hand. "But doesn't any kind of accident hurt the company?"

He glanced at her and smiled. At least her question didn't sound accusatory.

"Bello and Toale was notorious for taking risks. Financial gain versus possible risk of failure. Guess which one always won out?"

Jake nodded, digesting the information. "I assume the cheap equipment was painted or done up to look like the Grade Eight or

Nine bolts?"

Randall's eyes gleamed. "Very good. You know your stuff, for a man of academia."

Jake's jaw muscles clenched, but he said nothing. Many people assumed that his academia career meant that he was one of those who couldn't do, so he taught. But it was more than that. There were reasons he'd chosen academia over a nine-to-five job. Important reasons besides some cliché expression.

"Guess I need to study those bolts more. Not only on the cars, but on the track," Jake said.

"Look into the accounting practices of the company too. You'll be amazed."

Jake nodded. "Well, thanks for your time, sir. You've helped with my research."

"Glad to help a fellow engineer."

Amanda smiled and said good-bye, and then they sidestepped across the yard back to the vehicle.

Once inside the car, Jake let out a deep breath. "What he said makes sense, but I still want to find out more about this lawsuit. Let's go back to the inn, and I'll type out my notes."

"I think he's guilty," Amanda said.

CHAPTER TWELVE

"You what?" Jake stared at her incredulously before shoving the key into the ignition.

"The man reminds me of a scared dog. Twitchy, ready to bite any stranger."

"Did we just have the same conversation?"

She groaned. Why did Jake insist on the logical and never go with a sense of intuition? There needed to be a balance for things to work.

"Did you see how his hands shook when he talked about the bolts?"

"The man has arthritis. Why are you sneering at a man with a painful condition?"

"I'm not." She turned sideways to face Jake. "Catfish is a German shepherd. They're double-coated breeds, meaning this time of year they blow their coats. Yet Catfish was perfectly groomed. No loose brown fur, no clumps of hair coming out at the seams."

Jake frowned, and the stress lines on his forehead dug in deeper. "What are you talking about?"

"The man brushes that dog every few hours, I'll bet you money. If his arthritis is as painful as he claims, he wouldn't be able to thoroughly brush out Catfish's coat."

"That's the strangest example I've ever heard."

"Maybe, but it's true. If you want to study the bolts more, go ahead. I say the man is guilty. Wanted to get even with his employer for ending his contract."

"I don't buy it."

She shrugged. Maybe the ghosts at Zephyr Land would give her some more info on the mysterious Randall Kern.

Back at the Abandon Inn, Jake set up his laptop at the desk in the room and began to type in his notes. After freshening up her face, Amanda asked, "Do you care if I go wander around? I need to stretch my legs."

He looked up, smiled. "Sure. I may take a nap a little later. Care to join me?"

She could feel the heat rising to her face. Why did she always blush when he hinted at the two of them being in bed together?

"Maybe so," she said, using her flirty tone. "Or maybe I'll make you wait until tonight."

"Been waiting since I met you," he said. "So come back in an hour."

Smiling, she left him to type. Right now, she couldn't concentrate on how handsome Jake was or how much she wanted to be in his arms.

She needed to talk to Pearl. Get more info. Because one thing that would kill a romance faster than anything else—a restless bunch of souls who had nothing but time on their hands.

* * *

Amanda smiled when Pearl carried a pitcher of iced tea from the kitchen and placed it on the quiet table in the back dining area.

"Just what I need," Amanda said. "Are you sure you can take time away from the front desk?"

Pearl set down two glasses and grabbed an array of sugar and sweetener substitutes. "Honey, if I don't get some time away, I'll be certifiable."

"What's going on? Busy morning?"

"Clive woke up, dressed in his Confederate uniform, and walked out the front door with his gun. The crazy man thought today was one of his reenactments. I had to go chasing after him in my robe to get him to stop scaring everyone on the block."

Amanda tried not to laugh. "At least your marriage isn't boring?"

"That's the truth. The man is going to make me go postal one of these days." She tore open two sweeteners and stirred them in her tea.

"Has he ever wandered off where you can't find him? As funny as the story is, it must be dangerous with him walking around with a gun."

Pearl smiled wide. "I figure as long as he dresses up as a Confederate, he still knows some of the basics. At least he's not switching to being a Yankee just to win the war."

Amanda put some lemon in her tea, wondering what Jake would be like when he grew older. Probably more stubborn than he was now.

"How long have y'all been together?" Amanda asked.

"Thirty years. That's three decades." Pearl chuckled. "But I love the old fool. Now, tell me more about being gifted. What did you see at Zephyr Land?"

Stirring her tea carefully, Amanda met Pearl's eager gaze. "There's a ghost there named Declan. He says he is tasked with helping everyone who died that day cross over, but he can't do it without my help."

"What kind of help?"

"Bringing the man who killed everyone to justice."

Amanda waited a second to let that sink in. She wasn't sure how the entire town had reacted. Did everyone think it had been a freak accident all these years, especially since that's what the reports said? Or had Pearl known something else, seeing as how her sister, Opal, was killed, along with her daughters?

Pearl's eyes widened, and she smiled wide. This wasn't the reaction Amanda had expected.

"That's fantastic!"

"What?" Amanda glanced around, making sure they were still alone. "Why would you think someone murdering your sister and daughters was fantastic?"

Pearl leaned across the table, touched Amanda's hand. "Don't you see? This gives me answers. Answers to the unknowns for the last decade. The safety reports, the insurance companies—nobody could tell us the truth. With your gift to talk to the dead, you can help. Don't you see?"

"You sound like my aunt Anzhela."

"I like aunts. They tell it like it is."

Amanda smiled. Truer words were never spoken. Her aunt had been her confidante all those times her parents never understood.

"It's just that, with Jake…"

Pearl's eyes darkened. "You haven't told him about your ability yet."

"No." Amanda sighed, grateful she could be honest with Pearl.

"Honey, you might risk his laughing at you or disapproving of you, but you need to help those people." Pearl took a sip of tea, and then her eyebrows rose. "Wait a second. Did you meet everyone? I know you saw Sarah here. Did you meet Becca and my sister, Opal?"

Amanda bit her lip, reluctantly meeting Pearl's stare. "Yes. They want me to bring you to the park."

"This is wonderful! Do you know how long I've waited for someone like you?"

"Wait. Just wait."

"What? C'mon, we need to go to Zephyr Land. I'll drive."

Amanda thought of Jake, of his invitation to be intimate. How angry would he be if she took off with Pearl to go to the park?

"I can't—"

"Please? If Opal wants me there, I need to go. I can't get in the gate without you or Jake. Didn't y'all say you had some special permission?"

"Yes, we have a temporary key for the lock. Got it from the attorney's office."

"Then what's stopping you? I'll get Clive down for a nap, and we girls will go."

Everything was happening too fast. Too much.

"Pearl, I know you want this, but I can't leave Jake—"

"Then bring him along."

She tried to envision what that would be like. Her interpreting words between the living and the dead. All while not letting Jake know she had that ability, and his stern glares if she acted strange.

No. Not good.

"If you don't come with me, I'm going to tell Jake about your ability myself," Pearl said.

Amanda's pulse raced. "You wouldn't. I told you this in confidence!"

"Then come with me. I don't want to butt my nose into your relationship, but if you won't take me to go see my daughter and sister, well, I guess I'll have to."

Pearl grabbed her purse. "I'll text Mr. Langley, one of our regulars. He'll look in on Clive."

"But I…I mean, how did we get here?" This conversation had not gone as planned.

"Just slip in the room and get the key," Pearl said. "If he's anything like Clive, he won't even notice you're in there if he's sawing logs."

"Fine. Not that you're giving me much choice."

Pearl smiled. "It's called Southern stubbornness, my dear. And I'm afraid I have a bad case of it."

Amanda couldn't help but grin at Pearl's antics, even though the woman had clearly put her in a no-win situation. Maybe there was a way to get the key, go to the park with Pearl, and return back to the inn with plenty of time for a late afternoon interlude with Jake?

Only if he didn't wake up in the meantime.

Pearl grinned, tapped her foot, and began to hum the *Jeopardy* tune.

"Meet you in the parking lot," Amanda said, then slipped upstairs to retrieve the key. Her day had just become a hell of a lot more challenging. Something she didn't think was possible.

CHAPTER THIRTEEN

Amanda winced as she turned the old room key into their lock. *Don't wake up. Don't wake up.*

Stepping inside, she scanned the room for Jake's wallet. There. On the table. With quick-footed steps, she grabbed the leather billfold and opened it to where Jake had put the key in one of the credit card slots.

On the other side of the room, Jake grumbled and rolled over. She froze. Waited to see if he would wake up, notice her. The silence filled the air. Even the second hand on her watch sounded deafening.

Ten seconds passed. No movement from Jake. She exhaled, quickly dashed out of the room, and pulled the door shut. Stood outside, listening for any movement through the door. None.

Good. She could take care of the ghosts and Pearl and get back before Jake woke up.

Scurrying down the stairs, Amanda checked her watch for a time check. Three o'clock. She had an hour, give or take.

She hurried to the parking lot, where Pearl's Jeep pulled up to get her.

"Nice ride."

Pearl tapped the dash. "My Jeffrey here has taken good care of me."

"Jeffrey the Jeep?" Amanda had heard of people naming cars but didn't know anyone who actually did.

"He's a smooth ride. Took me on many mudding trips."

Amanda had also heard of mudding—the art of going off-road

in a vehicle and driving through the mud for fun—but never knew anyone who had actually done it. Maybe Pearl had also done the infamous cow tipping? She would need to find out someday.

Pearl pulled out of the lot and took the main highway toward Zephyr Land. "So what's the plan? Do you just see ghosts automatically? Can you get a message to Opal and Becca? How does it work?"

Amanda grinned. If only her ability had a logical side. A way to explain it to strangers.

"Let's just get to the park. Knowing Opal, she will find me."

Pearl turned in surprise. "That's her, all right. She's only a year older than me, but she was the bossiest older sister around. Always thinking she knew how to take care of my girls better than me. You got siblings?"

The question sent a pang straight into Amanda's heart. She turned and stared out the window for a quiet moment before answering. "A younger brother. He's five."

Pearl's eyes widened. "That's quite an age difference. Was he a whoops baby?"

Amanda glanced at the old sign welcoming them into Zephyr Land property. "I think he was more of a second-chance baby. My parents don't have the gift, only my two aunts. So they really didn't know what to do with me. My brother, Max, is the normal kid they'd always hoped for."

Her parents' frequent remarks rang shrill in her ears. How she was such a strange child who couldn't keep friends around for long.

How they couldn't send her to camp for fear she might see the dead and be sent home. How they always longed for normal and doubted the psychiatrists who claimed she didn't have a mental illness. Amanda swallowed a lump of hurt and tried to focus on the present.

Pearl slowed the Jeep and pulled up to the gate. "That's a shame. Parents not knowing how to relate to their own kids."

"Tell me about it. Max was their way of getting the child they always wanted."

A wave of sadness swept through her as she said the words. She hadn't thought about her brother in a long time. He was a sweet kid, albeit a bit spoiled. Mom and Dad had succeeded with him where they'd failed with her. So far, he had no indications of supernatural ability. He didn't talk to ghosts. Normal—just the way her family wanted things to be.

"You had parents who didn't appreciate you. I appreciated the hell out of my twins, and they were taken from me. Same day that our dog, Sam, died too. Right next to Sarah. He'd seemed to know she was sick and wouldn't leave her side that day. Maybe he died of a broken heart? He was old. We never knew why."

Amanda wondered about the dog for a moment but didn't ask. She only nodded and stepped out to unlock the gate. Once they entered and relatched the lock, she said, "I'm sorry about your daughters. For what it's worth, Becca and Sarah are both beautiful. Sweet girls."

Pearl drove to the boardwalk. "Thanks. Do I just park here?"

"Anywhere is fine." Amanda glanced around. Which soul would

appear first?

They got out of the car. Pearl glanced around, taking in the whole sinister scene.

"You said Opal has been trapped here since the derailment?"

"Yes."

"Do you see anyone?"

Amanda glanced around, scanning every ride and surface. Some swings creaked in the distance, but Becca wasn't there.

"Opal?" she called out. "Becca?"

A rustling wind blew through the pines. Pearl crossed her arms, shivering. "Breeze was cold."

"That usually means they're close by." Amanda walked out a few feet, keeping an even gaze on all the nooks and crannies where ghosts could hide.

"Amanda."

She turned to find Declan leaning against the doorframe to the log flume. "Declan, hi."

Pearl watched but didn't say anything.

"Who is she?"

"This is Pearl, owner of the Abandon Inn. Opal is her sister, and Becca is her daughter."

Pearl stepped closer to Amanda. "Is there a ghost talking to you now?"

"Yes. His name is Declan, the one who helps souls move on."

"Hello," Pearl said, facing the other direction than where Declan stood.

He chuckled. "Tell her hello. I'll get Opal and Becca for you. But I need to know if you decided to help us or not."

"You didn't give me much choice," Amanda said. "But yes, Jake and I went to the library and reviewed some records. We talked to witnesses, including Randall Kern—"

"That no-good, cheating, corrupt fool!" a male voice said from behind her.

Amanda spun around, facing a tall, executive-looking soul she hadn't seen before. "And you are?"

"Chester. I'm the one who hired Randall."

Maybe she could finally figure this out and release these spirits after all. "Randall said that your company took shortcuts to save money. You used lower-quality bolts."

Chester leaned back his head and laughed. "That no-good moron wouldn't know a decent bolt if it hit him in the head."

Amanda bit her tongue. Jake had talked so much about Randall's accomplishments, she knew the man wasn't an idiot by any means.

"Pearl, why don't you have a seat on the bench?" Amanda asked. "I'll let you know when Opal or Becca appear."

"Okay." Pearl walked right through Chester before sitting down.

"Excuse me," he said. "Most people watch where they're going."

"Stop it," Amanda said. "She can't see you."

"Then how come you can?"

Declan stepped forward. "Because she's gifted. She'll help us."

Why did everyone volunteer her without her permission? Did being gifted mean she automatically had no say in anything?

"Wait a second. I said I would help my boyfriend with his paper and research. I never said I would play police cop and take down the killer—"

"They need this." Declan marched up to her, his pale face and dark-green eyes only inches from her. "I need this. If you don't help, I can't finish my job. If that happens, I get sent to some awful part of the world in the worst weather for my next assignment."

"I understand—"

"No!" His sharp glare sent chills through her. "You don't know what it is like to spend ten years with Idaho winters. With Death Valley summers. I tried to be reasonable, ask you for help. I tried asking my boss for more time. I got nowhere. Stop being afraid of your gift. You need to help. End of story."

She glanced down at her feet, unable to endure his fierce green eyes. His words were sharp, but they were true.

With a heavy sigh, he added, "Amanda, look at me."

With a deep resolving breath, she met his gaze. Fury vanished into the background. Instead, compassion gleamed from those big eyes.

"I know it's hard to accept your gift. My sister, Brianna, has it too, and she went through agony to come to terms with herself."

"All I want is a normal life." She wrapped her arms around her, as she'd done on the carousel.

Declan glanced around the amusement park. "Normal is

overrated. I hate to tell you, but normal isn't in your reach."

"How'd your sister cope, then?"

"It took a long time, but she finally understood that to help others and herself, she couldn't ignore who she was. Quirky flaws, ability to the talk to the dead, everything. We don't get to pick and choose which gifts we get, but we can't waste the ones we have."

Amanda chuckled. "My aunt would say the same thing."

"Where do you think I got the speech?" he said, grinning.

Chester paced back and forth. "I'm sorry. Am I interrupting this tender moment for us to find out what the hell is going on?"

Declan shot him a cold glare. "Hey, Mr. Callous. Keep it civil."

The guy huffed and puffed and stormed off down the boardwalk.

"He'll be back. Just an impatient guy," Declan said. "What did you learn from the witnesses?"

Amanda reiterated everything she and Jake had learned that morning, including her suspicion that Randall Kern had something to do with the derailment.

"Good job," Declan said. "Thank you. Sincerely."

"So can you go get Opal and Becca? They wanted to see Pearl."

With a wide grin, Declan pointed to where Pearl sat. "They're already over there."

Amanda looked. Becca gripped tightly onto Pearl's leg, a child so happy to see her mama again. Opal sat next to her on the bench, a heartwarming smile on her face.

"See what you can have a part in doing?" Declan whispered.

"C'mon. You can't tell me that some part of your soul doesn't warm at that sight."

She relaxed and let her arms fall to her sides. She had to admit, seeing two souls reunited with the living—even if Pearl couldn't see them—did send a happy flutter through her.

"Maybe."

"Maybe? You're a tough crowd, Amanda Moss." He chuckled. "I better go check on the others."

"Quick question?"

"Yeah?"

She turned to face him. "Did your sister ever manage to date anyone who accepted her gift?"

"As a matter of fact, yes. She's married to him now, though the beginning was rough."

"So it's possible?"

"Of course. There's always hope, Amanda. Always."

And with that fortune cookie, he walked away, slowly fading out of sight.

CHAPTER FOURTEEN

Jake rolled over, and his face mushed into the soft down pillow. He'd been dreaming of roller coasters. Up, down, side jaunts and quick turns. The feeling had made him seasick.

No. Not comfy. He turned on his side, peered his eyelids open. Widened his eyes. Where had Amanda gone? He missed her, even if she was acting a little...odd.

Digging his palms into his eyes to wake up, he fumbled around for his cell phone. Almost four. Shouldn't she be done having tea with Pearl by now? He pressed the button to check for any text messages, any e-mails.

None from Amanda.

A bellowing voice echoed in the hallway. "Woo wee! We're going to Selma! Where's my canteen?"

What the hell? He got up, pulled on a T-shirt. Put jeans on over his boxers. Hopped over the various clothes and opened the door.

"Hello? Can I help you?"

A salt-and-pepper haired man dressed in a gray uniform danced up and down the hallway, lifting his flask and shouting with glee, "Gonna get me some Yankees today!"

"What's your name, sir?"

"General Robert E. Lee. Reporting for service, sir!"

Oh lord. "Are you Clive, by any chance?"

"On my normal days, yes, but not today."

"C'mon," Jake said, shutting the door behind him. "Let's go

find Pearl."

"She's out with the other ladies washing the linens. It's time for war!"

Jake held on to Clive's skinny but determined arm to hold him steady. "War is closed today. Let's get you back to Pearl."

After checking the upstairs and downstairs, Jake rang the front desk bell. "Pearl? Hello?"

Clive staggered over to one of the large recliners and plopped himself down. "I told ya, sonny. She's gone. She took Jeffrey and your gal, too."

"Wait. What?"

"She's gone. Off. Away. Took Jeffrey."

"Who is Jeffrey?"

Clive gawked at him like he had three heads. "The Jeep."

Jake tried to make rational sense out of Clive's words, which wasn't unlike building a shopping mall from a bunch of toothpicks and dirt.

"She took Amanda too? Why?"

Clive's voice became a half yodel, like he was dwindling down. "Got me, sonny. You know how those women gab when they get together. Ask Langley."

"Who's Langley?"

Clive shut his eyes, snoring in the chair.

"Clive!" Jake nudged the old man's shoulder. "Who's Langley?"

Between air bursts of snore and sniffle, Clive said, "Room two fifteen."

Jake took the silver flask from Clive's hand and set it on the adjacent table just as Clive's snoring rhythm picked up pace. Maybe the old guy could sleep off the crazy while Jake located Amanda.

He knocked on room 215 and waited. Seconds later, a middle-aged gentleman opened the door. "Yes?"

"Are you Langley?"

"Yes. How can I help you?"

"My name's Jake Mercer. Clive is downstairs—"

"Brussel sprouts and biscuits! He got away from me."

Jake arched his eyebrows. He wasn't familiar with that Southern term, but whatever. "He's fine. He's sleeping off his liquor."

"I'd better check on him."

"Clive said you knew where Pearl might be? Apparently Pearl took my girlfriend, Amanda, with her."

"Oh, yes. Nice girl. They went to the park."

Jake's pulse raced. "What park?"

"That ole abandoned one. What's the name of that place again?"

"Zephyr Land?" Jake exclaimed.

"That's the one."

"Shit!" He paced the hallway. Pounded his palm against the flat wall. "Thanks for your help." Why hadn't she checked with him? Abandoned places were a haven for unsavory characters. He would have gladly returned to the park, stayed by her side to protect her. What had she been thinking?

He stormed off to his room. He dug in his wallet, searching for the park key. It was gone. *Damn it, Amanda. Please don't be hurt. I'm on my way.*

CHAPTER FIFTEEN

Amanda strolled over to where Pearl sat on the bench. "Opal and Becca have been by your side for the last ten minutes," she whispered.

Pearl's eyes glistened. "I didn't want to presume anything, but it's like I can...*feel* them."

Becca's cherub cheeks held the happiest dimples around. "Thanks for getting my mama."

"You're welcome, sweetie." Amanda looked at Pearl. "Becca is holding on to your left leg. She's thanking me for bringing you here."

"Can she hear me when I speak? Or do I tell you what I want to say?"

Amanda glanced at Becca, who nodded she could hear. Sometimes ghosts could, other times not. Everything depended upon circumstance, just like in life.

"She can hear you."

Pearl started bawling. "Becca, my sweetheart. I miss you so much. Clive and I love you more than you can imagine."

"Love you too, Mommy."

Amanda spoke the translation, freeing the remaining tears to spill down Pearl's face. As she sat there, able to help mother and daughter connect across time and place, the energy coursing through her felt like a natural high.

"Is my sister here too?" Pearl asked through blubbering tears.

Opal patted Pearl's back, nodding yes. Amanda helped both sisters speak for a few moments, then gave Pearl some space to cry quietly.

Maybe she could do this, use her gift for good. Aunt Anzhela kept telling her to accept her talent. Declan said to stop being afraid of her own gift. She couldn't escape these ghosts, even if she tried. Why not just embrace the good she could do for a nice woman like Pearl?

"Amanda Moss!"

She spun around, her heart racing at being called by her full name. Even worse, she recognized the voice. Behind the main entrance gate was Jake, shooting daggers at her with his angry glare.

Coughing, she cleared her throat. "Jake? What are you doing here?"

"I might ask you the same question."

Crap. What to do now?

Pearl blew her nose. "We can go, hon. I don't want to be the cause of you and your boyfriend arguing."

"No, just give us a second."

Amanda walked over to the gate and unlocked it.

"Nice key. Where'd you get it?" Jake demanded.

"Jake, please—"

"Do you know how worried I was about you? You trust people too much. And you come here with Pearl, the two of you alone? What if some vagrant decided to murder both of you on his way through town?"

The ghosts would scare the person away? It didn't seem the best answer, even though it was true.

"I didn't mean to upset you—"

"You have a strange way of showing it."

"I'm sorry I worried you," she said. "Pearl wanted to see Zephyr Land, and you were sleeping. I didn't think."

Jake crossed his arms over his chest. Everything about him—his body language, his razor-sharp tone, his darkened eyes—radiated anger. She knew she'd upset him by putting herself at risk, but his attitude seemed a bit excessive.

"I thought you were going to come join me for a nap. Not go driving around alone where you're not safe."

"We're fine, honest." She glanced toward Pearl. "See? We're just fine."

He gripped her hand, squeezing it. "You have to stop making dangerous choices. What if you'd been hurt?"

"We've been careful—"

"That park key is my responsibility. If anything had happened to it while you two were running around—"

"Don't worry. I kept it safe. Sorry to have worried you."

He released her hand but held her gaze for a long minute. Those gorgeous blue-gray eyes of his turned stormy, as if he were Zeus ready to zap a lightning bolt aimed for her head.

"You always let feelings dictate your decisions. One of these days, that's going to hurt you. You have to use logic, think of what could happen." He ran his fingers through his hair and let out an exasperated sigh. "If anything happened to you…"

Beneath the bulging vein on the side of his neck, Amanda sensed his worry. Worry for her well-being. She'd frightened him. He didn't deserve that. Then again, she didn't deserve to be the brunt of his anger either.

"We're fine. I didn't mean to scare you." She stepped closer, put her hands on his shoulders. "Let me go have a quick word with Pearl. Then we'll go. I'll ride back to the inn with you, okay?"

"Fine," he mumbled.

Her heart racing in her chest, she turned her attention to Pearl. Becca and Opal remained nearby, and Pearl had a big smile on her face despite the tears.

"I need to go back to the inn with Jake," Amanda whispered.

"I got you into a heap of trouble, didn't I?"

"Don't worry about it." She turned to assess Jake's rigid posture. "We'll be okay. But we do need you to leave with us so we can lock the gate back up."

"Sure thing." Pearl stood up, breathing the air of her family in deep. "I'm ready."

Amanda smiled, returned to Jake, and handed him the key. "It's yours to lock up."

He cast her a sharp look as if to say, "Nice of you to notice," but to his credit, he said nothing as he locked the gate.

Amanda hugged Pearl and then stepped into the passenger side of Jake's car. He stormed around and got into the driver's seat. He stared straight ahead, his voice monotone.

"Why didn't you come join me for a nap? Why go off with Pearl?"

She shrugged. "You were sleeping so soundly. I figured I'd help Pearl see the park."

"I don't think you came to Zephyr Land because of me. This trip was supposed to be about us, Amanda. Since we got here, you've ignored your carousel research. Insisted on helping me, which I appreciate, but then you just take off on your own with the inn owner. It doesn't make sense."

She dropped eye contact and glanced out the window. They remained parked. It would be so much easier to look at passing trees and streams.

"I have a lot on my mind," she whispered. Did that sound as lame and cliché as she thought? "It's almost dinnertime. Want to have an early dinner and then hang out together tonight?"

His jaw twitched. "The mood's gone, trust me."

"I'm sorry."

He put the key in the ignition, started the car, and screeched out of the lot. "So am I."

CHAPTER SIXTEEN

Back in their hotel room, Jake's mind reeled from the day's events. Meeting the master of roller coasters, Randall Kern, only to see the hero of Jake's childhood turned into a wacky recluse. Even worse, Amanda thinking the guy could've killed all those people. Her refusing to come upstairs to snuggle with him, to finally make love like they'd talked about doing on this trip—only to have her sneak away with Pearl and steal his key.

Come to think of it, the worst parts of the day all connected to Amanda. Not to her, exactly, but to her strange behavior. She'd made every apology imaginable on the drive back to the inn, but he couldn't shake this nagging, itchy feeling crawling through his veins.

The feeling of being lied to.

"I'm going to get some ice and check out the vending machine," Amanda said, shaking him from his thoughts. "Can I bring you something back?"

"No."

The hopeful optimism in her smile vanished at his curt response. With a deep breath, he modified his answer. "Thanks, though."

Looking wounded like only she could, she said "Okay" and left the room. Guilt seeped into him. He hadn't meant to snap at her, to seem cold and unforgiving.

But why was she behaving so strangely? Time for an honest talk. Get answers. When she returned, he would insist.

Minutes ticked by. Ten minutes stretched into twenty. How long did it take to get something at the vending machine and then return?

He peered his head out the door. Empty hallway illuminated by artificial and flickering lights. No one around. He walked several doors down to the ice vending area. Nothing.

Crap. What now? Had she returned to Zephyr Land again?

He raced down the stairs. Stopped short at the landing just out of view from the lobby. Across the way, Amanda stood by the umbrella stand—alone. Yet she seemed to be talking.

Talking to whom? She didn't have a cell phone headset, so she couldn't be on the phone.

He continued to watch, to analyze her behavior. The same approach he'd used when his mother first went mentally ill. Watch, analyze, and then take action and heal. His mantra through his teen years.

Amanda knelt and continued talking, chatting with inanimate objects as if they were human. Her posture and demeanor suggested she was speaking to a child, but only the umbrella rack heard her words. Pearl and Clive were nowhere to be seen.

Shit. This was happening. He'd watched his own mother live with schizophrenia and the never-ending hallucinations. The suffering she endured, the horror the disease inflicted on the whole family. Especially him.

He stumbled backward, managing to break his fall. Blinked his eyes quickly to keep things in focus. The sharp pang in the pit of his stomach shifted into a wave of dry heaves. Any second, he'd be sick.

How could he not have seen this? His worst fear coming true. Amanda wasn't being superstitious, paranoid, or flaky. She'd seen things—and people—who weren't there. Just like his mother. He'd already fallen hard for Amanda. What was he supposed to do now?

* * *

At dinner in the nearby Abandon Café, Jake stabbed a carrot with his fork and ground his teeth as he chewed. Across from him, Amanda studied his every move, her round eyes watching him like a hawk.

"Please talk to me," she said.

He finished chewing. Did she really want to clear the air now, in this Southern diner while some 1950's song played on the jukebox?

She rested her elbows on the table, stared at him with those beautiful green eyes. "You can't give me the silent treatment forever."

Logically, he knew she was right. But did she understand his side? How difficult things could become when one partner was mentally ill?

Maybe she needed to know. He glanced around the empty diner. A cheesy jukebox in the corner, black-and-white checker tile floors, cherry-red booths with silver chrome. Behind the counter, an older woman wore a pink uniform and cleaned the equipment. Completely cliché, but at least the place was private.

"You really want to clear the air?" Jake asked.

Amanda sat back in her chair. "Yes."

"Who were you talking to in the lobby?"

The color drained from her face. "What?"

"I saw you. You stood facing the umbrella rack, then you knelt down like when you talk to a kid."

Amanda bit her lip. Reached for her drink and swallowed.

"No one was there," Jake said. "And I know you don't have a phone headset. So I repeat. Who were you talking to?"

Her mouth opened but nothing came out. Fine. He would do the talking.

"I told you about my mom. What I left out was the agony it put on my dad and me. The hysteria, wild hallucinations, getting her schizophrenia medication stabilized. When the cancer came, everything became worse—"

"Sorry."

"You're showing the same psychological symptoms she did." Jake leaned forward. "I can help get the medical care you need, but you can't lie anymore."

"Lie?"

"You have to admit that you're mentally ill to yourself first. Stop denying it. That's the first step to getting treatment." He reached for her hand and clasped it in his.

She glanced down at her tableware for several seconds. "I know I've been behaving strangely, but I don't have schizophrenia—"

"Then what the hell is up with you? You jump at things that aren't there in Zephyr Land, you talk to umbrella racks, and you just take off with Pearl earlier today."

The color returned to her cheeks. He didn't want to pressure her into answering, but he didn't want to give her time to dismiss him either.

"Your concern is sweet," she began. "I wouldn't want to put you through anything like what your mother did."

"Then let me help you get treatment. Don't dismiss me. Don't balk at science and logic."

"What...exactly...do you want from me?"

"Behave rationally for the duration of this trip. When we return to Georgia, you go see a psychiatrist and get on meds, agree to whatever treatment is prescribed."

Amanda's eyes narrowed. "I don't know that I can do that. I admit I'm acting strangely, but I have a lot on my mind. You know I want a new career. This carousel restoration proposal is my chance. If I act a little strange, forgive me? I don't have schizophrenia."

He stabbed another carrot and chewed. "I should be honest with you."

"Okay," she said, her voice dubious.

"I won't go through this again. I'm fine helping you seek treatment. I'll be there for you in any way I can—"

"But..."

"But I won't tolerate wild craziness from someone who refuses medication like my mom did. I wish I could, but I can't. It's a minefield I swore I'd never walk across again."

She nodded. "I understand."

Time for the moment of reckoning.

"So, will you agree to seek medical help when we return to Georgia? Meanwhile, you'll behave like the Amanda I know and love?"

"Y…yes."

He smiled, stood up, and walked to her side of the table and kissed her. Her lips tasted like sweet oranges, probably from the iced tea.

"Thank you. I'm glad to hear it."

She pulled on his shirt collar, tugged him toward her lips again. First she didn't want to nap with him, now she became amorous? Not that he was going to fight it.

"Let's go back to the inn," she said, that familiar gleam in her eyes.

"Amanda…" He wanted her as much as ever, but was that fair? He'd just insisted she get medical treatment, and now he would agree to sleep with her?

"I'm done making you worry," she said. "I love you, and I want us to be together."

"Trust me—I want that too." His lips released hers for a moment. "But it feels like I'm taking advantage."

Her hands cupped his face. All logic melted away. Only desire and longing remained.

"I want you. You're not taking advantage," she said. "Let's go."

He could barely look away from her beautiful face long enough to find the hostess.

"Check, please?"

CHAPTER SEVENTEEN

Amanda yanked Jake's shirt out of the buttons. A *pop* sounded as a rebellious button hurled across the room. Good. The more intense, the better. Anything to keep him in her arms. Focused on the love they had for each other, not the antagonism. Or worse, curiosity.

She stood facing him, looking into his admiring eyes.

"Arms up," he said with a wink. She willingly obeyed. He pulled off her shirt, took a minute to admire her purple lace bra. "Nice lace."

Grinning, she inched herself even closer to him. "The clasp is in the front. Your turn."

He undid the clasp with ease, slowly pulled the straps off her shoulders. "You're beautiful, Amanda Moss."

Heat flares spread across her chest and neck, up to her face. "I like it when you use my full name in a nice way."

He nodded, putting his hands along her waist and unbuttoning her jeans. She wasn't about to let him have all the fun, and her fingers worked their way to unhooking his belt, sliding off his slacks.

"University of Georgia boxers, eh?" she said, chuckling.

"Don't knock the Bulldogs. I'm a loyal fan."

She kicked off her loosened jeans, tossing them across the room with her feet. "Kiss me."

For once, color rose in his cheeks. Aha. So the engineer man blushed too. Nice.

Leaning in, his lips touched hers. He pressed against them, slow and soft. The touch of a man who knew the inner workings of things.

You need to tell him about your gift.

Crap. Her aunt's words invading her mind at a time like this. No. Go away.

She tugged him closer, pressed hard, and opened her mouth to his. Met his tongue and circled it with hers. Focused on their bodies, the heat between them. Forgot all rationale and logic.

He responded in kind, grabbing her and pulling her into him so no distance existed between their naked and willing bodies.

This close, she could smell the piney scent of his aftershave. She nibbled along his neck, inhaling deep. His arms were warm, secure muscles of comfort. Exactly what her soul needed.

As he kissed her, he slipped a hand to her breast and tickled little circles in her most sensitive spots. "Am I getting to you?" he asked.

Hot and breathless, she said, "Yes."

He nibbled along her collar bone, sending jolts of pleasure through her. She ran her fingers through his hair, tickling his ear before focusing on his chest.

Moaning, she continued tracing the light-brown hairs on his muscles to tease him even further. Oh yes. Her hands wandered down to his core pleasure. He was ready. She was more than ready.

This would be perfect.

* * *

Jake did everything in his power to hold steady when Amanda

first touched him. The sensation of her fingers exploring every part of his skin was almost more than he could contain. She'd consented to get treatment. He'd wanted her for weeks—now she was here. Everything would work out.

He did love her. No one could come close to her. She cared about him, didn't think he acted stuffy or boring. And this beauty wanted him! If he didn't take her soon, he would explode.

"On the bed," he whispered.

She sat down, inched back on her butt and hands with that longing gleam in her eyes. Damn, she looked like one of those sirens he'd read about in lit classes. Beautiful, charming, wanting him.

He crawled onto the bed, stopping to kiss her knees, her inner thighs. She whimpered under his touch, bringing the world's biggest grin to his face. He knew in that moment. The two of them could have fun forever, trying to pleasure the other one more.

A life he could see.

As if she could read his thoughts, she reached down and pulled him up on top of her. Her hair smelled like raspberry. He inhaled in the sweet scent.

"I want you, Jake Mercer," she said.

Holy moly. That was it. No more waiting. He kissed her collarbone, massaged her breast as he entered her. She moaned, dug her fingernails into his back. Damn. He never thought nails could feel amazing, but hers did.

"Come with me," she cooed.

He shuddered, filling her sacred place in one long, blissful moment. She held on, pulling him closer until they both collapsed into each other's arms.

* * *

Amanda rested her head on the pillow, Jake lying next to her. Their rapid breaths slowly returned to normal.

Every part of her body had a feeling of bliss, yet something inside her stomach began to ache. A pang from untold truths, omitted lies.

I told you, dear. You have to tell him about your gift. Lovemaking should be honest, no secrets.

Damn it, Aunt Anzhela. The woman's words found the most inopportune times to enter her consciousness. Yet her aunt had been right. Being with Jake physically had been incredible. His strong arms, tender kisses, and adoring eyes all sent her toes curling.

Yet emotionally? She'd held back, knowing her true self and being afraid to share it. Behind her eyes, fat tears pushed for release. Amanda blinked in rapid succession. No. Do not cry now.

Jake folded his hands behind his head and leaned back on the pillow. "You were amazing."

"You too," she said, her voice quivering in spite of her full effort to not do so.

He glanced over. "Amanda? Are you crying?"

Blink fast. Faster.

"I'm fine."

"No, you're crying. Why?"

She met his searching gaze. His yearning to know the inner

workings of her mind. And yet she didn't dare tell him. Hell, he already assumed she had schizophrenia. She'd even agreed to a medical checkup when they got home. What was she thinking? What was she supposed to tell a psychiatrist? No matter what explanation she gave, it would sound hokey.

Because the truth had to remain hidden.

"I've heard some women cry afterward," he said.

"I'm fine. Let's get some sleep."

He rolled over, kissed her lips softly one more time. "Night, Amanda."

She smiled at him. "Night."

In the darkness, her thoughts raced once again. The excuse of some women crying after sex had worked. She didn't have to tell him how guilty she felt for holding back her true self with him.

She could even deal with seeing a shrink when they returned home. No matter what, she would let Jake and anyone else come up with their logical excuses. Because in her world, being thought of as mentally ill was a lot better than being known as the freak who could see and talk to the dead.

CHAPTER EIGHTEEN

Amanda woke up the next morning feeling better. Today was a new day. A means of refocusing her efforts on why she'd come on this trip to begin with.

Spend time with Jake, work on the carousel project.

Enough time had been wasted with chasing ghosts—literally—and today she would return to her priorities.

Downstairs, she and Jake sat down for a quick breakfast.

"I can't wait to get to the carousel and document my findings," she said.

He winked at her with that wide grin, making dimples appear on his face. So damn handsome. "You'll do a great job. I'm going to remember my binoculars today so I can study the loop framework of the roller coaster."

Pearl walked over carrying a pot of coffee. "Anyone up for a refill?"

"Great, thanks," Jake said as he held out his cup.

Amanda declined but exchanged a quick glance with Pearl. "How's Clive this morning?"

"The old coot is still trying to find his canteen to do his reenactment. He hasn't been to one in ten years, but the man's mind isn't on full speed. Are y'all off to Zephyr Land this morning?"

"I need to do some documentation for the carousel work."

Pearl gave her a knowing wink. When Jake looked away, she mouthed, "Tell Opal and Becca hello for me."

Amanda nodded. She would pass that message along, no

problem. But no more letting ghosts run her day. Time for a new start.

An hour later, she entered the carousel tent. Thick humidity from the prior night made the entry flaps clammy. Inside, like a roasting oven. This wouldn't do. She found strands of rope on the ground—wonder where they came from?—and tied back the flaps so the entire carousel area could breathe.

First up. Photograph.

Pulling the wide-angle lens from her bag, she snapped it onto the camera body. Adjusted the aperture. She looked through the viewfinder and took several quick shots of the entire carousel to document the work as a whole.

There were tattered horses, chipped paint on animals, even an ostrich with a saddle and a smile. Each piece more unique than the last.

Time for some interesting angle shots. Fortunately, she'd done photography as a hobby and side business for more years than she could count. The key to intriguing photos, like movie camera shots, was to use a variety of angles and keep the viewer interested in the subject.

She knelt down, aiming the camera straight upward to give the effect of the carousel being part of the sky overhead. The tent ceiling provided the backdrop as she caught glimpses of large ostrich beaks, wild mustang manes, and proud war horses with gold bridles.

"There's a way to combine your gift with carousel restoration," a male voice said.

Heartbeat racing, she overcorrected the camera wobbling in her hands at the startling voice. In the process, she accidentally snapped a photo of one horse's foot.

"Declan. What are you doing here?"

He ran his hands along a horse's saddle before smiling at her. "I wanted to see how things were going."

She clenched her jaw. "No, you wanted to make sure I was still doing what you need. And the answer is no, not today. Today, I work on my career."

"The souls here are quite impatient. I don't know how much longer I can hold them off—"

"Not now. Give me one day without any ghosts. Otherwise, I'm not helping at all. It's not too much to ask."

His keen eyes studied her, seeming puzzled by her request. "I suppose it's not."

"Thank you."

"Just one thing, before I go…"

Of course. Men always needed to have the last word. Even when they died and became ghosts.

"Yes?"

"Carousels are about history. Not only the pieces themselves, but what the artisans put into each one."

Where was he going with this? Did he not think she knew these things?

"I know."

He ran his fingers across the chipped manes and once-fancy

bridles. "The craftspeople often put treasures inside the carousel pieces. Like a time capsule, something that signified their efforts."

She walked over to where he stood. "I've read about it."

"What do you think?"

Think? Why was he asking her this? She sought for an answer.

"It's romantic? Sad, in a way, but also beautiful how the artists put a piece of themselves into the final product. Whether it's their initials, a letter, or a piece of jewelry."

In truth, she found the idea more than romantic. Artistic creation and preservation were essential, if only to return the favor she'd known as a child. Give others a chance to escape on a galloping horse while lyrical music played. Her favorite memory: summers spent with her aunt when her parents needed their three months of normalcy. Every day, Aunt Anzhela took her to the park to ride the carousel. The glittery lights, the fat musical notes and whistles bobbing up and down just like the long-mane horse she always chose—the experience freed her from the torment of her everyday existence.

"Amanda," Declan began, his voice soft and empathetic. "These carousel pieces are bound to the people who created them."

And the people who rode them—like me. She waited for him to say something, but he stood silent. "Why are you telling me this?"

Declan's green eyes beamed. "Because you can use your gift to talk to those souls. Find out their stories. Share their passions with people today who ride the carousels they helped create."

Amanda blinked. Declan was giving out career advice? He had

an excellent point. If she did get the apprenticeship, she could help bring a voice to those artisans who created the carousels in the first place. But that would mean deliberately making use of her gift. Could she do that and hide her ability at the same time?

"Thank you," she murmured.

"I know I've asked a great deal of you, and I appreciate your help. Just trying to let you know a way you can use your gift for your own interests too."

He gave her a friendly salute and a smile before walking out the tent.

Leaving her alone with twenty carousel horses, all with untold stories to explore.

CHAPTER NINETEEN

Jake reached into his backpack and pulled out the binoculars. This time, he'd remembered to bring them. Looking through the two eyepieces, he examined the loops of the roller coaster. Every bolt had the same amount of thread showing along the track. Meaning not a single one was loose.

He aimed the binoculars at the second loop. Same thing. Some rust had worn down parts of the track, but every bolt and screw remained solidly in place.

Amanda's camera would come in handy. He could use her zoom lens to take pictures of the top loops, the bolt threads. To prove nothing had gone wrong in the coaster design. This also likely proved Bello and Toale hadn't used cheap bolts like Randall had claimed.

Based on his exam through binoculars, he had to agree with the published report. It didn't appear the track circuit had been the problem in the derailment. Something must have gone wrong with the roller coaster cars. And he needed to work his way through all that scrunched-up metal to find the answer.

As he stepped into the containing shed area where the roller coaster cars were kept, he exhaled with relief at his findings so far. Randall Kern might be kind of strange, but he wouldn't design anything to harm others. No way. Knowing this—seeing the perfection of how well the coaster circuit had endured—sent a wave of comfort through Jake. Engineering outlasted everything, if done right. Those thousands of people who'd built the Egyptian pyramids knew that, and Jake knew it too. And it looked like Bello and Toale had known it too.

Humidity swept through the park. Jake rubbed the sweat off his forehead. Now was not the time to be in an enclosed space examining hot scrap metal from the cars. He could find Amanda now and get photos outside for a while.

When he walked through the red-and-white tent flaps, he found Amanda crying on the base of the carousel. Stiffness shot through his bones. Nothing made him more uncomfortable than her crying.

"Hey," he said softly. "What's wrong?"

She wiped her eyes. "Nothing. I'm just happy with this carousel research. I hope I get the apprenticeship."

His throat tightened. Most women didn't cry happy tears. How was he supposed to react?

"You're crying because you're happy?" Confirm first, panic after.

She nodded, ran into his arms. The rushed force pushed him back, but he regained his footing. Patting her back, he reached for the only words he could think of.

"It's okay. Everything is going to work out fine."

He repeated the phrase a few times. Maybe saying it more than once would make the words work faster?

After what seemed an unbearable amount of time, she stopped crying. Looked up and smiled at him.

"How is your roller coaster research going? Did you find out anything for your paper?"

"The coaster framework, including the track, was securely built. No bolt failure. I'll examine the cars next, but it's so humid outside I thought I could borrow your photography expertise for a few minutes?"

"Sure." She stood on her toes and kissed him. "Let's go."

* * *

Amanda glanced up. The sky changed from cornflower blue to dark gray. An abrupt gust of wind prodded them forward with an invisible force.

"It's not supposed to rain, is it?" she asked.

"Nope. Sticky but otherwise ideal weather."

She glanced around and planned an escape route in case of a thunderstorm. The carousel tent was far behind them on the opposite end of the boardwalk. Up ahead, scraggly vines wrapped around the base of a structure.

"What's that?" Jake asked.

As they approached the half-overrun Kudzu box, she said, "It's one of those old fortune-teller booths."

Jake frowned. "Hokum. I'm surprised they don't have astrology machines here too."

She glanced at the glass panels of the booth. In its dark interior, purple beaded tapestry cloaked the background. A mannequin woman with dark hair and eerie eyes remained frozen, requiring payment before offering fortunes to the masses.

"I don't know. Sometimes fortunes and horoscopes can be right on target," Amanda said.

Jake looked squarely at her. "Hokum."

"Fine, be that way."

She hadn't been surprised by his reaction. How much worse would he become when he learned about her gift? If he had this much disdain for a fortune-teller booth? Could she really tell him the truth, or let him believe she needed a psych evaluation? She cringed inside. He'd said he wouldn't go "through this again"—supporting someone who wouldn't take medication for a mental illness...

Booming thunder echoed around them. She glanced to the right. "We can duck in the House of Mirrors. It's about to rain."

"No. Why don't we head back?"

"Look how dark it's become. I doubt we'll make it back to the car or even the carousel."

"I don't like the House of Mirrors," Jake said. Everything about his body language told her to back off. His posture stiffened. His smile vanished. He'd shifted from casual to strictly business.

"We can try, see how far we can get without getting caught in a downpour," Amanda said.

As if to argue, the spongy dark clouds released their wrath in that instant. Torrential rain pounded them like tiny arrows, splattered against the ground, and bounced from the impact.

"Not worth it. Let's do the House of Mirrors!" Jake yelled.

He grabbed her hand and ran inside, their clothes dripping from the sudden monsoon. Amanda wrapped her long hair, now heavy with the wet weight, in a rubber band behind her head.

"You okay?" Jake asked. He shook his head, and droplets of water fell from his hair.

"Fine." She glanced around at their surroundings. At least they were out of the rainstorm for a few minutes.

The House of Mirrors had ornate gold-leaf frames lining every wall. Each mirror showed distorted images. One turned her squatty and fat. Another, tall and powerful like an Amazon woman. She laughed as she walked between the two mirrors.

Jake gripped her hand. "Stop playing around. As soon as the storm clears, we need to get back to our priorities."

The tone in his voice reminded her of the strict schoolteachers she'd known as a kid. For some reason, Jake had passed his comfort zone.

"Why don't you like it here?"

He said nothing.

"Didn't you ever go into a House of Mirrors when you were a kid?"

He stared at her. "No."

Now he'd piqued her curiosity. Why would anyone have such visible animosity for a carnival ride? For someone so logical, Jake didn't make sense.

"Why not?"

He glanced outside, where the pounding rain continued to fall across the boardwalk, washing away debris like a giant Zamboni.

"We have time until the rain stops," she said.

Time to finish this conversation. Learn why he had such a deep-seated resentment for the supernatural or anything that manipulated people into denying logic. Maybe this rainstorm had been the sign she'd been waiting for, the chance to get answers.

"The roller coaster is one thing," he said. "Bolts, wheels, velocity, and motion. Concepts I respect and understand." He stood rigid, fists clenched.

"And the House of Mirrors isn't?"

"The House of Mirrors is nothing but trickery," Jake said.

"Tell me why."

"Why what?"

"I know you said your mom was schizophrenic, but what does that have to do with the House of Mirrors?" She leaned against the rail, attempting to relax even as he tensed.

He stared at her a long time before answering. "The rest of the place is just a showy manipulation. A way for charlatans to exploit people's imagination and need for entertainment."

"What's wrong with entertainment?"

"Nothing, as long as no one gets hurt."

Out of the corner of her eye, she noticed the mirror reflecting where she and Jake stood. This one had turned her into a squiggly figure with a giant head. His reflection made him appear like a miniature human. Or, more appropriately, a little boy.

His ambiguous answer begged the question. Finally, she decided to ask it.

"Did *you* get hurt?"

He peered outside. "I think the rain is beginning to let up."

"No, not yet. C'mon, Jake. Tell me why you have such a disdain for anything except the roller coaster."

"That's not fair. I like the carousel."

She smiled. "Okay, except the roller coaster and the carousel."

Shrugging, he said, "I guess I don't like anything that takes advantage of people with trusting personalities. The House of Mirrors isn't real. It cons people into paying money to see themselves in squiggly lines."

His words sounded like a foreign language. Why would anyone have a problem with things that were fun? If he didn't want to pay money for something, why be angry at someone else who wanted to enjoy the experience? Something deeper was going on here.

"People like to be entertained," she said. "What's wrong if they are fine with paying admission for the circus, the amusement park, whatever? I still don't understand."

Once again, he looked out at the pouring rain. "The weather never has been on my side."

She smiled, knowing full well that nature had her own agenda.

"Remember when I told you my mom was ill?" he asked, clasping her hand in his.

"Yes."

"Well, the part I didn't mention happened close to her death."

Amanda clasped his hand tighter to offer support. "What happened?"

"Some charlatans came through town. Promised all-natural healing, for a price. Everyone knows you can't cure cancer with snake oil, but Dad paid every cent. He abandoned all logic, all reason, to keep my mother alive for even one more day. The schizophrenia grew worse, and she was in pain."

"I'm sorry."

"Me too. Most of the money those con artists swindled was for my dad's retirement and my college education."

"What?"

He squeezed her hand before releasing it. "Yep. All their savings, Dad's reward for decades of hard work, and my future. My dad poured it down the guzzling drain to heal my mom. All so those damn charlatans could make money and head to the next town of suckers."

At a loss for words, Amanda stared at the ground for a long minute. Everything made more sense now. His disrespect for anything supernatural or what he called hokum. His lack of empathy when she showed faith in something. His following a career based on logic and reason.

"I'm so sorry that happened to you," she whispered.

"Yeah, well, I wound up getting loans for school. Still paying them off. That's why this department promotion will really help."

"I thought your paper was your way of staying on track for tenure."

"It is, but any raise will help lower my debt in the meantime. And no matter what, at least I know that you and I are different. We won't be fooled by the supernatural, by the con artists." He reached for her and hugged her close. "That's why I want you to see someone when we get home, if stress causes you do see things that you might not see otherwise."

She bit her lip as she hugged him back. Now, more than ever, she would need to make sure Jake never learned about her ability.

CHAPTER TWENTY

Declan held up his hands to quiet down the crowd of souls. "Hold it. One at a time, please."

"When can we leave this place?" Opal said, firm hands on her hips like always. "I thought the reason you showed up was to help us."

"True, but we need Amanda—"

"I thought you went to see her this morning," Chester said in a deep voice. He stepped to the front of the crowd. "We assumed you and her were square. So where do we stand?"

Declan cleared the back of his throat. He knew this gathering would not go well, but he had to manage the outcome.

"Things are progressing," he said. "And look good."

"What does that mean?" Andrew said. He stood shorter to Chester, kind of the mini-me of being the boss man.

"I need to speak to you and Chester privately for a few minutes. Other than that, we are giving Amanda today by herself—"

"You're doing what?" Opal bellowed.

"This is complicated, ma'am."

"To hell it is. We can't afford to sit around one more day. If you won't force that girl's hand, I will."

Others rumbled and mumbled their approval. Great. Opal leading the mob scene. Not how he wanted things to go.

"Listen, this is delicate. Trust me. I've dealt with these situations before. We can't force the gifted individual's hand. She's close. Tomorrow we will get our answers, and today I will speak to

Chester and Andrew for more information."

Opal shook her head. "If we don't get out of here soon, that girl will leave. Then how long will it be before another gifted human stops by Abandon, Alabama? Try never."

"I assure you—"

"Don't," Opal said. "Don't assure anything. Just get that girl to hurry up." She turned away, disgusted, muttering something about how she should have spoken up yesterday when she'd seen Amanda with Pearl...

"I will," he said, mainly to appease her. He hoped she wouldn't do anything stupid like taunt Amanda. Then Amanda really would leave and never come back.

"Chester and Andrew, please meet me over here by the picnic area. I have some questions for you both. Everyone else, remain calm."

Mumbles across the crowd again. Frowns all around. Declan took a deep breath. When would this assignment would be over? That day couldn't come soon enough.

* * *

Declan sat across from both company partners, studying their demeanor as well as their responses.

"You both need to come clean about your business practices. Did you use inferior equipment to save a buck?"

"Of course not," Chester said with the smooth, traveling-salesman voice.

"Any information I can give Amanda will help everyone be able to leave. You're dead. This isn't a trial. You won't be fined or arrested for any fraudulent or less-than-ethical actions."

Not right now anyway. Declan didn't say the last words out loud. Bottom line, everyone answered for their deeds after death, but these two corporate guys would find that out soon enough. Right now, better to use honey than vinegar to garner information.

"Well?" he prompted.

Both men stared at each other, each seeming to want the other to speak first. Declan didn't have time for this crap.

"Chester, did you use inferior equipment?"

Chester scratched his chin. "Every amusement park costs a ton of money. We only cut corners where there was no danger to the public—"

"Stop." Declan rolled his eyes. "I didn't ask you for the Miss America speech or what you told your stockholders. Tell me the truth."

He glanced at Andrew, who had a more honest face. "Anything you want to say?"

Andrew shrugged. "I'll admit, we considered using lower-grade bolts for the upstop wheels."

"Did you?"

"No. One of our employees found out."

"Good. Now we're getting somewhere," Declan said. "Who was that employee? Is he or she here?"

"Randall Kern," Chester said as if uttering the most grotesque word in the English language. He said it with the same tone as "regurgitate."

"Where is Randall now?"

Chester looked away. Andrew shrugged. "He's probably still alive, living in town. He always said he'd never leave this area of Alabama."

"What happened when he found out about the bolts? Did he bribe or threaten you?"

With a sneering glare, Chester said, "No. That little pissant could never have taken on our company."

"So what happened?"

Andrew clasped his hands together on the table. "Randall went crazy. Said we couldn't use those bolts. Told us he'd go to the press if we didn't change them back to his original specs."

"And did you?"

"No," Chester spat. "My grandfather built this company, and I was not about to let some redneck ruin its reputation."

Declan sighed. "I know I'm going to regret asking this, but what did you do?"

Chester's icy glare spoke volumes. "We fired him."

"You what?"

Andrew quickly added, "To be fair, Randall had other performance issues."

Declan studied both of these men. One preppy and greedy, the other kind of second fiddle and needing attention. A match made in hell.

"Tell me what happened. Did you use the subpar equipment

after you fired him?"

"No." Chester cleared his throat. "After we axed Randall, he sued us. Dragged us all into a legal and paperwork mess. We had to show good intent, so we ordered only the best bolts for our coaster. At a financial loss."

"The bolts didn't cause the derailment."

"No," Andrew answered, a proud smile on his face.

Declan shook his head. He didn't trust these bastards for a second. "How did the lawsuit end?"

"We won, of course," Chester said. "Randall received the blame for everything. We even managed to pin the ordering subpar bolts on him and his lack of performance."

Declan narrowed his eyes. "It never occurred to you that he might seek revenge for ruining his career?"

"Our firm's stock went up by fifty cents a share," Andrew added. "Well, I'm guessing, until the derailment."

"Gentlemen," Declan began, albeit using the term loosely, "you smeared this man's reputation, and you fired and belittled him in the public eye. Haven't you ever heard the phrase 'don't poke at a hornet's nest'?"

Chester laughed. "That stupid jerk wouldn't have the nerve to kill us. Besides, my guys were in place by the coaster the day of the ride. Randall was nowhere nearby."

"Then how is he a witness to the derailment?"

Andrew and Chester exchanged glances before Andrew spoke. "He lives right near the park. Probably saw and heard the accident from his front lawn."

Declan tried to organize his thoughts. Greed, jealousy, betrayal. The big three motives for murder. These two corporate clones seemed to think they were above such things. Morons.

"Andrew, do you think Randall could have sabotaged the coaster?"

"Randall is a strange one, but I can't see him wanting to hurt anyone. He'd never hurt women and children."

Declan's eyes widened. "But the original debut roller coaster ride was supposed to only be the two of you in the front car, according to what you told me earlier."

That did it. Got their attention. Chester's eyes grew dark. Andrew's mouth formed an *O*.

"You two are a piece of work," Declan said. He stood up, what semblance of a ghost pulse he had remaining racing at top speed. "You're so focused on promos and money that you admit your intention of bringing harm to the public to save a buck. Seems to me, Randall uncovering your intent makes him the good guy. Except you two fired him, then ruined his life in open court. Lord knows what the man could've done."

Chester folded his arms across his chest. Andrew's eyes reeled with the possibilities as the color drained from his already-pale face.

"If my boss wouldn't kick my ass to Idaho," Declan said, "I'd like to deck both of you in the jaw right now. I don't know if this Randall character tried to kill you or not, but it seems to me you both handed him a great motive for revenge on a silver platter."

CHAPTER TWENTY-ONE

Amanda peered out the exit to the House of Mirrors. To her horror, the exit was a gigantic clown's mouth. In the monsoon, she hadn't noticed. With the rain now a fine mist, she cringed as she pressed her hand against dark crimson lips of a creepy clown.

"Let's hurry back to the car."

Jake scanned the clouds, the park surroundings. "We should return to the library, research that lawsuit Mary told us about."

Amanda's breath caught in her throat. The library? Where her aunt Anzhela had appeared last time, unnerving her as always with tidbits of wisdom about self-acceptance?

"I'm sure the Internet will have some info. Why don't we head over to the Abandon Inn?"

He stepped out into the gray misty air. "C'mon. We didn't come here to spend all our time at the hotel."

"But you're fine spending it at the library?"

The second the words left her lips, she knew how idiotic she sounded. But what other way could she prevent them from returning? That was one trait about Jake—once he had his mind made up, he became the stubborn one.

"What is it with you and the library?" he asked, holding out his hands to check the rain. "C'mon. It's fine."

She stepped out, escaping the clown's mouth only get into Jake's car and head to another uncomfortable place—the library.

Ten minutes later, dreading what might be inside, she asked, "Where should we search for the lawsuit records? They have the

Internet in libraries—"

"They also have librarians," he said with a smile.

"Right." Like there was any chance she could forget such a fact. Okay. Deep breath.

He pulled open the library door and held it for her. She walked inside and immediately scanned the room to see if Aunt Anzhela was nearby. Nothing so far, just a gray-haired woman behind the desk. Maybe Aunt Anzhela wasn't around today?

"It's a new woman," Jake whispered. "I'm sure she can help us though."

Amanda followed his beeline sprint to the desk. While he asked where lawsuit and local legal notices would be kept, she scanned the back area to check for signs of anyone else. The graying woman appeared to be the only one there. Whew.

"Right over there against the wall, sir," the librarian said with a pointing wrinkled finger.

"Thanks, ma'am." Jake turned to Amanda and beamed. "Let's go check it out."

Each time she passed a bookshelf with no sign of her aunt, she felt like she'd accomplished something major. Like getting a first down at a football game. Not down the field yet, but there was hope. There was always—

"Hello there. I see y'all have returned."

Crap.

Jake paused in his trek and smiled. "Nice to see you again, ma'am. I was expecting to find you at the front desk."

Amanda stared at her feet. She knew her aunt's voice. She'd sung lullabies to Amanda as a child. She'd prodded her niece to acknowledge her gift. She wouldn't leave Amanda alone about telling Jake the truth… Oh yes, her voice was annoyingly familiar.

"Thank you, young man," Anzhela said. "And your lady friend is with you today too."

Jake bumped Amanda's elbow, urging her to say hello. Like a kid prodded to say thank you and please.

"Hi," Amanda said with a knowing glance. *Why are you here?*

Able to decipher any cryptic message, Anzhela casually mentioned, "They have me at the legal desk today so Rosella could be up front. Anything in particular you two are looking for?"

"The lawsuit that Randall Kern filed against Bello and Toale," Amanda said. "I think the man is guilty of sabotaging the roller coaster that killed those people."

"Amanda!" Jake said, eyes narrowed. His judging tone didn't even register on her emotional meter. Right now she only hoped her aunt wouldn't spill the beans about their family.

"What? I think the man has something to hide."

With a quick glare, Jake turned to her aunt. "Ma'am, I'm sorry for my friend here and her superstitions. We simply want to do research."

"You know what they say," Anzhela said. "Superstitions got their origins from a kernel of truth."

"Be that as it may, can we see the file?" Amanda said. *Be quiet, Aunt Anzhela. Don't ruin things for me and Jake.*

Anzhela reached out and tied the blue scarf around her auburn curls tighter. "To answer your question, however, those legal papers are right here." She handed him a file folder about three inches thick. The papers were barely holding on to the metal clips that bound them to the file. "I found quite a bit more information after your last visit that I thought you might find helpful."

"Wow. That's a lot of info," Jake said.

"Yes. Quite the big case here in Abandon many years ago."

Her aunt shot Amanda a discerning glance.

"Yes," Amanda said. "Jake, why don't you start in on the file? I'll see if there are more legal notices here." That was pretty flimsy, as that file was thick, and she didn't even know what was in it. But he fell for it.

His eyes were already gleaming from the analysis work to be done on the files. An engineer in hog heaven. Analyzing something from every angle. That would at least keep him busy.

When he pulled out a chair at a far wall table, Amanda turned to her aunt. "What are you doing? Keeping tabs on me?"

Anzhela only glanced up with those big and knowing eyes. "Someone needs to, dear."

"I appreciate your concern, but I need you to keep your mouth shut where Jake is concerned. He doesn't understand gifts like we have. His mother was schizophrenic. I don't want him to continue to think I am mentally ill."

"There's a difference between the mind being ill and the mind using the talents given to it," she said. "Until you tell him, he's falling in love with a facade."

Amanda's face flushed hot. "You think he's falling in love with me?"

With a stern cocked eyebrow mastered over the years, Anzhela said, "Yes. You need to make sure you put your gifts and talents to good use. That comes first, before your supposed love interest."

Supposed? Amanda clenched her fists into tiny balls. "Is that why you sent Declan to bother me? To insist I help spirits who have nothing to do with my life?"

Anzhela smiled. "I don't *send* Declan anywhere. He reports to forces higher than me."

What higher forces? She wondered for a minute before responding.

"He keeps quoting the same old lines you do."

"Maybe you should take the hints the Universe is giving you." Anzhela lowered her voice. "Do you know how complex some of my situations were when I was a girl? At least your boyfriend has a similar interest in finding out what happened to those people. You can tag along and do this job for Declan in your sleep."

"I need to focus on my work."

"Yes, you do."

Groaning, Amanda said, "No, I didn't mean supernatural work. I meant my carousel work. That apprenticeship is the chance for me to get an artistic career—my dream. Right now I'm a glorified secretary, and I hate it."

"Yes." Her aunt's Southern drawl gave the one-syllable word at least three. "Isn't it interesting that doing something you love often fits with what you're meant to do?"

"Argh! You're impossible." Amanda turned, looking at Jake to make sure he didn't have eavesdropping radar.

"Listen to me," Anzhela said. "Our gifted kind doesn't get the luxury of saying no to those beings who need us. We were blessed with these talents for a reason. Whether you accept yourself and your gift is up to you, but you can't turn your back on your duty to others."

"I'm fine dealing with this gift so long as I can keep it to myself. Jake never needs to know."

Her aunt's long stare pierced into Amanda's heart.

"Sooner or later, you need to give your young man a chance to accept you. All of you."

Amanda crossed her arms over her chest. "I'm not ready."

"Fair enough, but remember everything is connected. Maybe using your gift to help Declan—who is a great man, by the way—and helping Jake with his research is also a way to help yourself. Did you ever consider that? By using this ability you hate so much, you can help yourself?"

Amanda thought for a long moment. If what Anzhela said was true, then a decent future was possible. But what if it wasn't? History was filled with stories of those individuals who could never accept anything different. And Jake had already made it clear he despised supernatural "hokum."

The way to survive had *always* been to blend in, not stand out.

CHAPTER TWENTY-TWO

Jake paged through the thick legalese documents that comprised the Randall Kern lawsuit. There was enough reading material for a decade.

"Hey, find anything?" Amanda asked, taking a seat across from him.

"Where have you been?"

Her throat turned red. "Just…talking."

He narrowed his eyes. "To the librarian you don't admit to being chatty with?"

"She said this lawsuit was the gossip of the community when it happened. After you review the file details, we should go back to Mary Galden's house, talk to her."

"Good idea." He passed fifty pages across the table. "Start reading these. Anything about Randall Kern getting fired or the company claiming fraudulent or subpar equipment policies is of interest."

"Um, sure."

Minutes ticked by, the silent hum of the air-conditioning providing the only sound besides Amanda's slow breathing.

"Man, they really screwed Randall over," he said. "The guy had a bright future, great opportunities."

"Yeah?"

He nodded. "Until the execs at this company, Bello and Toale, fired him. They accused him of swapping out required standard materials and trying to embezzle the money saved." Jake shook his head. "Poor guy."

His hero. The father of roller coaster design. And these bastards ruined him. No wonder the guy became a freaky recluse. If the engineering department at UGA conspired to ruin Jake's reputation, he wouldn't have a chance. People in academia had elephant memory. No way would he survive even a false accusation.

Surely the company that fired Randall had falsely accused him. No way would any self-respecting engineer create something that would harm people. Not deliberately.

Amanda snuck her hand across the table, reached for his. "You want to go see Randall again, don't you?"

Jake shrugged. "Is it that obvious?"

"Like I said, Jake Mercer. You're an open book."

He smiled and lifted her hand to his mouth and kissed it. "I wish I could read you as easily as you seem to read me."

She lowered her gaze. "I'm complicated."

"You're a challenge, Amanda Moss. A challenge."

* * *

Jake placed the pertinent copies he'd made of the Randall Kern lawsuit in the backseat of his Honda Civic.

"You have everything you need? We should spend more time at Zephyr Land and interviewing witnesses so we don't have to return to the library," Amanda said. She'd used her factual voice, one he only heard on rare occasions.

He slid into the driver's seat and started the ignition. "Are you ever going to tell me what you have against this place?"

Her hazel eyes glanced away before returning to meet his gaze. "Nothing. We just need to keep our focus."

"What about your carousel project?" he asked. "How come you're talking to me about focus?"

"Fair enough."

Her lips drew into a tight line, with one edge of her mouth curled upward. She was pretending to be upset, but that little upswing told him she wasn't truly angry. Just playing.

He drove out of the parking lot, keeping his gaze on the road to Mary Galden's place. "I'm only saying you have a problem with that gypsy-looking librarian, and I'd like to know why."

Amanda sighed loud enough to wake the possums dangling from nearby trees on either side of the highway.

"Can we just say I would rather we do our own research? Leave it at that?"

"No. Not this time. You've always been mysterious. I usually like it."

She put one leg under her other one and sat watching him as they drove. "But not now."

"Exactly."

Was she beginning to see his point of view, or was he imagining things again? One thing he'd learned: most women didn't make sense. That's what he loved about Amanda when she wasn't in her superstitious moods. She did make sense.

She opened her mouth as if to speak, but kept quiet. Time to get to the bottom of this.

He pulled off the main road into a widened side lane and parked.

"I feel like you're lying to me when you're this mysterious."

She turned in surprise, her black pupils growing big. "Lying? That isn't my intention."

Leaning back, he got comfortable. Obviously this conversation would take a few minutes.

"Back in Athens, you're carefree, fun, full of life. More than that," he said, "you're a smart woman who's honest with me. Since we came here, you seem to be keeping secrets."

Her lower lip tucked under her upper one, and she flexed her jaw muscles.

"I don't want to pressure you, but don't you think we should be open with each other? I don't understand what's so secretive about a librarian—"

"She's my aunt." Amanda gave a simple smile, one of happy resignation.

He opened his mouth to speak—nothing came out. He'd expected any number of her odd explanations, but saying the woman had been a relative? Not one of his top ten.

"Okay. Then why not introduce her as such?"

With a sigh, Amanda ran her hands through her wiry curls and pulled her hair back.

"Aunt Anzhela and I...we're...different. There are things about us I don't want you—or anyone—to know. And trust me—she's the type to spill the beans to strangers."

"Then why be so secretive? Your explanation makes logical

sense. We all have skeletons in the closet, along with those family members who are excessively talkative. Why not just tell me?"

"I'm trying," she whispered. "But anytime she and I were alone, she'd start in on the lectures and things I should be doing with my life—"

"Ah. One of *those* aunts. I know the kind."

Her cheeks flushed pink, and she smiled at him. "Yes. I'm sorry I didn't tell you. You were so interested in talking to her, and I was worried she'd tell you things about us that you wouldn't like—"

"Amanda."

She kept her gaze on the floor.

"Look at me," he said gently.

Slowly, she lifted those beautiful greenish pools with the black eyelashes. "Yes?"

Reaching for her hand, he took it and squeezed. "There may be things I don't understand about you, but I like everything."

She sniffled. Eyes brimming with tears. No. No. Don't cry.

"I'm sorry...for lying...for not telling you the truth..." Her voice trailed off with her quiet sobbing.

Dear lord, don't cry.

"It's okay. We're fine, all right?"

She nodded quickly.

"Thanks for telling me about your aunt. We have enough info from the files. We won't return to the library unless you want to. Okay?"

She beamed at him, her pink cheeks dripping with tears.

"Thanks."

"You ready to go interview Mary again? Get some details?"

"Yes."

"Good." He adjusted his rearview mirror. "And afterward, I want you to focus on your project. Don't let my paper overshadow the work you need to be doing."

With a half smile, she said, "Will do."

Great. He'd had a breakthrough with her. Now they could both forge ahead. Logic would be their arsenal, not superstition.

CHAPTER TWENTY-THREE

Amanda wiped away the rogue tears streaming from her eyes. Stupid. She'd been an idiot to seem mysterious about Aunt Anzhela. Then she'd been a bigger idiot to try and hide everything.

Jake was a genius. Of course he would figure something was awry. At least her explanation—completely true—had made sense to his logical mind. Why hadn't she thought of telling him that basic fact sooner? Would have saved heaps of worry.

He pulled into Mary Galden's driveway. The gravel stones crunched under the tires, reminding her of the many rural places she and her aunt had lived during the summers.

Amanda couldn't remember spending even one summer with her parents. Seemed the moment school let out, they shipped her off to her aunt's to satisfy their own need to be normal and respected in the community. At least those summer memories with Aunt Anzhela had been happy, providing the much-needed time away from parents who never understood her.

"Let me do the talking," Jake said, knocking her out of her reminiscing.

"Sure."

This time, she meant it. From now on, she would listen. Garner information. Bring it to Declan. Let him do some of the heavy lifting where investigative talents were concerned.

Mary opened the door, though this time confusion reeled in her eyes. "Hello, again?"

"Sorry to bug you," Jake said. "We were able to do some

research on the lawsuit and had a few follow-up questions for you."

Amanda studied Mary's face. Something about it. Was she afraid? Nervous? Last time, she'd been relaxed and welcoming. This time, she seemed—what was the word—paranoid.

"This isn't the best time," Mary said, her voice an octave higher.

"Oh, I'm sorry ma'am." Jake glanced at his watch. "When would be a good time to come back?"

Mary peeked her head out of the doorway, darted her gaze left and right. "Oh, fine. Come in now. Quick."

Amanda stepped quickly behind Jake to get inside.

"Is everything okay?" she asked.

Mary walked over to the teapot. "I've received some weird phone calls lately. Since I talked to both of you."

"What kind of calls, ma'am?" Jake asked, his eyes narrowed and ready to take action.

She placed two cups of tea, along with a container of milk and sugar, on a silver tray and brought it into the living room.

"Help yourselves," Mary said.

Jake sat down, elbows on his knees, his posture hunched forward, ready for an answer.

"What type of calls?" he repeated.

Mary shrugged. "Let's see. Hang ups, with no caller ID. Or a caller ID of a pharmacy, so I pick it up to see if it's about my prescriptions, but there's someone with a breathy voice on the other line saying I better keep quiet."

"Threats?"

"Yes." Mary inched the tea tray closer to Jake and Amanda, her shaking fingers almost toppling it off the table in the process.

"Whoa," Amanda said, steadying the tea tray. "We're fine, thank you. Just tell us what happened."

"The calls at all hours of night, someone rapping on my back door in the early morning—"

"Do you know or suspect anyone?" Jake asked. "Have you told the police?"

Mary's eyes turned dark as she shook her head. "During the lawsuit, the same things happened. I was the one who had the papers for our attorneys. I delivered them to the courthouse to file."

"Go on."

"Little things. Footsteps behind me in the parking deck, only to find no one was there. My tires were slashed one night." Mary paused, blinking back tears. "My house got ransacked. They took my mother's broach. All I had left of her memory."

"I'm sorry, ma'am," Jake said. "Did the police tell you anything when you did speak with them?"

Amanda stood up, went to Mary's side, and patted her hand. "You must be frightened to talk to any strangers like us. We're sorry if we put you in this position."

Jake glanced at her, his eyebrow raised for a moment as if trying to figure out her strategy. This was her talent. She knew people and emotions. He knew logic and reason. Mary seemed to need the former.

"The cops didn't find anything," Mary said. "They told me it must be neighbor kids playing a joke."

Amanda knew better. The timing was no coincidence. Whoever had tried to shut Mary up must have had some connection to the lawsuit. But who? Which side? This recluse Randall guy? Or the company?

"Tell us about the day the lawsuit was resolved," Amanda said. "You said your firm won, meaning Randall Kern lost."

Mary nodded, reaching down to take a sip of tea.

"How did Randall take the news?" Jake asked.

"Not well. He started shouting in the courtroom. Saying he was innocent, the firm had been at fault, and he would eventually prove the truth."

Amanda sat forward. "What about after? Do you think those were just rants, or did he try suing again? Going to the press?"

"No," Mary said. "Actually, the opposite. He kept to himself, retired, went back to daily life. He occasionally volunteers for the fire department, but otherwise he became how he is now. An old man who wants to live alone. I've kind of adopted the don't-speak-until-spoken-to policy with him."

Someone with so much anger, living as a recluse, might justify trying to show how the firm was at fault.

"Do you think he'd talk to us again? I know he likes his privacy," Jake said.

Mary shook her head. "I wouldn't. He called me after y'all visited the first time, said it got him to thinking all about the accident. I don't know if he can go back to the dark place without crawling into a bottle again."

"He drank heavily?" Jake asked.

"Wouldn't you?"

Jake nodded. "If something ruined my career, yes, ma'am, I believe I would."

Amanda poured another cup of tea for Mary. "Have there been any problems since the news about the lawsuit died down?"

"No. Randall went back to living a quiet life. Our firm closed after the execs were killed on the roller coaster. I wound up doing administrative work for the local bank branch until last year, when I decided to retire."

"If you think of anything else," Jake said, "please call us at the Abandon Inn. Do you need the number?"

Mary glanced up and smiled. "Only hotel in a small town? No, I know Pearl. She's in my sewing circle."

"Thanks again for speaking to us," Amanda said, giving Jake the "let's get out of here" glance. They didn't need to make Mary any antsier than she already was.

When they stepped out her door, five locks clicked into place with loud noises. "She's frightened, Jake. Should we be?"

He turned to face her. "Us? Why?"

"Someone got to her between our last visit and today. This is a small town. Everyone must know we're studying the derailment at Zephyr Land. You heard her. The Abandon Inn is the only hotel in town. What if the derailment was sabotage? If the person who did it is still living here and comes after us?"

"Don't get paranoid on me," he said. "We have permission to be here, and we're going to stay until we get enough info for me to defend a theory in my position paper."

He opened her car door, let her in, and walked around the back of the car to enter on his side. Before he did, she let out a soft whisper, "Just because I'm paranoid doesn't mean someone isn't really after us."

CHAPTER TWENTY-FOUR

Randall's jaw clenched. He ducked behind a thick curtain, getting out of those kids' line of sight. What the hell did they want with Mary? Asking more questions about the derailment? About him?

No. That guy Jake was all about hero worship, a real fan of his past accomplishments. But he didn't trust the blonde. Amanda? That witchy one—he'd seen green eyes like hers before. Eyes that knew things.

She might discover what really happened at Zephyr Land that day. He wasn't about to let that happen.

Catfish padded his way over and stood by Randall's side. "Good boy. Don't let us be seen."

The dog snuffled and kept a steady panting rhythm. That was the thing about dogs. They never betrayed. Not like those bastards at the company.

Once the Civic left Mary's driveway, Randall put on his working boots. Laced them up. He poured some dog food for Catfish and then walked to Mary's house.

"Who is it?" a timid voice asked.

"Randall Kern."

Silence.

"Mary, I know you're in there. C'mon now. Open up."

Slowly, she pulled the door open. "What can I do for you? You out of grits again?"

He leaned one hand against her doorframe. "Nah, I got plenty of corn grits. Enough to last six months."

"Stocking up for winter?"

"Yeah." He cleared his throat. "I don't mean to push into your business, but I couldn't help but notice the strange car in your driveway earlier. I wanted to make sure you were okay."

She crossed her arms in front of her chest, holding on to her arms like bracing against a cold wind. "Oh, that was Jake and Amanda. I'm fine. They were just asking questions about the firm, the coaster. I think Jake is writing some paper for academic purposes."

"Yeah, about that…"

"What?"

"These two youngsters. They show up out of nowhere. Jake claims to have followed my career. He knew most of the highlights. All of a sudden, they're interested in the derailment, and they want to know more?"

"That's right. I think he's working on a paper for his college department, and she's doing a study on the carousel."

Randall took a deep breath. How could he get Mary to see his side of things? This had to be done carefully.

"Would you mind if we visited for a little bit? My back is killing me from lifting heavy equipment in the yard."

Her mouth twitched, but she opened the door wider. "For a few minutes, sure."

"Much obliged." He hobbled in for effect and sat in the corner chair of the front room.

"Want some lemonade or tea?"

"No, no, thank you." He situated a small couch cushion against his lower back. "As I was saying, those kids came knocking on my door. But we're a small town. We've never seen these two before. How do we know they are who they say?"

"Why wouldn't they be?" Mary asked, ever the naïve Southern lady.

"I'm not casting false words on them," he said, keeping his accent slow and Southern. "But we need to be careful, Mary. What if they're reporters? What if they represent some grandson of Chester and Andrew, here to get more money?"

Mary waved a dismissive hand. "Oh, Randall. You're being paranoid."

"I think we should just make sure they have a right to be here. Jake told me he had permission to go into Zephyr Land. But how does a twenty-something guy get access to a park that's been closed off for a decade? Don't you think something is suspicious?"

She shrugged. "What do you think we should do?"

"Maybe get the sheriff to check it out? Ask them for their permission papers to get into the park, at least?"

"I don't know. They seem like such sweet kids—"

"Doesn't mean they won't jump at the chance to ruin this town with reporters, false accusations. You don't want more people burdening you with questions about the derailment, do you?"

She nodded. "You're right on that. Someone's been crank calling me. No caller ID so I can't find out who."

"I've experienced the same thing. One thing is for certain—the strange occurrences began when those two arrived in Abandon."

"What do you want me to do? Call the sheriff? I don't know that he'll find anything."

"You know no one trusts me in this town anymore," Randall said. "You're one of the few people who continue to speak to me."

"I was brought up to see the good in everyone," she whispered.

"Good Christian woman," he said. "Right now, I'm asking that you use your head and keep this area safe. The sheriff won't take anything I say seriously, but he'll listen to you."

"If you think it best," Mary said. "But I'm going to call the nonemergency line. I don't think being suspicious of two youngsters is worthy of calling 9-1-1."

"However you see fit."

Randall smiled. Mission accomplished. Time to find out what Jake and Amanda were really doing in the town of Abandon, Alabama.

CHAPTER TWENTY-FIVE

Amanda stared out at the highway in front of them. "Are we going back to Zephyr Land?"

Jake kept a steady gaze on the road. "Yep. Unless you think we should hire some personal bodyguards or something."

She socked him in the arm. "Hey, I'm only trying to keep us safe. You have to admit. A creepy abandoned amusement park. A woman who seems scared for no reason, over something that happened ten years ago."

"I don't call that anything but what it is. Coincidence."

Glancing out the passenger window, she bit her lip. Some things weren't worth arguing over. Especially when there would be no winning side, not with Jake. One sacrifice for having what she wanted—a normal relationship. With this man. The one who understood and listened to her more than any other boyfriend had.

The minutes ticked by, along with the miles.

"I'm tired," Amanda said. "And it's late. Can we go back to the inn? Catch up on our research and return to Zephyr Land tomorrow?"

Jake shrugged. "I can always use time to type up my notes, but didn't you want to get in a few hours of analyzing the carousel?"

Right. The carousel. A reason she had come on this trip with Jake to begin with.

Time to get some career focus. Ever since the ghosts showed up and the derailment news had rattled her mind, her goal of changing her career had taken a backseat. Why couldn't her gift keep its nose out of her career plans? Instead, the two seemed to be in a perpetual war.

"Good idea, but let's grab something to eat at the inn first," she said. "Then we can see the park at sunset."

"Now you're talking."

* * *

An hour later when Amanda and Jake returned to the park, the large pink sun began its descent behind the cypress trees. Tiny glints of light poked through the web of Spanish moss dangling from the oaks.

"Look at this," Jake said, moving about ten paces to his right. "Check out the silhouette of the roller coaster."

She moved closer to him, then saw the coiling track arch in silhouette against the sun. "Beautiful."

"Let's make sure everything is fine in the carousel tent, then I'll leave you to your work," he said. "I need to inspect the roller coaster cars."

A warm feeling surged through her. "You're concerned about me, eh?"

He squeezed her hand. "I am."

She squeezed back. "I think I like dating a Southern gentleman."

With a wink, he flashed her a charming smile. "Anyone would do the same. It's twilight. We should make sure there aren't any stray animals or trespassers in the tent."

Stray raccoons weren't her concern. Declan and a mob of impatient ghosts, however? Definitely.

Jake yanked open the flaps to the carousel tent. Three crows whooshed past, barely inches above his head.

"What the—"

"Just birds needing shelter from the rain earlier," Amanda said, surprised at her own voice of reason. That's when she spotted Declan sitting on the ostrich carousel piece, waiting for her.

Jake dusted himself off while Declan said, "We need to talk."

She turned away. Was not going to have two conversations at once again.

"I think the place is secure," she said. "You'll be near the roller coaster car shed?"

"Yeah. I'll use my cell phone as a camera tonight, but if I find anything that needs macro ultra-close-up shots, can I borrow your camera tomorrow?"

"No problem."

Once he left, she let out a deep breath. "Declan. What are you doing here?"

He leapt off the ostrich like it was a real animal he'd tamed in some rugged terrain. Who knows? Maybe before coming to bother her, he used to talk to other gifted people in the outback.

"The natives are restless," he said with a smile. "I need your help. I know you want to deny your gift—"

"Only in front of Jake." She peered out the flaps and ensured Jake had walked away. "But yes, with the research he's doing, I am helping." She propped herself against the side of the carousel, looking up at Declan.

"I talked to Chester and Andrew, the two execs from Bello and Toale. They admit that Randall Kern might have had the motive to kill them." Declan looked down from his stance near the ostrich.

"I'm suspicious of Randall myself," Amanda said. "But we don't have any proof. Jake scoured the library, researched the lawsuit. Randall had his life ruined by those guys, but there's no evidence that he sabotaged the ride. He didn't even step foot back onto company property once the lawsuit ended."

"But the cops questioned him as a witness to the derailment."

"Only because he lives near the park," she said. "We went to see him—"

"You what?" Declan's eyes darkened. Amanda didn't even know ghosts' eyes could darken. "You talked with him?"

"I thought you wanted me to bring these ghosts' killer to justice. Of course we talked with him. Jake wanted to meet him for his reputation alone, and I figured I could make heads or tails as to whether he was guilty."

"And?"

"I think he's guilty, but that's just intuition. Something tells me he didn't intend for things to happen the way they did, but I'm fairly sure he is responsible."

Declan paced between the horses, ostriches, and the giant bear figurine on the carousel. "I do too, but you're right. We need proof for you to call the police."

"Why did those execs set him up, anyway? Not that I condone murdering your ex-boss, but Randall definitely has the biggest motive. I can't blame the guy for being angry at how they ruined him."

Declan smiled at her, put his hands in his pockets, and leaned against one of the flag horses. "You're preaching to the choir. Those guys are jerks. I'm trying to get all the info I can to help them reach their next realm so I can move on to my next job."

She tilted her head. "Tell me what the next realm is like. Are these two going to go off into the sunset, rewarded for the greed and lies they forged?"

"No. More like, they'll go through standard orientation and then become civil servants in the afterlife."

She laughed. "At least there's some justice in the world. Or, the world after."

"I hope so." His eyes stared into hers. "For Tweedle Dum and Tweedle Dee, as well as whoever hurt the women and children. Speaking of which, Becca made me promise—or should I say pinky swear—that you would say hello to Sarah and Pearl for her."

Amanda smiled at the words *pinky swear*. Some things were purely from a child's mind. "Sure. I'll manage to make some time alone in the lobby so I can talk to them."

Declan jumped off the carousel base and onto the ground. "Tell me something."

His gaze seemed so intent, she wondered what subject he would bring up. She braced for whatever it could be.

"What's that?" she asked.

"Why are you so intent on fitting in to a world, and with a guy, that doesn't know the real you?"

"Don't start—"

"I'm serious. How do you think this will end, Amanda? You might get the cops to arrest the killer, the ghosts and I will be gone, but then what? You return to your life and continue to ignore—worse, deny—that you have a talent given to so few?"

She closed her eyes tight.

"What are you doing?" Declan asked.

"Hoping that if I click my heels together, you'll disappear. Or at least stop talking."

"Ha-ha. Things could be worse. I could sing off tune for hours."

She opened her eyes and smiled at the persistent ghost. "I know you mean well, but I'm tired of people lecturing me about my gift. You, my aunt, random ghosts, even Pearl. Just let me be."

"I can't. Besides, Jake's not an idiot," Declan began. "One day, he's bound to find out. Some slip up. Don't you think it will be better for both of you to hear it from your lips? He expects you to get on medication and seek treatment, perhaps inpatient, for crying out loud. Don't let him convince you to do that."

"How do you know that about Jake?"

"I have ways of finding out information."

"Obviously." What other things did Declan know about?

"Trust me—you don't want to be in a psych ward. My sister spent time in one. I know what's in your future if you don't tell Jake the truth."

Amanda tried to imagine the horrors of a psych ward. The

regular world wasn't exactly accepting of the supernatural. But a mental institution? Talk about zero tolerance.

"I'm sorry to hear about your sister," she said.

Declan crossed his arms, his jaw tightening as he hissed out the words, "They stuck Brianna with needles, did shock therapy, and numerous other things not to be spoken of."

"Because she could see ghosts, like me?"

He stared off at one of the horse pieces. "Yes, though at the time she could only hear them. My parents were good people. They thought they were doing what was best for her, but—"

"But no one deserves that," Amanda said, reaching for his semitransparent hand. Coolness swept across her arm as she tried to hold him but couldn't.

"Not much contact between the dead and the living, not without prior permission," Declan said.

"From whom?"

Her aunt had told her there were numerous types of spirits walking the Earth at any given time. Ghosts, fairies, and others. Forces from good and evil. So who would give permission for things such as holding a hand?

"The powers that be," Declan said, declining to elaborate further. "My point, I don't want to see you wind up being overmedicated or put in a mental hospital."

Amanda nodded. "I appreciate your concern, but I'll be okay. Jake wants assurance I won't turn into his mother, that's all. I'll figure it out."

"How? You need to plan to tell him, Amanda. No matter what his reaction, he deserves to know the truth. The real you." Declan paused a moment. "We aren't the only ghosts who need your help."

His words sunk in slowly, set off alarm bells in her mind. "Wait a second. You told me that these ghosts would cross over if I helped you." She wanted to shake him. If only she could put her hands on his shoulders...

"I did."

"But now you're saying there are more jobs you need help with?"

Nausea pushed through her stomach. She choked back the urge to throw up as the dizziness washed over her.

"I'm saying you have the gift of helping the dead. Your aunt has the gift of moving place to place without being seen. Those gifts will need to be utilized throughout your lives. Jake may not like or understand how you can talk to the dead, but if you want a life with him..."

"Then he needs to accept me. That's what you were going to say, right?"

Declan's green eyes met her own. "Yes."

"Then I decide when to tell him. Not you, not Aunt Anzhela. Deal?"

He gave a half grin. "Agreed."

While his answer offered comfort, she wasn't so sure about the look in his eyes.

CHAPTER TWENTY-SIX

Jake shone his flashlight on the misshapen metal of the first derailed car on the roller coaster train. This would have been the car to take the hardest hits, based on the insurance investigation's reconstruction of the trajectory as the coaster flew off the tracks.

The critical bolt assemblies on all three wheel types had been bashed in from the derailment. He couldn't see any threads, no part of the shank or hexagonal bolt head. The head was where the grade markings were. If cheap equipment had been used, he would know once he could find a decent bolt to examine.

Checking the second car, he found the same result.

One of these damn cars had to have some evidence. Right?

He tried the third. The upstop wheels were missing some hardware, but the guide wheels on the side of the car had a few bolts intact. Taking out his cell, he snapped a few photos. He would need Amanda's macro lens for clearer images. Hell, he needed her, even if her behavior alarmed him lately. But he couldn't let his mind wander now...

On the road wheels, the hex head bolts looked like they'd survived the carnage. Perfect. This was his chance to determine the validity of the bolt. Not to mention the road wheels were the easiest to access since they were on the top. He wouldn't have to turn over any of the cars to analyze them. Not yet, anyway.

He rubbed his thumb over the steel head, wiping off dust and dirt. Numerous scratches and some flaky substance covered the hex head. Jake leaned in closer, needing to know the difference between existing markings and standard wear and tear.

Then he counted at least three markings. Sign of a Grade Five bolt, not up to standard for roller coasters. Would they really have been so stupid as to use cheap equipment?

He took the bottom edge of his T-shirt and rubbed and polished the bolt more. Ah. Now he could see there were six lines on the hex head. They had used Grade Eight Premium bolts and stainless steel safety wire. Whatever accusations had been made in the Randall Kern lawsuit, these bolts were premium grade, and the safety wire remained intact. No foul play on equipment.

Damn. What had caused the derailment? Looked like he needed to turn over the cars after all, get a closer look at the upstop wheels.

"Hey, anyone in there?" a loud voice bellowed.

Jake's breath caught in his throat. The voice had been male, definitely not Amanda's.

"Abandon County sheriff," the man said again. "Speak up if you're inside."

"Yes, sir," Jake said, keeping his voice as calm as he could. Why would the sheriff be here at this time of evening?

"Come out, please."

Jake snapped a few more photos of the proof of Grade Eight premium bolts, then stood up and slowly exited the car storage area.

A rotund man wearing a tan shirt and navy pants stood about ten feet away. Gripping Amanda's arm. Her pupils had dilated so much, the black had pushed away any sign of her hazel coloring.

Jake wanted to lunge. Reach out and teach this backwoods man to unhand Amanda. They weren't behaving in a threatening way. There was no need to put his hands on her.

The sheriff rested his other hand on his waist, near his night stick. Jake swallowed hard. As much as he liked the South, they were in a small town in Alabama. Some places didn't have the prettiest history. Maybe the best way out of this predicament was to offer respect and find out what the problem might be.

"Good evening, Officer. I'm Jake Mercer, and you're holding my girlfriend Amanda Moss's arm. What seems to be the problem?"

"Problem is, I've asked Ms. Moss for proof that you two are allowed to be in Zephyr Land. She can't seem to produce any, which means you're trespassing. How'd you get in here anyway?"

All of this because of suspicion of trespassing? Good lord, what did this state do to jaywalkers?

"We do have permission, Officer. A written letter from the law offices of Hunter and Reid. We were also given the key. They granted us permission to be here for the week."

The sheriff stared at Jake like he was an insect, one he'd like to pluck the feelers out of and burn under a microscope. "How 'bout you show me this so-called permission letter?"

Jake reached into his back pocket. No. God, no. Checked his backpack. Felt like he was in the hot sun getting his feelers burned off already. Yesterday, he forgot the binoculars but had the letter. Today, he remembered the binoculars but left the letter back at the inn?

"I seem to have left it at the Abandon Inn, where we're staying.

I have the key here though."

With indignation, the sheriff released Amanda's arm and strutted over to inspect the key. Amanda rubbed her arm with her other hand and grimaced.

"How do I know this isn't a copy you made? Maybe you broke in and stole the key to make a copy? Thought you'd spray some graffiti?"

Jake took a deep breath. Obviously, the sheriff did not trust outsiders.

"Sir, I assure you it's not a copy I made. We can call the law offices, if you wish. Or perhaps call Pearl at the inn, get her to find the documentation in our room?"

"We can get all that taken care of," the sheriff said.

For a minute, Jake breathed easier. Amanda's hazel eyes returned to their normal color.

"After I arrest you both for trespassing in the first degree," the sheriff added.

"What?" Jake and Amanda cried in unison. She moved toward Jake, and he pulled her into the circle of one arm. Earlier, he'd yelled at her royally for coming to the park by herself. Now she was going to jail because she was there with him!

"Call Pearl at the inn," Jake said. This was getting ridiculous!

"We aren't the phone company. You'll be able to call Pearl, your lawyer, the law offices, whoever you like once I bring you both in."

"Sir, this is ridiculous," Amanda said. "Please, can't you call the law offices?"

The guy looked at his watch. "It's after eight. No one's going to answer the phones. Don't worry—trespass in the first degree is a misdemeanor. If what you say is true, we'll get it all cleared up at the station."

Jake's mind reeled. Misdemeanor? That kind of thing didn't look good for eventual tenure, for any professor job he applied for going forward. Zephyr Land had become beneficial and horrible for his career in less than a week. Never mind what it was doing to his relationship with Amanda.

"I'm going to put zip-cuffs on both of you," the sheriff said. "And we'll straighten this out downtown. Worst case, you spend one night in the holding cell until we can confirm your story tomorrow."

"Jail?" Amanda repeated, her voice cracking.

"Hands behind your back," he ordered.

Jake stared, unable to say anything else. With every fiber in his being, he wanted to stop this situation. Everything seemed like a bad dream. If only he could pinch himself, he'd wake up.

But when the rotund sheriff zip-tied both their hands and put them in the back of his squad car, Jake knew this was no dream. It was a nightmare.

CHAPTER TWENTY-SEVEN

Amanda shuddered as the jail cell door slammed into the locked position, trapping her and Jake for the unforeseeable future. At least they were together, not in adjoining cages. One good thing about Abandon, Alabama. Not much room in the small-town jail.

Jake gripped the bars as if he could change their fate. She sat on the cot and buried her face in her hands.

If only they hadn't returned to Zephyr Land at sunset. Had they returned to the inn, she'd be giving Pearl and Sarah hello messages from Becca right now. Instead, she and Jake were stuck in a jail cell. For the night, at least.

"You okay?" she asked. His fingers had grown white from gripping the bars.

He turned halfway around, staring at the floor in her direction. "Fine. I just want to get us out of here."

"Me too, but it won't happen tonight."

He groaned, released the bars, and sat on the cot next to her. "I'm sorry about this. It was stupid of me to not have the letter from the lawyers in my possession every second—"

"Don't blame yourself. People forget things. It happens."

"Not to me." The fury in his gaze hadn't waivered.

"We'll get our phone call in the morning," she said. "The law offices *will* clear us, right?"

"Of course." He reached out, put his hand on her knee. "I'm sorry. I feel like a jerk with all this."

She'd never seen him with such self-loathing. Had he really gone his entire life without having made a serious mistake? That sense of nonfailure twenty-four seven had to be exhausting. Maybe more so than keeping secrets about ghost abilities.

"What happens tomorrow? Will we need bail?" she asked.

"If they confirm with the law office first thing, the charges will be dropped, and we'll be released. I doubt bail will be involved."

She nodded, grateful for one piece of good news. "My aunt can come get us, if we need it."

Jake flashed her a smile. "The crazy aunt who you don't want to see much? Nah, we'll be okay. Take a cab back to Zephyr Land. If we can get a few decent hours sleep, then tomorrow won't be a wasted day. We can continue working."

She nodded. "Did you make any progress on the roller coaster? Did the company use cheap equipment?"

His eyes brightened. "No. Many bolts were too banged up to inspect, but the ones I could see had premium markings on them. So subpar bolts didn't cause the derailment."

She glanced around the stark room. One cot, one ugly toilet that she didn't dare use. In simplicity, things had become clear.

"So Randall Kern might just be a disgruntled employee. He may not have sabotaged the roller coaster like we thought."

"Like *you* thought," Jake said.

She half smiled at him. "Fine, like I thought."

"That's true. I still need to inspect the upstop wheels, the ones that keep the cars on the track. And unless I find something strange, the derailment might be what it's been called all these years. An accident."

He frowned when he spoke, and a tiny pang struck her heart. He'd put so much forethought and stock into this research. To not learn what really caused the derailment must be hard to swallow.

"Maybe the remaining bolts and wheels will provide enough proof to pinpoint the cause." She used as much hope in her voice as she could muster, given their circumstances.

"Perhaps. If not, I can still document my findings. Between the photos you've taken and Randall's interview…" Jake patted her knee. "At least I've been able to garner more info than anyone else in the last ten years. That has to count for something."

She leaned in and kissed him on the cheek. "I'm sure it will."

* * *

Amanda struggled to raise her eyelids. They were so heavy, like someone held them down. Random din noises echoed through the hallway outside. Keys jingling, computers pinging as people logged in, and the smell of strong coffee wafted into the cell.

"I want some," she moaned.

"Jake Mercer and Amanda Moss," an authoritative voice said.

She shook Jake's shoulder. "Wake up."

Jake moaned, glanced up. "What?"

"The officer called our names." She pointed to outside the cell, where a deputy waited.

Jake stood up, wiping the sleep from his eyes. "Officer?"

"Yes. You're Jake Mercer?"

"Yes, sir."

"And Amanda Moss?"

"Yes, sir."

The deputy stretched his keys from his belt and unlocked their cell. "We cleared everything with your trespassing charge. Charges have been dropped."

Amanda breathed a sigh of relief and squeezed Jake's hand. "Thank you."

Maybe she imagined it, but the air felt different once they'd left the holding cell. Freer, though perhaps the feeling was psychological. Either way, she'd take it.

"Sign here," the deputy said, handing over his clipboard.

Amanda scribbled her name on the form, followed by Jake.

"Let's get cleaned up, grab some breakfast," he said. "Then go to the park, where we are allowed to be."

She chuckled at how he said the last few words with emphasis just so the deputies standing nearby could hear him. Their night in jail was over. Time to get back to work.

When they entered the Abandon Inn lobby, Pearl panted as her heavyset frame chased Clive around the room.

"I told you, the reenactment isn't today! You haven't been to one for ten years," Pearl said, her voice loud and desperate.

Clive, who sported a Confederate uniform complete with the hat, grinned wide. "Woman, we're going to Selma!"

"No we're not, you old fool! If I ever get a watchdog, I'm gonna make certain he keeps you in line."

Pearl picked up her pace and set her hand on his shoulder. "Come on now. Let me refill your canteen. How 'bout you come with me to the office?"

Clive waggled his eyebrows. "Trying to get in my good graces, eh?"

Amanda watched the two of them back and forth like a bad tennis match. "Can we help you with anything?"

Pearl rolled her eyes, letting out an exasperated sigh. "I'm just trying to contain Clive. He's gone around the bend this time."

Before Amanda could reply, Jake stepped in front of Clive and saluted.

"General Robert E. Lee here," Jake said, his voice serious and deep.

Clive snapped to attention, held a firm salute. "Yes, sir. What are your orders?"

"Let the woman refill your canteen. We're holding back on our mission until tomorrow."

"Yes, General!" Clive nodded, stepped back, and went with Pearl to the back room without complaint or argument.

Pearl waved a chubby arm of thanks before disappearing into the back room.

Amanda chuckled. "You certainly have the touch, Jake Mercer."

With a wink, he said, "Do I now?"

"If you ever give up engineering, you'd be great with elderly folks."

Jake shrugged. "He reminds me of my grandfather. Crazy old

coot, just like Clive."

Amanda rested a hand on his forearm. "I thought you did great." She glanced around the room. No sign of Sarah, not even by the umbrella rack. Amanda sighed. Guess she would give Pearl and Sarah the hello from Becca later.

"Let's get cleaned up," Amanda said. "Get some breakfast before going to Zephyr Land."

"Yep. C'mon, beautiful. I predict you'll join me for a quick shower."

"You think so, huh?"

His eyes sparkled. "I have a way with words."

"You do, do you?"

"My girl told me so," Jake said with a smile.

The rising heat in her cheeks seemed to flood her face all at once. Damn her blushing nature. She probably looked like a clown. There was never a need to wear blush for makeup. Her rosy cheeks and tendency to blush always added color to her face.

"Race you upstairs," she said. Then she leapt past him to ascend the staircase first.

"No fair. I wasn't ready."

"Too bad, General Lee."

He laughed. "I may be from the South, but honestly, it's the only name I could think of. I'm fairly certain Lee never went to Selma, but I hoped Clive would buy the excuse."

She reached the room door first, turned around, and welcomed him a few seconds later with open arms.

"What does the lady wish for first prize?" he whispered.

To keep my secrets forever. Stop. I have to tell him sometime. Just not now.

With a coy voice, she said, "I'm sure I'll think of something."

Once they entered the room, he eased up behind her and curled his arms around her waist. Resting his chin on her shoulder, he nuzzled her neck.

She shivered. Every cell in her being trembled with him being so close.

"I'm going to put the shower on," he whispered. "Care to join me?"

Knots formed in her stomach, combined with a fluttery feeling. Quick. Think of a coy response to stall the inevitable decision. Did his invitation to shower with him mean he expected they'd make love? Or did he simply want to be close?

Their first time had been wonderful, but the post-togetherness guilt? Not so much. She couldn't go through the agony of experiencing that distance between them again. Before they made love again, she had to tell him about her supernatural abilities. And right now, on the verge of a twosome shower, wasn't ideal.

"Amanda?" he prompted, his voice low and sexy.

"Seems to me you already predicted I'd join you."

"Predicted, yes, but never demanded. But I did hope, Amanda Moss. Hoped."

His hot breath on her skin sent jolts of electricity through her. It was intoxicating to be free, young, and in love. No more jail cells.

No more horror.

She wanted to be close. Near him.

Jake's kiss was slow and deep. One by one, every strand of their clothing was unbuttoned, unzipped. Until it all fell to the floor in colorful piles. The whisk of the shower curtain marked the next step. Steam clouds rose from the shower, making Jake's eyes appear even bluer against his tan skin.

"Ladies first?"

She stepped inside, her bare feet touching the mosaic tile base. He joined her, leaning his face into the jet stream to dampen his hair.

In that instant, she rediscovered why she'd been attracted to him in the first place. Droplets of water clung to his angular chin, not wanting to fall from the hairs on his chest. If she were one of those droplets, she'd have held on for dear life too. Just to be near the man for another second.

Jake Mercer, an absolutely gorgeous man. And he was here, in Abandon, with her.

With a wink, Jake said, "Lean back. Get your hair wet."

"What?"

"I want to wash your hair," he said plainly. "So get your hair wet."

Not what she expected, but maybe he only wanted to be close too? Maybe she wouldn't have to make love now. This was only the perfect opportunity to be together without the guilt.

She let the surging water soak into her scalp and through her long curls, then brushed the water off her face with her hands.

Jake poured a spoonful of peachy-smelling shampoo into his hands. "Turn around so your back is to me."

She turned and faced the showerhead and let the water drip down the front of her. Suddenly, every cell in her body tingled. Holy cow. Jake massaged her scalp, moved his magical fingers in circles. A sweet peach scent hovered in the air between them. She closed her eyes and made a low moan.

"I thought you might like this," he said, his breath warm on her shoulder.

She managed to get out a few intelligible words. "You have amazing hands."

"All the better to touch you, my dear."

For several long seconds, she closed her eyes. Allowed Jake's hands to work through her long curls. The pulse of the hot water, the smell of peaches, the smell of Jake...

"Time to rinse," he said.

"Hmm?"

"Rinse," he repeated, pointing at the showerhead. "You don't want soap in your hair or eyes, do you?"

"Guess not."

She stepped forward, carefully placing her feet. Let the hot water whoosh away the peach smells of the shampoo as it traveled down her hair to the ends and dropped to the tile below.

Once rinsed, she turned around to face him. "Your turn."

He gave a cocky smile. Placed his wet hand on her cheek. Caressed one side of her face, then leaned in and pressed his lips to hers.

The steam seemed to increase in that instant. Was it her imagination, or had their kiss somehow turned water into its alternative form?

Jake pressed tiny kisses onto her lips, the split second of each one making her yearn for more.

"You're teasing me, Jake Mercer."

With a knowing grin, he said, "All's fair in love and war."

Love? Had the man just said love?

As if he could read her mind, he quickly dropped eye contact. Picked up the shampoo bottle, reached for her hand, and poured some.

"My turn."

As the word *love* spun around in her mind like some mathematical equation to be solved, she did her best to return the awesome feeling of having one's hair washed by someone else.

"You're not so bad yourself," Jake said as she dug her nails deeper to wash his scalp.

Love?

Her hands paused as the word seemed to fill her mind with neon lights. Granted, he hadn't said the three words—I love you—but he had referred to the word all the same. But how could he love her when he didn't even know the real her?

Guilt crept back in, washed over her faster than the showerhead's pump.

"Don't leave me half soapy here," Jake said. He tilted his head to her like a dog prompting its owner for a good petting.

"Sure." She continued to scrub, then switched places with him so he could rinse.

"Feels good," he said, placing his face and hair in the middle of the shower stream. "Want me to wash your back?"

"Sure." She planted her feet solidly on the tile. Last thing she needed was for her knees to wobble from his touch.

He moved the soap in tiny circles along her back. She breathed deep, knowing where this could lead. No matter what, she needed to keep them close but not get intimate. Not now. Maybe she could tell him about her gift tonight?

His smooth hands traced over the soap to increase the lather on her shoulders. She leaned her head back on his chest, and he bent in and kissed her ear.

"Jake..."

"Yeah?"

I can see and talk to the dead.

No. Not the time. But she couldn't be intimate again until she told him.

"Want me to do your back?" she finally said. Anything to keep his navigating hands above her waistline. Once they dipped below, she wouldn't be able to stop without him becoming upset.

"Sure."

His chest brushed against hers as they exchanged positions once more. With the water pounding on her back, she soaped the area between his muscular shoulders. Then down his arms. As she approached his waist, her hands began to tremble.

"You okay?" he asked.

"Yeah. Just give me a second."

She quickly washed herself, knowing if they crossed the line into intimacy, there would be no turning back, and she needed to be clean.

Jake turned, saw her rinsing, and frowned. "You should've saved the fun parts for me."

"I...um..."

His blue-eyed gaze seemed to stare right into her soul. Inside those blues, she saw passion. Admiration. With a tweak of sadness.

"So we aren't doing calisthenics this morning?" he added.

What could she say? She didn't want to turn him down, but she couldn't bear the guilt again. Damn her aunt Anzhela for being right all along. Especially once Jake had said the word *love*, even in passing conversation.

"We've had a rough night," Amanda said. "I want to enjoy being close to you. It's wonderful, but let's stay focused. Get ourselves clean and to the park."

He shot her one of his mischievous grins, the kind where dimples shone bright from his face. "Showers get people clean, Amanda."

Heat flared in her cheeks. "I know. I just—"

"Yeah, I get it."

Had there been a hint of anger in his voice? Or had she imagined it?

She lifted the soap, started to rub it across his well-defined chest.

"Nah, let me," he said, taking the soap from her. "Probably safer if we aren't going to go further."

"I didn't mean—"

"I *will* hold you to a raincheck," he said.

She exhaled a long breath of relief. "Absolutely." *After I tell you everything.*

CHAPTER TWENTY-EIGHT

Jake reluctantly finished his shower and wrapped a towel around his waist. The shower had fogged over the mirror. He wiped it down with a washcloth and brushed his teeth. Amazing how the simple things could feel incredible. Like brushing his teeth after a night in jail.

If only Amanda hadn't freaked out, he might have enjoyed a few other sensations. She'd leapt from the shower like a cat avoiding water.

What had that been about? He combed his hair, got dressed. Although he hated to admit it, he respected her drive to stay focused and get their work done. At the same time, he wished she'd have let things progress in the shower. Maybe they could have their raincheck tonight. Work, then play.

Yes. Better.

When he stepped out of the bathroom, an already-groomed Amanda stood by the window, taking in the view Zephyr Land in the distance.

"Why don't we get something to eat downstairs, then go to the park?" he asked. "Stay most of the day?"

She turned, offering a kind smile. "Sounds good."

He walked closer to her and brushed her lips with his in a quick kiss. "Don't forget—raincheck comes due tonight."

"If we aren't in jail again," Amanda said.

"Trust me. I'm going to keep our permission slip with me at all times from now on."

"If it happens again, you can always use your lock-picking talents to escape the cuffs."

He shrugged. "Doubt the cops would appreciate my little hobby."

"Maybe not, but I think it's a handy trick."

"Either way, we'll be prepared next time."

Amanda sighed. "Let's hope there isn't a next time."

"Amen to that." He winked at her, grabbed their things, and went downstairs for breakfast.

* * *

Before starting the car, Jake double-checked his backpack. Good. The permission letter from the law office, and proof they had a right to be in Zephyr Land, was in the side pocket. Not that he anticipated any further complications from the sheriff, but better safe than sorry.

He started the ignition and drove them the short distance to Zephyr Land and parked. Between last night's incarceration and this morning's frustration with Amanda, he needed to focus on work.

Reaching for his backpack, he and Amanda exited the car and went through the gate. He half expected some pudgy-bellied cop to come along and arrest them again, but the only sound came from tree frogs chirping in the distance.

"Can I borrow your camera? I need to get some shots of the premium bolt heads on the cars. If you don't need it."

"I'm good," she said. "For any shots I might need, I'll get them with my cell and use my camera later. You go ahead."

"You sure?"

She looked at the bright-blue sky blanketing Zephyr Land. "I'm sure."

"Thanks." He took the camera bag and walked her to the carousel tent.

"I'm fine if you want to go to the coaster," she said.

Not after last night. He needed to make sure they were safe at all times. "A quick glance inside the tent, then I'll go."

She squeezed his hand. "You can't take the gentleman out of the guy."

"No ma'am," he said with a smile.

They entered the tent. He pulled back the flaps to let air into the humid pocket and did a quick walk around the carousel. "Everything looks good."

"Told ya. I'll come find you at the roller coaster when I'm done," she said. "Good luck with your findings."

"You too."

Jake wandered over to the coaster car area. Today, he would find out why the coaster derailed. Lack of premium bolts had been ruled out. Bello and Toale had, whatever the original intention, made good on the safety equipment.

Now it was his job to determine what else could've been the cause.

He went car by car. Some were too mangled to see anything, just a reminder of the wreckage that had shut down Zephyr Land. The riding wheels, guide wheels, all good. Premium bolts, correctly installed safety wire, nothing out of place.

The key to the derailment had to be the upstop wheels, the bottom ones that held the train on the track. First car, upstop wheels damaged. Second car, upstop wheels bent to hell. He went through each one until he noticed the bolts on the second-to-last car hadn't been torn up.

Finally.

When he looked at the underside of the car, something was amiss. The bolts seemed to be installed correctly, but why was the safety wire rusted? The wire appeared to be situated in the right pattern and wound so it pulled the bolts tighter. The twists where the ends of the wires were attached looked textbook perfect.

The safety wire for the upstop wheels should have the same appearance as for the other wheels—a dull silver color. Normal discoloration for stainless steel after being abandoned for ten years.

Instead, on the most crucial roller coaster wheels, the safety wire had rusted and had a dingy color. There was only one explanation: the safety wire for these wheels wasn't made from stainless steel. This wire had been regular steel, which would've rusted over a decade in the humid salt air of the Gulf Coast.

Corruption or cheapness on the part of Bello and Toale, the designers? Doubtful. Why use stainless steel on two sets of wheel types, but not on the upstop ones? No, this was something else.

These wheels had been tampered with.

Bello and Toale would've known that stainless steel safety wire could only be purchased from aircraft maintenance suppliers. Since

9/11, the safety wire had been on a list of materials whose sales were recorded. Basic mechanic's wire, available at any hardware store, looked the same as stainless steel wire, at least for the first several months. Probably appeared that way for the insurance inspectors after the derailment.

But here, now? Ten years after the fact? The crappy wire would've rusted, just like the sight Jake was looking directly at.

Time to get some photos. When he looked through the viewfinder of the camera and under the magnification of the lens, he could see that parts of the hex head of the bolts had scratches from being tightened. They didn't look any different from any of other bolt heads, but even overtightening would not damage the bolt heads. He would have to look deeper.

He snapped pictures of one of the bolts from every angle he could think of, to show exactly how he had found it. Then he took a pair of wire cutters from his backpack supplies and carefully cut the ersatz safety wire. Unfortunately, he didn't have the right size socket to remove the bolt, but he had a decent-sized pair of Channellock pliers that would do the trick.

Worth a try. If his effort didn't succeed, he could purchase the right wrench at the Abandon hardware store later. Gripping the bolt head with the pliers, he placed one foot against the car for leverage. Then pulled with all his might.

He immediately landed on his ass, several feet away from the roller coaster car. The huge resistance he'd expected never came, leaving him in violation of several of Newton's laws. Fabulous. His reward for hard work? A bruised backside.

He looked at the partial bolt that had landed next to him. The head and part of the shank were intact, but the threaded part was apparently still attached to the coaster. As he looked at the end of the broken bolt, he could see the telltale markings of a bolt that has been severely overtightened. Most of the broken end of the bolt was slightly rusted, but a small portion of the end was dull metallic colored. The bolt had been broken almost in two, leaving only that small portion of the bolt to carry the whole load. For a bolt of this size and grade to have broken like this, it would have to have been torqued way past the specification.

No way could this have been an accident or mistake. This was sabotage. And murder.

Damn. He'd solved what happened. Only two questions remained. Why? And who?

Had the bolts been overtorqued from the beginning? During construction? Some jerk during the assembly thinking it would be a fun joke? No. And why was proper safety wire not used just on the bolts for the upstop wheels? The safety inspection would have failed. Unless the inspector accepted a bribe, but why would the company pay to risk an accident?

Then again, according to the lawsuit, the company had planned to use subpar equipment and Randall had become the whistle-blower. Then they'd ruined him for doing so.

Or had someone overtorqued by accident? No way, based on even a cursory examination of the broken bolt Jake had found. Any engineer worth his salt would've known the correct torque for this size bolt and would never have specified such overtightening.

Especially Randall Kern…

Amanda thought Randall was guilty from minute one, but she relied on emotion and intuition. Unstable resources.

Jake shook off the thought. No. The father of engineering couldn't have anything to do with the derailment that killed thirty-plus people. Besides, Randall had been fired by the time the bolts went onto the cars. By logic, the overtorqueing had been done after the safety inspection, before the first and fatal ride.

Amanda must be wrong. Randall Kern couldn't have done this.

Which left the burning question: Who did?

For his position paper, once he had the cause for the derailment, he didn't need to know who'd been responsible. Then again, he and Amanda had until the weekend to remain in Abandon. Maybe he could find bonus material for his conclusions while Amanda finished up her carousel analysis.

That work promotion was his. He could feel it.

CHAPTER TWENTY-NINE

Amanda double-checked the carousel tent to ensure no stray ghosts were around. No Declan, no Opal. Good. A break, for once.

She began with the most tattered-looking horse. It was a jumper, meaning none of its hooves touched the base of the carousel when the piece moved up and down during the ride. Checking the hooves, she noted on her pad: silver paint chipped on horseshoes.

Moving her hand across the horse's muscled legs, she felt for any divots or cracks. A few places could use some sanding, but overall the legs were in good shape. The horse's body was another story. Over the years, being abandoned, cracks formed in the paint and revealed bare wood underneath. Hmm. They must not have used primer on this horse. Not a good practice. She made a note with her recommendation for consistent primer in her notes.

That's when her phone rang. "Hello?"

"Yes, I'm looking for Amanda Moss?" the woman's voice said.

"This is she."

"This is Bette at the Carousel Restoration Institute."

Amanda's pulse quickened. "Yes, I'm planning to submit my entry on your website by Monday morning. I'm actually standing next to the carousel in question right now."

Bette cleared her throat. "Er, yes, about that…"

Amanda held her breath. *Please don't tell me the apprenticeship is no longer available. Or that I'm ineligible. Or that I have to answer phones and play secretary for the rest of my career.*

"Ms. Moss, are you there?" Bette asked.

Barely.

"Yes, I'm here. You were talking about the apprenticeship. Is there a problem?" Amanda asked.

"Not a problem so much as a modification. Lena Cole, the main judge of the entries, has to go to France to do some consulting on the Parisian carousel. She will be leaving the country on Saturday and won't be available to judge the entries on Monday."

"So what does that mean?"

"We need your entry by Friday noon," Bette said. "I trust this won't be a problem?"

"Problem?"

Amanda wasn't sure if she repeated the word to continue the conversation or just to state what it was. Of course this was a problem! Today was Wednesday. She had photographic evidence that was complete, but she'd planned a thirty-page paper to submit with all her theories, and she'd only just started.

"No, no problem at all." She choked back the rising panic in her throat. "Friday noon. I'll have it submitted on your website by then."

"Excellent. Lena looks forward to everyone's entries."

"Can you...I mean, is there a way to know how many people plan to enter? Are you allowed to tell me?"

"I'm sorry. We keep entries confidential."

"Yes, of course."

I'm an idiot for even asking. How could I have let the words slip from my mouth?

"Glad you understand. So we'll look forward to your entry by Friday noon."

"Yes, thanks," she said, bobbing her head up and down even though Bette couldn't see her. Maybe the visual would make it clearer to her own mind she needed to get the carousel report done.

By noon Friday.

She tapped the End button. How was she supposed to get everything documented and submitted by Friday at noon? She had to tell Jake the truth about her abilities at some point, meaning there needed to be time set aside for arguments and negotiating that no, she wouldn't need a psychiatric evaluation.

Then there was the issue of the ghosts. Just because Declan hadn't bothered her in the last day or two didn't mean he wouldn't— and in full force.

Friday, noon? Really?

She rubbed her temples. Already, a headache began to form. Okay. She could calm down. First step, deep breaths. Second, complete the analysis of the horse piece. At least she'd already taken most of the photos, but she would need to resize and format them for the online report.

Returning to the horse piece, she continued her analysis. Every pole sleeved in brass had tarnished down to a dullish green-black color. The back of one horse's mane had chipped paint, revealing damaged wood underneath. She traced the ebb and flow of the black mane, making notes as she went.

Wait a moment. Was there a hole in the design? She shifted her stance and examined the opposite side of the horse's mane where it brushed close to the back. There was a two-inch gap between the mane and the horse. Likely a breakdown of the glue. In this Gulf Coast weather, particularly being abandoned for ten years, the wood must have expanded and contracted enough to cause such a gap. Regluing and replacement of the wood would be needed for restoration.

Getting a flashlight from her bag, she shone it down the dark opening inside the horse. Could this be one of those time capsules Declan told her about, that she'd read about? Original builders sometimes put treasures inside the pieces they built for carousels.

A faded piece of paper had been placed inside the horse's neck area. She tried to reach in and grab it but couldn't stretch her fingers far enough.

"Want to know what it says?"

Amanda turned and saw Opal standing there with a knowing smile. The ghosts staying away for a brief time had been too good to be true.

"Yes. Do you know?"

Nodding, Opal approached her. "That horse was contracted out to a place in Louisiana. They wanted it to resemble the old style like the carousel in City Park."

"What does it say?"

Opal fixated her gaze on Amanda. "High-level summation? Life is too short to keep secrets."

Amanda frowned. She was on the verge of opening one of the

time-capsule treasures she'd read about, that sounded so exciting, and the content was the same as what Aunt Anzhela and Declan had been spouting off at the mouth for a week?

"Is that what it really says?" Amanda asked.

"Yes. Why?"

"Because people keep giving me fortune cookies on how I'm supposed to embrace my ability to talk to the dead."

Opal shrugged. "Be that as it may, I knew the man who built this piece."

Amanda studied Opal's semitransparent face, trying to ascertain if she was being truthful. "Who built it? Help me get the notebook paper out so I can read it."

"A man named Grayson crafted this piece." Opal looked around. Spying an open drawer in a work cabinet, she went to the corner and pulled out a set of pliers. "Will this work?"

"Perfect." Amanda grabbed the narrow pliers and stuck them inside the hole. A few seconds of patience and she'd managed to grip the yellowing parchment and pull it out.

"I'm telling you the truth," Opal said. "The man had a tragic life. He built only ten pieces for carousels before he died from heartbreak."

"Heartbreak? How can someone die from heartbreak?"

Opal fixed her hair and walked to the exit of the tent. "Read and find out."

Amanda carefully unfolded the piece of paper. Time, humidity, and being inside a carousel horse for years had given the ordinarily crisp paper more of a fabric feel. She stepped out of the tent, longing for some hint of a breeze to cool her down.

She brushed away some scraggly vines overtaking a bench and sat down to read. First, she glanced around at the vast quiet. Reading what had been kept secret so long felt like she was looking into the past, into something she didn't have any right to see.

My name is Grayson Lowell. This carousel piece is my final contribution to a world that lost two of its brightest souls, my wife and son.

The cancer spread too quickly. Even now, I feel the aching in my very bones. What's worse, I kept the disease from my family. Reasons escape me now, except I didn't want to be a burden. Radiation kept my health in check for a time. I maintained a brave face, continued to be the proud provider for everyone.

Stupid ego.

One day I got a phone call, the worst of my life. My wife and child were killed in a car wreck. Quick. Sudden. No chance to say good-bye. No chance to tell them how much I loved them, how sorry I was for not being honest.

This carousel piece remained unfinished for months, a half-carved wooden horse gathering dust in the far corner of the garage. Then one day, something changed. I couldn't bring my family back, couldn't watch my son giggle as I set him on the horse's back while holding him steady.

But I could finish what I started. That's what kept me moving forward many a day. Completing a task I set out to do.

So this piece, now complete, will have my truth hidden inside of it. Should anyone discover this note years from now, I only ask this of the reader: don't keep secrets. Share your life with those you love. Give them the opportunity to do the same. And always finish what you start.

Here's hoping this one piece of a carousel brings joy to children as it did to my son.

Sincerely

Grayson

Amanda stared at the letter. Every word seemed to wiggle and swirl on the page. Her trembling hands didn't help matters. The man had etched his soul onto the paper inside his carousel piece.

Don't keep secrets from those you love. And right now, she was keeping a big one from Jake.

CHAPTER THIRTY

Jake finished his round of photos, put one of the paint-chipped bolts into his pocket for evidence, and went to check on Amanda.

When he stepped into the red-and-white tent, he found her sitting on one of the jumper horses. Staring into space.

"Is this some form of analyzing I haven't seen before?" he asked.

A long second passed before she turned her gaze to him. "Jake. Hi."

"Hi." He walked closer and put his hand on her knee. "You imagining what the carousel would've been like in its prime?"

He hoped that guess was what she was doing. Sitting on a wooden horse and staring into space for no reason didn't seem a viable alternative, not when she had a job to do. Same as him.

"I found a letter inside this horse," she whispered. "A powerful letter."

"What did it say?"

Her big hazel eyes flickered with hints of green. "To live life to the fullest. Let those we love know how much they mean to us."

He smiled. "Sage advice."

"We should talk," she whispered, then cleared her throat.

"Not here. I need to use the hotel's printer to print out these digital photos I took, then get my findings documented. If you don't have any further analysis to do here today, let's return to the inn and get our work done."

"That works, but I'm on a tight time frame. The restoration

company called. They need my proposal by Friday," she said, her voice cracking toward the end in a clear moment of panic.

"Friday?" He shook his head. "Why the change?"

"The judge will be leaving the country. She wants the weekend to review our entries."

"Then we can stay here until the light goes. Anything I can do to help?"

"No. Let's go back to the inn and talk. I have a large part of my analysis done, and I should start working on the paper. If need be, we'll come back later this evening."

"You sure? I don't want to interfere with your work," Jake said.

"Positive, as long as I can have a full day tomorrow."

"Works for me. Besides," Jake said with a wink, "that'll give us time to make good on the raincheck. A chance for some relaxation. C'mon. Let's go to the car."

On the walk to the parking lot, Jake shared his findings and suspicions about the overtorque and how that may have caused the derailment. The midafternoon sun cast slanted shadows of the two of them along the boardwalk, hand in hand.

When they approached the gate, Jake stopped short. "Son of a bitch!"

"What's the matter?"

He ran to the car and confirmed what he thought he'd seen. Both tires on the passenger side had been slashed, and enough air had escaped to set the rims against the concrete pavement. He raced to the driver's side. Same thing. Big, thick slashes through the black rubber.

"Damn it!" He held up his hands in resignation. "All four tires have been slashed."

Amanda didn't scream, didn't yell. She just stood there, folding her arms across her chest and staring at him with those wide greenish eyes. "One flat tire is coincidence, but four? I think we might be in danger."

"Why would anyone want to slash our tires? Do you think this was some cop, upset that we had permission to be here after all?"

"No. I think this might be someone who doesn't like us digging into the accident," she said. "Either way, it's a definite message. We need to be careful. First the sheriff shows up out of the blue wanting to know why we're at Zephyr Land. Do you think he randomly happened to know where we were?"

Jake's pulse raced as he tried to piece together what had happened, what they needed to do next.

"What are you saying?" he asked.

"I'm saying four slashed tires is a powerful message. That maybe someone called the sheriff, asked him to check us out."

"Why would anyone care?" Jake asked. "It's an abandoned park."

She glanced back toward the carousel, appearing lost in her thoughts. If he didn't know better, he swore she might be exchanging eye contact with someone else.

"Well?" Jake prompted.

"I don't know. Someone obviously doesn't like that we're here.

It's been ten years, but over thirty people plummeted to their death in Zephyr Land. Maybe the person who caused the overtorque is still nearby. There's not a statute of limitations on murder. He or she might want to scare us enough that we'll stop investigating?"

"I wish I could argue your logic, but I can't," Jake said. "Four slashed tires is definitely a message. But from who, and why?"

Amanda shrugged. "I'm not sure. Either way, let's get out of here now. Should we call the inn, ask them to send a cab?"

"Yeah. That will be quicker than getting the rental company out here. We can contact them later, fill out the paperwork to get a vehicle."

"Okay. I'll call," Amanda said. She reached for her cell and called Pearl.

Jake walked the perimeter of the vehicle one more time. The amount of force to slash big tires like these must have required strong arms and one hell of a knife. Kneeling down, he ran his hand around the tire to inspect the entry and exit point of the slash.

Knots formed in his stomach. As much as he didn't want to think about it, one thought kept coming back into his mind like a boomerang.

What if the person who slashed the tires was watching them? Waiting, planning to use that giant knife on him and Amanda? He needed to have his Honda towed to a tire store right away. He hoped Abandon had one.

CHAPTER THIRTY-ONE

Amanda blinked twice, gawking at what the rural town of Abandon called a cab. It was a PT Cruiser, painted black, and looked more like a hearse. But the spray-painted image of a gold lamé Elvis Presley on the front hood made this particular cab stand out among all others.

"I suppose we can't be picky about transportation when we have no other option?"

She hoped her half-humorous comment would put Jake in a better mood. He'd barely said two words since they'd discovered the lacerated tires. He just stood there, his fists tightening while the vein in his neck bulged.

"Jake?"

A long minute passed, and then he finally turned to meet her gaze. "Yeah?"

"You okay? The cab is here."

As if he hadn't even seen the spectacle before them, he nodded, said nothing, and reached to open the door for her.

"Thanks," she mumbled.

Maybe Jake would feel better once they'd returned to the Abandon Inn.

"Evening, folks," the driver said. "My name's JT. I'm your cabbie for the evening. Pearl says y'all need a ride back to the inn."

He appeared to be in his sixties, wore a plaid shirt and blue jeans, and had the look of someone who'd rather be on a dock fishing for trout.

"Yes," Amanda said. She slid inside. Immediately noticed the lime-green shag carpet. Shag carpet, in a cab?

"Interesting cab," she said, trying to spur conversation. She'd heard of bizarre people living across the South, but had never seen such an ugly shade of green. And shag? Wouldn't it be hard to keep clean?

JT slowly pulled onto the main road. "Oh yeah. Elvis's Graceland home has a room decked out with the green stuff. Kind of my tribute to the King."

Jake stared out his window, apparently not wanting to talk or make eye contact.

Amanda cleared her throat. "That explains the spray-painted hood. I take it you're an Elvis fan?"

"Oh yes, ma'am. I go to Graceland at least four times a year."

"I've never been," Amanda said.

"Are you kidding me? You have to go!"

She smiled at his insistence. "Maybe someday."

JT paused before the main road to the Abandon Inn, turned around, and gave a half smile. "I know the shag green carpet in the cab is a bit overkill, but I thought it'd be fun for the locals."

Amanda nodded. "Definitely memorable."

JT continued to drone on about Memphis, the sights, and trivia on Elvis that most people never knew. Or would care to know.

Meanwhile, Amanda rested her hand on Jake's knee. A gesture of checking in.

He glanced at her and gave a polite smile. No reaching for her hand. No other communication.

Was he seriously freaked out about the tire slashing, or was he upset about something else?

Thank goodness the drive to the Abandon Inn wasn't a long one. When they arrived, Amanda thanked JT, who handed her a brochure titled *Southern Elvis Impersonators*. She stuck it in her pocket, for a souvenir more than information.

Once she and Jake were in the lobby, Jake turned and said, "We should pack up. Leave tonight."

"What? I can't. I mean, I have most of the information I need, but we still need to finish our projects."

He grasped her hand. "I'm done with mine. I know you're almost done with yours. So let's pack up tonight, spend half a day at the park tomorrow, then get out of this forsaken town."

The enlarged black pupils in his eyes gave away his true emotion: fear. He always seemed so logical, but now he'd become worried, panicked.

"You're freaked out about the tires. I get it—"

"I need to protect us. I've been thinking about what you said. Whoever trashed our car is obviously not happy that we're investigating the derailment. I have what I need. You're almost done with your research."

"And you want to leave?" She thought about the ghosts. About them being stuck at Zephyr Land for another ten years. And worse, the many ways other spirits could taunt her if she didn't help the ones at the park.

"Don't you?" Jake asked. "Why stick around if there's danger and we don't need any more info?"

"But I do need more," Amanda said. "At least another full day. You know the deadline for my apprenticeship entry got pushed up. I have photos of all the carousel pieces, but I still need to analyze each one, propose my steps for restoration, and give my suggestions."

His lips formed into a straight line. "Can you get everything you need with one more day?"

She glanced at the reservation desk, where Pearl stood scribbling into a notebook and pretended not to hear their conversation.

"I don't know," Amanda said. "But I will know by the end of tomorrow where things stand."

He sighed. "We need to stay safe. Some things aren't worth the trouble."

A sharp pang struck her heart in that instant. Did he consider his work to be more important than hers? This trip was supposed to help both their career paths. The thought nagged at her, along with what he would say about her once she told him the truth about herself. Would he presume *she* was not worth the trouble?

"I need some time alone," she whispered.

"What?"

"Give me a few minutes to gather my thoughts," she said, using every bit of firmness her voice could muster. "You go on upstairs, get started on your paper. I'll be up in a little while."

Jake glanced around the lobby. "You're just going to hang out here, alone?"

No. I need to talk to a five-year-old little girl who happens to be dead.

"I'll grab some iced tea and sit in the dining area. Just...please?"

With another concerned gaze, he relented. "Come up soon, okay?"

"I will."

Once he'd ascended the stairs and was out of earshot, Pearl's knowing eyes looked over her spectacles. "That was interesting."

"Yeah, well. He's spooked about someone slashing our tires."

"And you're not?" Pearl set her glasses down on the counter. "Seems like someone doesn't like you and your boyfriend snooping around. Small towns keep to themselves by default, but in the case of the derailment—"

"I know, but if I leave now, things will be worse. I can feel it."

"Worse than hauling you to jail or leaving you stranded at Zephyr Land?"

Amanda thought a moment. "You have a good point, but believe me, ghosts can make my life a living hell. If not these ghosts, others will come along." She sighed. "No, I have to finish what I started. I'm in too deep now."

"Sounds like you need some sweet tea and a bit of relaxation."

Amanda smiled. "Maybe for ten minutes, max. I have so much analysis and typing to do for my restoration report."

Pearl set out the bell on the desk in case anyone needed her assistance, and then she carried two sweet teas into the dining area. "Here we go."

"Thanks." Amanda took a sip. "That's amazing."

"I add fresh mint sprigs when I'm steeping the tea. Gives it a nice down-home touch."

Amanda took another few sips, savoring the mint and sweet flavor on her tongue. "I think I need to tell Jake about my gift. I'm sure as hell not looking forward to that conversation."

Pearl stirred her tea, rattling the ice cubes against the glass. "What made you change your mind, hon?"

"He keeps wanting to be intimate. And we have been before, but afterward…"

Nodding, Pearl said, "Not the same when a secret becomes a brick wall between lovers."

"Exactly." Amanda loved how this wacky inn owner seemed to understand so much. How Pearl even managed to survive after both her children died was beyond comprehension. She'd obviously had them after she'd been married quite a few years, and Clive was…a handful.

"How did Sarah die, if you don't mind me asking? She wasn't at Zephyr Land, was she?"

Pearl blotted one of her eyes, perhaps to keep tears away. "No, my sister, Opal, wanted to take them both to the park, but Sarah had a fever, so I kept her here that day."

"Did she die from an illness?"

"We aren't sure. Opal had been so insistent on spending time with the girls. Thought she could have been a better mother than me, thought I was crazy for raising two youngsters in a bed-and-breakfast inn."

"It's not like you were raising them in a dangerous place."

"Exactly," Pearl said. "Anyway, I kept Sarah here, but Opal was angry as a pig that was denied mud."

Yet another strange Southern saying. Amanda smiled to herself. "So when, or how, did Sarah die?"

"Later in the evening. We were packed full of guests that weekend. Everyone having anything to do with the park was here. The press from out of town, architects flown in from Austin, you name it. And I was so frantic."

Pearl shook her head, blotted away a few hints of tears. "Sarah was resting in one of the rooms. Clive was off at one of his reenactments, so when I went to check on her, she'd stopped breathing. Sam lay on the floor beside the bed…"

The fact that both twins died the same day—one of them not even being at the park—was too unique to be a coincidence.

"Had the fever made her worse? Had she been cut or bruised?" Amanda asked.

Pearl shook her head. "Sarah just lay there peacefully. I didn't have the heart to have those doctors slice her up in an autopsy, so her death was ruled natural causes since no one found anything."

"No trace of poison?" Amanda asked. There were a number of substances that could've been used, ones no one could detect. And if there were tons of people coming and going in the lobby, it wouldn't be too difficult to slip in and out.

"No, and she hadn't eaten much that day anyway. What she did eat, the rest of the guests had eaten too. They were all fine."

Amanda nodded. "Thanks for the info."

"So, you said Sarah remains here? Her spirit is in the inn?"

"Yes. Near the umbrella rack is where I see her most often. Becca is at the park, usually by Opal's side."

Pearl drank the rest of her tea in several swigs. "You tell both my girls how much I love them. And good luck with your fella."

"Thanks, and I will. They ask about you all the time, Pearl. You were lucky to have two such beautiful little girls."

Smiling, Pearl nodded and started to gather their tea glasses. "I miss them every day, but I always thought I could sense little Sarah near the hat rack. Funny thing was, we used to hang coats there. Sarah loved playing hide and seek in the thick coats dangling from the hooks. Guess she still likes the area."

"Makes sense," Amanda said. "At least my gift can bring you some comfort. Even if it gets me dumped by Jake. Or worse, committed. He wants me to check myself into the psych hospital when we return to Georgia."

Pearl reached out, touched Amanda's hand. "You're not crazy. A shame folks can't see that."

With a resigned sigh, Amanda whispered, "Jake might disagree."

CHAPTER THIRTY-TWO

On the way to the room, Amanda passed by the umbrella rack, where Sarah stood on her tiptoes in a ballerina pose.

"Hi there," Amanda whispered.

"I'm a dancer."

"Yes, you are. I just had tea with your mom. She loves and misses you so much."

Sarah's big blue eyes turned and stared. "Mom seems happier since you took her to Zephyr Land. You're helping Mom and Aunt Opal, aren't you?"

Sarah's tiny voice struck right into Amanda's heart.

"I'm trying to," Amanda whispered. "But it's complicated—"

"That's what grown-ups say when it's too hard."

Amanda smiled. Out of the mouths of babes.

"I'm going to do my absolute best," she said. "But I need to find out why they died first. The same person may be trying to stop me and Jake."

"Didn't the bad man kill them too?"

"Bad man?"

Sarah nodded. "The one who killed me."

"What?"

Amanda knelt down. "Come sit next to me for a minute. Take a break from your pirouette."

Sarah sat cross-legged on the floor with an enthusiastic smile and energy only a five-year-old could have.

"Your mom said you died of natural causes," Amanda began.

"You had a fever that day—"

"Nope. The bad man came in to tell me a story."

This was news. Amanda's pulse raced. She hadn't thought of questioning Sarah before, because Sarah's spirit remained at the inn. Made no sense to connect her death to those at Zephyr Land until Pearl mentioned Sarah had died the same day as Becca.

"Tell me what happened. Did he give you anything to eat or drink?"

"Yes. He said it was pineapple juice, but it tasted funny." She paused. "Sam wouldn't quit barking. The man poured some juice on the floor, and Sam licked it up."

Poison. Just like she thought.

"What did the man look like?" Amanda asked. "Tall, thin? Heavier? What color hair?"

"Thin. He looked tall, but I was lying down."

"Did he have straight or wavy hair? Brown? Blond?"

Sarah shook her head, making her black ponytails swish in the air. "Wavy hair. It was red."

Red. The only person on their suspicion list so far with red hair was Randall Kern. She knew it had to be him. Pulling out her cell phone, she Googled some photos of Randall from when he was in his glory days as a roller coaster designer.

"Sarah, I need you to listen to me carefully. I'm going to show you a picture of someone. You need to look closely. Tell me if he is the bad man who came into your room that night. Okay?"

She nodded.

Amanda expanded the picture of Randall Kern and held out her phone for Sarah to see. Sarah gasped and shrunk away upon seeing the image.

"That's him," she whimpered. "He's the one."

"He poisoned you, sweetie. Whatever he gave you didn't show up on a tox screen."

Amanda kept talking out loud, explaining her theory. Perhaps to practice for when she would tell Jake.

"Your mom didn't want an autopsy done, so they declared your death an accident. I don't know why Randall Kern wanted you dead—"

"I do."

"You do? Why? You weren't at the park, so why come to the inn and kill you?"

"Because Becca and I are twins."

"I don't get it," Amanda said. She looked around, making sure Jake—or another inn guest—wasn't watching her talking to the…air…and waving her phone around.

"After I drank the juice, he said twins knew things about each other. Could feel things. He didn't want me to say anything to anyone. And I didn't, until you came along. You're the first one who has been able to hear me."

Amanda's eyes began to water. She was the first gifted person who had spoken to Sarah, and she'd been spending all her time trying to deny it. But if she could help people like Pearl and Sarah, why fight something that could help families?

Time for a reassessment.

"Thank you, sweetie," Amanda said. "I know what I have to do now."

"What?"

Amanda stood up, breathed in a breath of resilience. "I have to talk to Jake."

CHAPTER THIRTY-THREE

Amanda knocked on their room door and waited for Jake to answer. He had the key, and she'd forgotten her spare on the night table after her quick exit from the shower this morning.

"It's me," she said.

Jake opened the door to reveal his suitcase, nearly packed, sitting on the end of the bed. "Hey."

She stared at the suitcase. "We should talk."

"It would make me feel better if you packed first. Tomorrow, we check out, toss our luggage in the trunk, go to the park as long as you need. But tomorrow by sundown, we leave."

Amanda held up her hand. "Jake, sit down. We really need to talk."

With a heavy sigh, he plunked down in one of the side chairs with his back to the window view. "What's going on?"

She sat on the edge of the bed, facing him. "First, let's not panic."

"I want to keep us safe. We don't need to risk our lives for our careers."

"You say that because you have everything you need. I may not. But that's not what I came up here to say."

He leaned back, cracked his neck in both directions. "What's on your mind?"

I see dead people? How could she say that without sounding like a line from a movie? Maybe she could start with her family history. Tell him about her aunt, how the gift was often passed down by one relative to another. Yes. Good approach.

"What is it, Amanda?"

She reached for his hand, held it in hers. "I haven't been fully honest with you about myself. About things in my past—"

"Wait," he said, his eyes narrowing. "Are you about to tell me you have an STD? Or you've been stepping out on me?"

"No, nothing like that." She breathed a sigh of relief. Maybe her abilities wouldn't seem so strange, given she wasn't about to give the news he had originally expected.

"Then what?"

"There's this…ability I have. It's been passed down through many generations of dozens of families." Maybe mentioning the generational angle would bring a semblance of respect for what she was about to tell him?

"My aunt Anzhela had the gift," Amanda said. "That's why I didn't want you getting too close to her, or you would learn the truth about me."

Jake tilted his head slightly, his face puzzled. "What gift? What are you talking about?"

Just spit it out. It's the aftermath discussion that will be hell.

"I can see, and hear, spirits who have passed on." She paused, waiting for some flicker of understanding to reflect back in his eyes.

"Spirits?" he asked.

"Those who have died. Doesn't matter how long ago. Sometimes it's a ghost from the Revolutionary War. Other times, like now, it's those thirty people who died from the roller coaster derailment."

"Stop. You're talking crazy. Why are you doing this?"

She let out a long, sad sigh. "I can't continue to keep this secret from you. At first I was scared you'd dump me, so I never said anything. Then you started to suspect things, and I blew it off like it was nothing—"

"Like when you were talking to someone who wasn't there in the lobby."

His voice remained calm, even-keeled. Almost like he was performing an analysis, gathering data to tell the men in white coats exactly what kind of padded cell she would need.

"Yes," she replied. "Please don't tune me out right now. I know what I'm saying sounds crazy."

"I'm glad to hear you're self-aware."

She gave him a half smile. "Trust me. I was kicked out of enough day-camp activities as a kid to know that the world isn't ready to deal with someone who can talk to their dead relatives."

"I don't believe in ghosts, supernatural things. You know this—"

"I do. That's why I've avoided telling you until now. I know you're logical, hate the supernatural—"

"I have damn good reason to," Jake said, his jaw flexing in anger.

"I know. Trust me. And when we made love, it was wonderful, but I felt like there was a wall between us because you never knew about the real me. I was too frightened to tell you, worried you would leave."

His lips remained in a straight line. He crossed one leg over his knee. His normally beaming eyes had shifted to blank.

"So why tell me now?"

She couldn't tell if his tone had traces of resentment or confusion. Probably both.

"That letter I found today, in the body of the horse carousel piece. The man who wrote it said he'd kept things from his family and he always regretted it. I wanted to make love with you this morning in the shower, but I couldn't bear to feel the guilt again. I swore I would tell you the truth, tell you about this—side—of me before we made love again."

He avoided eye contact, just turned his head and stared out at the sky turning pink toward sunset. Finally, after an agonizing silence, he whispered, "What am I supposed to say here, Amanda? I have no idea what you want."

She cleared her throat. "I wanted to be honest with you so you know about this part of me. Some of the souls at Zephyr Land have talked to me. Along with Pearl's deceased daughter Sarah, whose presence is restricted to the Abandon Inn lobby. Sarah claims she was poisoned. She identified Randall Kern as the man who killed her."

Jake stood up and threw his hands in the air. "What kind of crazy joke are you playing?"

"I'm not. Jake, I know he's your idol, but according to the people killed in the so-called accident, he caused the derailment.

Then he poisoned Sarah because she might have known what happened to her twin."

"Stop it! Just stop talking." His eyes wide, he ran his fingers through his hair. "We need to pack. Get you out of here. Once we're back in Georgia, you're going to a psychiatric facility so you can get the treatment you need."

Even though she'd expected this, his adamant and controlling attitude set her nerves on edge. She liked him, maybe loved him. His reaction, while expected, sent a painful jab right through her.

"I can't agree to that."

"What? You said you would seek treatment. I told you I wouldn't tolerate another relationship where the person slowly goes insane without talking to a doctor."

"Jake, I appreciate and fully understand this is a lot to take in, but you can't keep comparing me to your mother. My own parents still haven't accepted my…whatever you want to call it. Ability? The sight? A gift? No matter the term, I've already been through every kind of psychological evaluation there is, and there's nothing wrong with me."

"Impossible. You're claiming you talk to dead people. Based on that fantasy, you've assigned blame to someone who couldn't have murdered those people—"

"He *did* murder them, Jake. I'm sorry, but it's the truth. I've been exhausted, keeping this from you. But now my talents can help you with your paper—"

"Are you kidding? No way in hell will I notate ghost proof

explanations in an academic paper. Not only won't my university give me tenure, they'll blackball me in every university across the South!"

She took a deep breath. Tried to understand how difficult this must be for him.

"Let's just chill out for now. You work on your paper. I'll work on mine. Tomorrow, we'll go to Zephyr Land, and I'll prove to you that I can talk to ghosts."

"No!" He edged his way past her and grabbed his wallet. "I'm not going to get caught up in your delusion. We're done."

She'd been wrong. He didn't listen this time. Her heart ached, but a sense of relief still flooded her. At least he knew the truth.

"What do you mean, we're done? I know this is hard to accept, but I can help us both—"

"Not with your psychotic-break behavior, you can't." He flung the door open, turned back, and glared at her. "I need some time alone."

And with that, he stormed out and slammed the door behind him.

CHAPTER THIRTY-FOUR

Jake raced to the lobby, taking two stairs at a time. The faster he could get out of the Abandon Inn, the better.

An animated Clive, dressed to the hilt in the red-trimmed Confederate artillery soldier's uniform, waved his canteen in one hand and the hotel sign-in book in the other. He hooted and hollered about gunpowder, laughing as Pearl attempted to corral him into the back office. Jake grinned at the spectacle but didn't stop. He had enough relationship trouble at the moment. No sense intervening in Pearl's nightly routine.

Picking up his pace, he went outside. Then stopped in the parking lot. Crap. No car. The car agency rep said she would bring a car first thing tomorrow morning. In the meantime, he had no transport.

Or did he?

He returned to the lobby. "Pearl, do you have the phone number for that cabbie JT, the one who picked us up from Zephyr Land?"

She'd managed to grab the canteen and held it over her head like a youngster's game of keep-away. "No, Clive! I said get your butt back into your office!"

Jake waited for her to break free from the insanity. Hmm. Insanity. Was this a glimpse into his future with Amanda? Hanging out on Friday nights, her spotting ghosts under the trees and talking to beings who weren't there? At least Clive had a sense of humor about things, had the decency to not dress like a carpetbagger. Jake couldn't fault the guy.

"Just a moment, Jake. I'd be happy to get JT's number for you," Pearl said, all the while shooing Clive through the rear doorway into the office.

Minutes later, an exasperated Pearl came out, smoothing her beehive hairdo. "Sorry about that."

Jake smiled. "Another normal night, eh?"

"That man is gonna drive me to drink. If I could find myself a mason jar, I'd pour some moonshine right now."

Jake coughed. "You *have* moonshine?"

"Daddy made it in the woods near Fairhope. I kept a canister or two," she said with a mischievous wink. "Looks like you could use a drink yourself."

"Amen to that." Jake sighed. "But I want a change of scenery. I figured JT could drive me to the nearest town. Any pubs you'd recommend?"

She scribbled down the phone number on an index card and handed it over. "Raw McShuckums Tavern is about nine miles north of here, on the way to Fairhope."

Jake bit back a laugh. Southern pubs had strange names, even back in his hometown of Athens, Georgia. How did someone come up with the idea?

"If they have drinks, it sounds like the place. Not a rough redneck fest though, right?"

Pearl shook her head, then pivoted around when she heard Clive start hollering again. "I've got to go. You call JT. He'll take you around."

"Thanks."

Jake went outside to escape the latest Pearl-Clive show and dialed the cabbie's number.

"The King lives on. This is JT."

Chuckling at the Elvis fanfare, Jake gave him the pickup details.

"I'll be there in five," JT said. "The rest of my shift has died down, so good timing."

"See you then."

Jake tapped End. He glanced back at the glowing window lights from the Abandon Inn. Amanda's shadowy curves moved behind one set of blinds. Was she peering out at him? Or had she remained stuck in her delusion?

No matter. He needed to get away. Forget about Amanda's crazy talk.

Minutes later, JT pulled into the parking lot with his window rolled down. "Evening. Where we headed?"

Jake slipped in the back. "Someplace outside of Abandon. I need a drink."

"Sounds serious." JT adjusted the air vents. "Any kind of place you prefer?"

"Pearl said something about an oyster? I don't know. Just a quiet place for a stiff drink."

"Raw McShuckums," JT said, nodding. "Good choice."

They drove in silence as the small town of Abandon faded behind them. Even the air seemed clearer outside of Abandon. Or perhaps Jake was imagining things.

JT fiddled with the music player. "How about some music from the King?" The Elvis tune "Are You Lonesome Tonight" started to play.

Not this song, please. Enough about loneliness. Jake searched his mind for a more accurate Elvis song for the occasion. "How about 'Hard Headed Woman'?"

"Sure thing." JT kept driving, glancing up into the rearview with large brown eyes. "Lady trouble tonight?"

"You could say that." Jake stared out the window at the silhouettes of pine needles against the full moon overhead.

"She stepping out on you?"

"Nah, nothing like that."

"Tell you what. I'm at the tail end of my shift, and I know I'm going to need to drive you back. What's say I join you for a drink?"

Jake shrugged. As much as he wanted a quiet place alone to sip on some bourbon, JT was strange enough to make any conversation interesting.

"Sure thing."

Raw McShuckums was more of a shack in the middle of the woods. Dark walls inside, a few rooms with pool tables, and in the main room a long bar with a mirror behind it so patrons could see their reflections.

Jake took a corner seat. JT sat two stools down. Both of them kept an eye on the mirror to make eye contact rather than turning to talk to each other. Maybe it seemed less intimidating this way, a means to chat or get feedback from someone without looking him directly in the eye.

The bartender, a young waif with maroon streaks in her blonde hair and tats down her arms, set out napkins in front of them. "What are we drinking?"

"Bourbon," Jake muttered.

"And you?" the waif asked, addressing JT.

"Same."

A few seconds later, she plunked the two shots in front of them and moved seamlessly to the other end of the counter to help other customers.

"You know," JT began. "We've all had women trouble."

Jake sipped his bourbon. "This is different."

JT gave a knowing nod, took a healthy swig of his drink. "That's what everyone says."

Glancing at the mirror, at JT's curious stare, Jake figured, why not? Easier to talk to a stranger whom he'd never see again.

"Amanda claims she can see and talk to dead people."

JT continued to stare, his expression unfazed by Jake's answer. "Yeah, and?"

Jake twirled his shot glass between his fingers. "What do you mean, *and*? She's delusional. She honestly believes she can talk to the dead."

"So? You're in the South. People have all kinds of bizarre quirks here. I see Elvis at least once a month over at the Piggly Wiggly."

Jake bit his lip, picking up his shot glass of bourbon. Apparently everyone in Abandon had mental issues?

"The Piggly Wiggly?" he asked.

"Sure enough," JT said. "Buying bread and peanut butter. On sale."

Jake chuckled. "But you know it's not real, right? I mean, he died in nineteen…"

"Seventy-seven," JT said. "That's the rumor, yes."

"Then how can Elvis be at the Piggly Wiggly, taking note of grocery sales, if he died over three decades ago? It's not logical."

JT laughed, kept a wide grin on his face. "That's your trouble right there. You won't find logic in these parts."

"I'm an engineering professor. Logic comes with the territory. Elvis can't be alive if he died—"

"How do you explain all those sightings?" JT asked. "Every rumor has a kernel of truth. I think it's completely feasible Elvis got too overwhelmed by fame. Faked his death and continues to roam the South."

Jake gestured to the bartender. "Can I get another, please? Double?"

"Sure thing." She got his drink, then looked at JT. "How about you?"

"Just a decaf coffee, please. I'm driving this one back to Abandon."

Tat-woman poured him a coffee and sauntered away to help others. Despite her harsh appearance, Jake liked her. She wasn't one of those bartenders who hovered, like some.

"Where were we?" JT asked, ever the cabbie of talkative chatter.

"You were asking why there have been tons of Elvis sightings since his death," Jake said.

"Right. So, how do you explain it?"

"Easy. It's hokum."

JT poured some sugar in his coffee, stirred, and took a sip. "There's all kinds of mysterious things in this world—"

"Yeah, but I don't believe in things that can't be quantified. Elvis sightings? No. The guy's dead, sorry to say. Ghosts and dead spirits? It's a brain imbalance or something. She needs to be taking medication, not defending her psychosis."

"Well, you can have all the logic in the world, but some things just can't be quantified. Doesn't mean they aren't real. Look at the wind, for example. You can't see it, but you know it's there. Many people have found comfort knowing their loved ones are in a better place."

Jake shook his head. "The people selling that dream are charlatans. They're after as many bucks as they can get for their tapestry of lies."

JT broke eye contact with the mirror and turned to Jake instead. "With every profession, there are always those who take advantage. Don't have to talk to the dead to know that. There's honest contractors and pure thieves."

"True."

"I'm not defending the crooks," JT said. "But some folks,

particularly in the South, are known to see things most people can't put a label on. For me, I know Elvis is alive and well. Folks may call me crazy, but what harm I am doing?"

Jake thought a long moment. "You're harming the truth? The honest explanation?"

"So the hell what?" JT took a swig of coffee. "Is your girl hurting anyone? Taking anybody's money in exchange for her gift? I'd imagine telling you something like that had to be hard for her. Chances are, she's trying to help those ghosts with something. Did she give any of that information to you?"

"I didn't stick around to find out. The news of her delusion sent me running from the Abandon Inn. Literally." He had the grace to look down. He wondered now what she thought about him tearing out on her like that.

JT leaned back in his chair. "So she's back there, alone, after she told you something that probably scared her to confess?"

Jake turned, stunned by JT's direct question. "Yeah."

JT chuckled. "And you call *her* crazy. Seems to me you got two choices. Accept her version of things, or be alone."

Neither option had appeal. He hadn't known anyone he could be more comfortable around than Amanda—when she wasn't talking to air or accusing Randall Kern of murder, that is. Dump her and be alone? Not his favorite choice. But to accept her delusion? How? He envisioned their lives several years from now. She'd be on his arm at a faculty party to celebrate his tenure. Then she'd tell his esteemed colleagues how she speaks to the recently departed on a daily basis.

Not a good ice breaker. Not at all.

"You're saying I should not be bothered by her delusion?" Jake asked.

JT shrugged. "What's your alternative?"

"Get her the help she needs."

"And that's your job, is it?" JT asked, then finished his coffee. "Let me tell you something. We all have to be responsible for our own selves. You can't legally commit her. Maybe you can convince her to see a shrink—"

"Amanda swore she would go. Now she's changed her mind. Said she knows she's not mentally ill, she just sees ghosts. She said it like she was talking about what color carpet to buy. Matter of fact. Not like the hokum it is."

"Personally, I believe in gifted people, but that's me. I see Elvis, for heaven's sake. But y'all seem like sweet kids. I'd hate to see things break apart because of something that ain't hurting anyone."

Jake didn't speak for a long moment, just listened to the knocking of the billiards in the next room. He'd spent his entire life on a logical path, had vowed never again to get involved with delusionary tactics. Charlatans had robbed his family, his birthright.

Was Amanda trying to rob anything? No. Not really. She wasn't committing the evil those snake-oil salesmen had all those years ago. But to accept that Amanda talked to spirits who had died? He wasn't sure he could do that either.

JT gestured for a coffee refill. "Lots of pros and cons for either side, but it all boils down to a simple choice."

"What's that?"

"Do you want the girl, or not?"

Jake finished his drink and made mental notes of the pros and cons.

"Well?" JT prompted.

"Yes. I want the girl."

"Then it's simple. Go to her. Accept her oddities. All of them. You won't be as alone as you think. Everyone south of the Mason-Dixon Line has some form of family secret. Comes with the territory."

Jake nodded. He'd heard as much, though his deepest secret had been the agony his own mother went through. Wait a second. His mother.

"What if I asked Amanda for proof?"

JT narrowed his eyes. "Proof?"

"Evidence that she can do what she claims. I'll ask her to talk to my mom. Figure out a way to ask my mom something only she and I would know," Jake said. "Then Amanda will be forced to admit this isn't real."

"Not so sure I'd go with that approach," JT said. "Women can see through tests like that."

"If Amanda claims she can talk to the dead, why wouldn't she be able to prove it?"

Jake smiled wide. Finally. A logical way to handle this dilemma. Once Amanda understood her own psychosis, she'd be forced to seek help when they returned to Georgia.

"Drink up, JT. Things just got better."

CHAPTER THIRTY-FIVE

Amanda glared at the clock for the tenth time in the last half hour. Where was Jake? She shuddered when she remembered how angry he was, how he stormed out in such a hurry. Understandably, he'd been upset at hearing the news about her paranormal ability—but to walk out and not return? They didn't even have their rental vehicle yet.

So where the hell had he gone?

She attempted to read, keep her mind occupied, but tossed the book across the room. Moisture mask on her face? Done and done.

One thing was for certain: she couldn't continue to sit and wait.

After grabbing her purse and phone, she sprinted to the lobby. Sarah peered out from behind a colorful pink umbrella.

"Did you and your boyfriend have a fight?" Sarah asked.

"It's complicated."

"His shoes make a lot of noise when he stomps," she said.

Amanda knelt down, met Sarah eye to eye. "Did he say where he was going after he finished stomping?"

"No. Some weird cab picked him up."

The cabbie from earlier, with the Elvis fascination? She wouldn't put it past Jake to want to get away for a while. But would he return tonight, or did he plan on staying elsewhere until it was time to go back to Georgia? After all, he had what he needed for his project. She still needed to go to Zephyr Land and finish her research.

"Thanks, Sarah. I'm going to go look for him."

Amanda rang the bell at the front desk. Scuffled sounds came from the back room. Seconds later, Pearl appeared.

"Hey, hon. What can I do you for?"

"Did Jake call our cabbie from earlier? Do you know where he might have gone?"

Pearl frowned. The crow's feet on her eyes crinkled even more, giving her face a saggy appearance. Amanda guessed that Pearl had spent one too many evenings chasing Clive out of his many adventures.

"Yes, the PT Cruiser. Your boyfriend said he wanted to go to the next town for a bit," Pearl said. "Needed to get away from Abandon."

Amanda bit her lip. "Oh."

"You two okay?"

The burning tears threatened to pour out of her eyes. No. Resist. "I told him about my ability."

Pearl's eyes widened, stretching the crow's feet until they were almost invisible. "I see. I take it he didn't respond well?"

"No. He stormed out. I figured he would've taken a walk, but he's gone to the next town?"

"We have other cab contacts, sugar. I can call one for you."

Amanda shook her head. "Thanks, but I'm going to try calling my aunt. She can probably come get me."

"You need anything, you let me know," Pearl said with a smile.

"Thanks." Amanda walked outside for better phone reception and to avoid crying in front of Pearl.

Dialing her aunt's number, she waited and took deep breaths.

"Hello? Amanda?"

"Aunt Anzhela? It's me."

"You sound upset, dear. Are you all right?"

"N...no," Amanda stammered. "Are you still in Abandon?"

"Yes. I hadn't planned on returning to Savannah until next week."

"Can you come pick me up at the Abandon Inn? Our car tires got slashed. Jake left to go the next town." She blinked back the surge of tears. "I need to talk to someone."

"Of course, dear."

Usually the dear that followed all of Aunt Anzhela's sentences grated on Amanda's nerves, but right now, the word was a welcome term of kindness.

"Thanks."

"Be there in ten minutes."

Amanda shut her phone and took a calming breath. She didn't blame Jake for being upset, but she wished he hadn't walked out like he had. At least Aunt Anzhela was still in Abandon. The woman could change locations in a blink of an eye. Many times, she did.

Ten minutes later, her aunt pulled up in her blue Prius. Amanda slipped inside and immediately noticed the box of tissues on the console between them.

"Guess you knew I would need these?" Amanda took one and blew her nose.

"I don't have to be clairvoyant to know my favorite niece is upset."

Amanda smiled. "I'm your only niece."

Anzhela patted her hand. "You're still my favorite, dear."

They drove north of Abandon toward Fairhope. Fifteen minutes later, Anzhela jerked the car off the main road and drove between two narrow sets of trees.

"Where the hell are we going?" Amanda sat up straighter, tensing her muscles in case her aunt had suddenly lost control of the car.

"This is beautiful Alabama, dear. Plenty of good things to find if people just get off the main road."

Amanda's throat remained tight. She kept a watchful eye on her aunt's steady hands.

"I guess I didn't expect such a sudden turnoff."

Anzhela smiled wide. "Inertia keeps people going down the long flat path of the interstate. I thought you and I could go someplace more private. Talk. Look at the stars."

Gripping the passenger-side hook on the door handle for safety, Amanda nodded. At least she'd be ready in case her aunt decided to pull any other sudden stunts.

Minutes later, they came upon the edge to an empty field. Tall trees surrounded this hidden meadow carpeted with lush green grass.

"What do you think of the alternate destination?" her aunt asked.

"Beautiful. The Spanish moss dangling from the oak trees almost twinkles under the full moon's rays. How long have you known about this place?"

"I discovered it during my first week here as the librarian." Anzhela put the car in park and stepped out. "It's safe. C'mon, let's sit on the hood and look up at the stars."

Amanda loved how her aunt acted like a teenager more than a stuffy older relative. She must have been quite the fun friend in her youth.

They situated themselves on the hood, both lying on their backs starting at the vast night sky.

"I've never seen so many stars," Anzhela said. "Not even in Savannah."

"You aren't kidding."

For a few minutes, Amanda let her eyes adjust to the darkness and the zillions of twinkling stars overhead.

"You said you needed to talk to someone, dear," her aunt said. "What's going on?"

Amanda turned her head to meet her aunt's curious gaze. "I told Jake about my gift. Told him I didn't need a psychiatric hospital. I know what I am, and I know who murdered all those people at Zephyr Land."

"I'm guessing he didn't take the news well."

"Nope. I think he's done with me, Aunt Anzhela. I'm not even sure if he'll return to the inn. What if he doesn't? Our car's tires were slashed. I'd need to find another way home—"

"Don't get ahead of yourself, dear. You know the regular humans need time to adjust."

"Adjust, yes." Amanda sighed. "Jake's mom was mentally ill, according to him. Who knows? Maybe she was able to see things like we can."

"Perhaps, but it's difficult to tell." Anzhela adjusted the peach-colored hairband keeping all her curls in check. "Either way, sounds like he has a predisposition to dislike things beyond the norm."

"Yes. The man is humanized logic. Like I mentioned before, I'm not sure if he can ever accept me. It's why I kept my ability secret for this long."

Aunt Anzhela reached for her hand and squeezed. "Jake's reaction is his business. You're only responsible for telling him the truth about yourself."

Her wise aunt made sense, but sometimes her logic bordered on the simplistic. Anzhela could get away with being carefree, different, the breath of fresh air in a new town. She could wear paranormal abilities with the same ease as her flowing gypsy-like skirts.

But Amanda? Trying to dress with a carefree personality who could see and talk to the dead was more like wearing a Bavarian yodeling outfit in front of a large crowd at a soiree. Ridiculous, prone to being laughed at, and not comfortable for anyone.

"I know. What am I supposed to do if he doesn't want to see me anymore?"

"Aren't you in Abandon to work on your career?"

"Yes, to submit the proposal to the carousel restoration company."

Anzhela's eyes gleamed in the moonlight when she spoke, her

words slicing reality into the darkness between them. "Focus on your career. Welcome every experience. And don't worry about Jake's reaction until it occurs. Give him some time to adjust. People need that, but most of them eventually come around."

Amanda shifted her gaze back to a random shooting star soaring across the night sky. "I'm not sure Jake will change his mind. Even with time to adjust."

"You must give him the chance. If he fails, you move on. But you're not even giving him the opportunity to come through for you, dear."

Amanda's throat went tight. She choked back the tears beginning to form. Her aunt had described every relationship Amanda had been through in her life—only she'd run away from all of them.

Now she was assuming Jake would be like all the others, even preparing for him to leave.

It never occurred to her to consider the alternative. What if Jake, for some wild unknown rhyme or reason, decided to stay?

CHAPTER THIRTY-SIX

Jake paid JT a hefty tip and his cab fare as he stepped out into the Abandon Inn parking lot.

"Thanks, man."

JT adjusted his ball cap. "Nice hanging out. Good luck with your girl."

"Thanks. Let's hope I won't need luck." Jake waved and went inside the inn lobby.

Pearl stood quietly behind the desk and glanced up at him over her glasses. "Did you have a fun time at Raw McShuckums?"

"I did indeed. Thanks for getting me JT's number."

"You have a good night. See y'all in the morning."

He waved, practically sprinting up the stairs to their room. When he entered, no one was there.

"Amanda?"

Maybe she had stepped into the restroom? He checked. No one there. Not in the closet, nowhere to be found. Her suitcase remained in the same place, so she hadn't left.

A sinking feeling punched him in the gut. What if she'd gone back to Zephyr Land, and alone? He scrambled to get his cell from his pocket and called her.

His call went to voicemail, where he left a brief—and he hoped not as panicked as he felt—message. Picking up the hotel phone, he began to call downstairs to ask Pearl if she'd seen Amanda leave.

That's when a knock came at the door. "Hello?"

"It's Amanda."

Relief flooded through his veins. Good. She'd returned. Safe. He flung open the door and hugged her.

"Hi?" she asked. "What's going on?"

He released her, sat on the bed, and gestured for her to sit beside him. "When I returned and saw you weren't here, I worried you'd returned to Zephyr Land. Thought you might be in danger again."

"No, nothing like that." She brushed her hair back nonchalantly with her fingers. "I couldn't bear to stay alone in the room anymore."

"I'm sorry about the way I stormed out—"

"I shouldn't have dumped on you like that," she said. "I know it's a great deal to process. Most people don't even stick around to find out the details."

"I'm glad you're safe, is all." It was the most honest comment he could think of, because he didn't want to give the impression he believed in her supernatural tales. But thankful she was safe and in one piece? Absolutely.

"Thanks. You too," Amanda said.

"Wait a minute. Where did you go?"

She shrugged. "I called my aunt. We went stargazing in Fairhope."

"Stargazing?"

"What about you? You did run out of here pretty damn quick," she said.

"JT took me to a pub called Raw McShuckums. Pretty cool spot. Had a drink."

She stood up and went to wash her face. Was she avoiding him or waiting for him to spur the conversation on?

When the silence had moved to deafening, he spoke up. "Listen, JT the cabbie had some good things to say. So while I'm not really thrilled with your claim to supernatural ability, I thought maybe, if you provide some proof, I can try to understand."

She settled on the bed beside him. Her eyes flickered with...skepticism? "Proof?"

"Yes. If you can see and talk to the dead, I want to have a conversation with my mother."

"Jake, it doesn't exactly work that way..."

Here came the excuses. "Why not?"

"Spirits are tied to different places. I can't just go talk to John F. Kennedy and ask who really shot him. Not that he knows anyway. Or your mom, or anyone who died in another place or time."

He rubbed his temples, trying to keep the sarcastic comments to himself. "Then how does it work? I don't understand." She rubbed her hand along his arm. It didn't comfort him, and he resisted the urge to push it aside.

"Where did your mom die?"

His stomach clenched at the memory. "Park Hospital in Atlanta."

"I couldn't guarantee it, but if you wanted to speak to her, we would need to go there. I'd need to be close to the area where she left this place—"

"You do understand why it's difficult to believe anything you say about this?"

Her hazel eyes shifted to brown, the color they turned when she guarded her feelings. Most of the time, they were a shade of green, but not now. He swallowed hard, unsure what her next comment might be.

"For every relationship I had in the past, the minute they found out about my gift and freaked out, I ran. I never gave anyone the chance to understand. I don't want to run away from you. I hope you don't want to run away from me."

He absorbed her words, let them enter his psyche. She had a good point, but he wasn't about to start believing in ghosts now.

"I don't want to run," he said. His statement was true. He wanted to seek help for her, get her to understand her delusions. "However, some form of proof would be good."

"How about if I tell you, yet again, that Randall Kern is the one who sabotaged the roller coaster? That Pearl had two daughters who died. One on the coaster. One who hangs out in the lobby."

For a split second, he felt inclined to believe her. Ghosts who hung out in a hotel lobby? Even the most imaginative mind couldn't make up that shit, could it?

"Why the lobby?" he asked. For curiosity, and to keep the two of them talking.

"Sarah said Randall poisoned her. Gave her something to drink when Pearl and Clive weren't looking, and she died."

Jake clenched his jaw. He didn't want to get into another big fight, not after they'd already spent the night apart. But her accusations were verging on the ridiculous.

"Why would Randall poison a young girl?" he asked with as calm a voice as possible.

"Because she was a twin, he figured she might have known something about her sister being killed on the coaster," Amanda said. "So he wanted to make sure she kept her mouth shut."

"And she did, except now her ghost is telling you Randall killed her?"

Amanda gave an exasperated sigh. "I know it sounds strange, but yes. I'm telling you the truth."

"I believe that…" How could he word his thoughts? "I think you believe something you think is true—"

"Don't be an ass. You don't have to accept my supernatural ability, but don't treat me like someone in a rubber room." She scooted away from him.

"I'm trying not to, but your explanations are unexplainable."

She glared at him with dark-brown eyes, every hint of green disappearing. "I know I'm not crazy. Stop treating me like a child."

The words "then stop acting like one" were on his tongue, but he held them back. He had been the one to storm out earlier, the one who lost his temper first. Not her. He wouldn't make that mistake twice.

He took a deep breath. "Listen, we're not going to resolve this tonight." With a tentative hand, he reached out and touched hers. She didn't yank it away. Good. "Let's get some sleep. We'll spend as much time tomorrow at Zephyr Land as you need for your report."

A flicker of green entered her stern gaze. "And after that?"

"We leave town, hopefully in a car with its tires intact. No more safety hazards to threaten us."

She turned away, spoke to the window overlooking the moon hanging in the sky rather than to him.

"Tomorrow night is Thursday. I'm not sure I can leave by then. Definitely by Friday noon, though, once my report is turned in."

Some things weren't worth splitting hairs over. If he could keep an eye on them both, ensure they remained safe for the next day—or worst case, two days—then he could live with that option.

"Okay. Tomorrow night or the next day, depending on how your research goes," he said. "Are we agreed?"

She turned to face him. The glints of moonlight shining across her face made her appear like an angel. How could he stay angry at her for long?

"Agreed," she whispered.

He leaned in, kissed her cheek. "Good. And about your ability…the proof I need…"

"Yes?"

"We can discuss some options later."

She smiled and stood up to get dressed for bed. Tonight, he would give her some space. Tomorrow, he'd keep an eye on her and ensure their safety. Then, when the time came for them to leave Abandon and return to Georgia, he would need to find a way to get her a psychiatric evaluation. Get her the help she needed, once and for all.

The thought she might be telling the truth, that she might not need help, niggled at the back of his mind. With a resolved breath, he pushed it down. Of course she needed help.

CHAPTER THIRTY-SEVEN

Under the full moon's glow, Declan gently pushed Becca on the Zephyr Land swings. His thoughts leapt back to a time when he would do the same for his younger sister, back in Boston. How was Brianna doing now? Just like Amanda, his sister went through a period when she didn't trust herself. Didn't believe in her instincts until danger forced her to start.

He didn't want Amanda to get herself into danger just to believe in the talents she possessed. She seemed more than ready to help, but he needed more info.

Maybe she'd had issues with her boyfriend. One thing about the living, they always got overly concerned about the opposite sex. In truth, when he'd played the role of cocky air force pilot, so had he.

"Declan, push harder," Becca said.

Her tiny voice forced him back to reality, where apparently he'd let his push-her-on-the-swing duty lapse into nothingness and she could no longer soar as high.

"Sorry. I'm lost in thought."

"Why don't you ask for directions?" Becca quipped. Quite the kid.

He laughed. "Men don't ask for directions. Not even when we're dead."

"That's silly."

"Maybe so."

Declan turned his head at the sudden gust of wind in the trees.

Coincidence? He stared down at his hands. They were fading, even from his semitransparent form. No. Not now!

"What's happening?" Becca asked, her voice trembling.

I'm about to get yelled at.

"Don't be afraid, sweetheart," he said. "I'm being summoned by my boss. I'll be back soon."

She let out a scream as he faded from sight. Everything instantly shot past his peripheral vision, like entering an infinite spiral of colors.

Seconds later, he stood on the front lawn of the Alabama plantation. He walked between the arrays of oaks, searching for Connell. Why had the boss summoned him now? Last time they'd spoken, Connell had sounded too busy to even answer questions.

Declan rounded the next tree and stopped short. Connell sat atop Thunder, the majestic black ghost horse.

"Where's your carriage and other horse?" Declan asked.

"Helping out with the war." Connell leapt off his horse with a fluid jump. "So, how much longer are you going to take on this assignment? I need progress."

Declan still wondered what war Connell spoke of, but he knew better than to ask questions the boss would not answer.

"Amanda has agreed to help. She is gathering info on who caused the derailment."

Connell glared at him. "That's it? You haven't made any more progress than that?"

Declan swallowed hard. "I had to spend time convincing her to

help us. Then she had to research and agree to share info with me."
His mind grasped for words like a desperate reaching for straws.
"She was supposed to meet me at the carousel a few nights ago, but
she didn't show."

"Why didn't you go find her? Tell her she needs to hurry? You
have an entire abandoned park and all the props at your disposal to
scare her into helping you. Why haven't you made more progress?"

He stared at the ground. Why didn't upper management ever
understand the pressure that some of these assignments created?
Things were not as simple as being able to get Amanda to move
faster. Humans—especially female humans—were complicated and
took some time to gain trust.

"I appreciate our time frame," Declan began. "I've been doing
my best to gain Amanda's help while dealing with thirty people who
are pissed off they were left to rot for ten years."

Connell's stern gaze softened a bit. "I need you in Louisiana.
Soon."

"What's the assignment? More people we forgot about?" As
soon as the words left his tongue, Declan yearned to take them back.

Connell took two forceful steps forward and placed himself
inches from Declan's face. "Excuse me?"

"I'm sorry," Declan said. "My impatience got the best of me."

Angry cold eyes glared at him for what seemed an eternity.
"Next time my impatience gets the best of me, I'm coldcocking you
to the ground. Then I'll put in a request to send you to Death Valley
in summer. Understand?"

"Yes, Boss." He cleared his throat, exhaling the breath he'd been holding.

Connell stepped back, put a foot in the stirrup, and mounted his horse. "You have thirty-six hours to get these souls moved across. After that, I can't hold Liam back any longer. He'll do with you what he wishes."

A knot formed in the pit of Declan's stomach. Now he was at the mercy of some new boss, Liam, to get this assignment complete in less than two days? He'd been helping souls into the next realm for over fifteen years now. Didn't seniority count for anything?

"What's going on, Connell? Who is this Liam guy? I haven't heard his name in five years. Now you say he may toss me to some crappy assignment?"

Connell looked down on him—literally, from his horse—and sighed. "He runs things now. I can only protect my own people for so long, so take in my words, Declan. Get this job finished, or the next job will finish you."

Two minutes later, Connell had disappeared, and Declan was back in Zephyr Land. Only he'd returned two steps closer than where he'd vanished from. A second later, Becca's high-flying swing hit him in the face. Declan fell to the ground and held his aching jaw.

"I guess you got in your punches after all, Connell," he muttered as he stood up.

Wind rustled in the trees, and Declan swore he heard laughter.

CHAPTER THIRTY-EIGHT

The following morning, Amanda woke up early. Truth be told, she hadn't slept much. How could she relax after yesterday's tumultuous events?

Things could have been worse. She said the words aloud to convince herself. Jake could have abandoned her in Abandon—an irony she definitely didn't need. Instead, he'd stuck around. He hadn't tried to haul her off to the psych ward in Mobile during the night.

Maybe Aunt Anzhela had been right. Amanda and Jake could have a life together.

Of course, his need for proof of her gift—talking to his mother—sounded like the midterm exam from hell. Once they returned to Georgia, she could certainly try to contact his mother near the place where she'd passed on. But if the woman had crossed into her next realm, she couldn't be found, not even for family. Family relationships were complex when it came to the dead. Same as the living.

Maybe Declan could help get Jake the proof he needed? She didn't know, but kept the idea at the back of her mind.

She slipped out of bed, showered quickly, and dressed. Jake kept a pillow over his face as the floor creaked under her footsteps.

Just as she turned the knob to go downstairs, his voice called from behind her.

"Amanda? Where are you going?"

Crap. She'd hoped he would remain asleep.

"Hi. I'm craving coffee, so I'm going downstairs," she whispered.

"Give me a minute. I'll go too."

"You sleep for now. I'm just going to drink a cup, and I'll bring one up for you. How's that?"

Revealing a cute case of bed head, he nodded. "Cream and sugar. Thanks."

She shut the door and scurried downstairs for coffee. At this early hour, no other guests had come into the dining area yet. Just a sleepy-eyed Pearl with her enormous mug.

"Morning," Amanda said. She gathered the fixings for her caffeine fix.

"Look who's up early. Did you and your aunt have fun last night?"

Amanda nodded and sat at a bistro table across from Pearl. She told the older woman all about stargazing in the empty field.

"Heavens, yes," Pearl said, setting her mug down. "Why do you think I own Jeffrey the Jeep? Off-roading is what I used to live for."

The way Pearl had said "used to" made Amanda wonder. She had to ask.

"And now? What do you live for now?"

Pearl offered a half smile and held up her mug. "Coffee and a few minutes peace where I'm not chasing Clive. He sleeps till nine or so. I make sure to get up with the sun so I get time to myself."

Amanda sipped her coffee. Ahh, she felt more awake already.

"Guess it must be hard. When did Clive become…" What was the right word to use?

"A crazy old coot?" Pearl asked, providing the term Amanda sought.

"Yes."

The smile from Pearl's face vanished. "He was always a little nutty, but his condition worsened after Becca and Sarah died."

A hard knot pressed against the back of Amanda's throat. "I…I didn't realize…I know the death of a child had to have been heartbreaking, but I didn't know it could cause—"

"Insane behavior? I didn't know either." Pearl reached out, touched Amanda's hand. "But we learn new things every day. I did tell him I'd talked to Becca recently."

"You did?"

"I figured Clive is already strange. He wouldn't think me odd for talking to our little girl who's no longer here."

"I wish more people were like Clive," Amanda said. "Well, without all the hooting and hollering about reenactments."

Pearl laughed, and her eyelids crinkled all the way to her smile. "I'm afraid he was a die-hard fan of those things even before we met. Just got worse once our girls were gone."

"What did he say when you told him you'd spoken to Becca?"

"He talked about when he showed her how to ride a bike, just like it was yesterday." Pearl took a sip of coffee. "His eyes gleamed when he said her name, and for several hours afterward, he didn't seem as bad off as usual."

Amanda nodded and took a sip of coffee to fill the void of words. She had no idea that using her gift could help someone so much. Like giving Pearl a peace of mind, or giving Clive a tiny sliver of his mind back—if only for a few hours.

Pearl sat forward, seeming to know what Amanda had been thinking. "That's why I urged you to not deny the talent you have. It truly is a gift, something that can help people. Not just me and Clive. What I wouldn't give for a gift like that…"

Wiping away the threat of tears, Amanda said, "Most days, I wish I didn't have it."

"Honey, why would you not want something that could mean so much to people?"

"Makes for a difficult childhood."

"We've all had those," Pearl said. "Did people mistreat you? Ridicule you?" She patted Amanda's hand, and Amanda took comfort from the caring touch.

Amanda nodded. "I learned to live with the teasing. Like the old saying goes, words can't hurt me, right?"

Pearl's eyes brimmed over with concern. "But they did hurt you, didn't they?"

A rebellious tear forced its way out of her eyes and down Amanda's cheek. "Kids would leave voodoo dolls in my locker with a knife struck to the heart, saying I was a witch. Day camps kicked me out after I told someone I saw her grandmother standing next to her. Church groups tried to perform exorcisms on me, and my parents, well…"

"That must have been hard on you," Pearl whispered.

"My parents couldn't deal with any of it. They sent me to shrinks, teen hospitals. Put me on meds that wigged me out—you name it."

"I'm sorry. No one should have to be forced to be normal," Pearl said. "We embrace the abnormal in the South, you know."

Amanda smiled. "You were a great mom to Becca and Sarah, weren't you?"

Now it was Pearl's turn to cry, and cry she did. Big blubbery tears before she stood up, walked around the table, and embraced Amanda in a big mama-bear hug.

"Thank you for bringing my girls back to me," Pearl whispered.

"Glad I could help," she said, sniffling. "Guess it's my turn to cry now."

"Nothing wrong with tears…or special gifts," Pearl said, squeezing tighter.

Amanda reveled in Pearl's big Southern bear hug and enjoyed having a mother figure care about her again—it had been far too long. Something deep inside told her she needed to appreciate this feeling while she still could.

CHAPTER THIRTY-NINE

Jake tossed off the sheets. Hopped in the shower, dressed. Looked at the clock. Amanda had gone downstairs over forty minutes ago. Did it take that long to make coffee and bring back a cup?

Wherever she might be, he needed caffeine of his own. Locking the door behind him, he sprinted downstairs and into the dining area.

Amanda and Pearl stood in the center of the room, hugging. He opened his mouth to say something, yet suddenly felt like an intruder. The same feeling whenever Amanda asked him to grab something from inside her purse. Women's purses were the black hole of mysterious sources of power. Some things, men didn't need to know about.

He shifted the weight of his feet and stared at the floor for what seemed an eternal minute. Then he glanced up. They hadn't moved. Damn, women hugged for a long time. He gave them several seconds more before finally speaking up.

"Morning."

Both pairs of feet jumped about an inch as the women released their hold on each other and turned to him.

"Jake, hi," Amanda said. "Sorry, I was coming up soon with your coffee."

"No worries. I'll grab a cup now." He went to the nearby table and fixed up his cup. "Morning, Pearl."

"Jake," Pearl said, nodding. "Your girl and I were just having one of those emotional chats. Sorry we kept you from your coffee."

"Not a problem."

He kept his mouth shut on how long women hug. That wouldn't go over well except to a male audience.

After pouring the right amount of cream and sugar, he sat down at the table where Amanda's purse lay. Pearl daintily touched her hands to her beehive hairdo and made her excuses to leave, saying she had to go check on some things.

Amanda sat across from Jake. "I guess you couldn't sleep any longer."

"Nope. The need for caffeine surpassed everything else."

He briefly imagined how nice it would've been for Amanda to wake him up slowly, fill another need by being in each other's arms.

Nope. Focus. *She thinks she can talk to the dead, and you both need to get out of Abandon as soon as she's done with her carousel research.*

He took a few big sips of coffee. Hell, he'd have injected the stuff if he could. Today would be a long day, and he needed every alert brain cell to cooperate.

"So, do you think getting in most of today at Zephyr Land, we can be ready to leave tonight?"

Those large hazel eyes shifted, moved from her coffee mug to glare at him. "I told you, I need at least a full day noting the restoration needed on the fixtures and the estimated cost. Then I need to type everything up. The report is due at noon tomorrow."

Her voice had an edge, one he'd rarely heard. "I didn't mean to upset you. I'm only thinking of our safety, of a way to stop overnight on our way back to Georgia."

"We don't know who slashed our tires, and I don't think we need to abandon ship—no pun intended—and leave just yet. Let's spend today at Zephyr Land. Give me until tomorrow morning to write up my paper, and we can leave by lunch."

"I checked the parking lot," he said. "The car rental company brought us a vehicle, and they left the keys at the front desk. Our car will be delivered by the shop by end of day today, so we're good in terms of transport—"

"Great. So we can't dash out of here without abandoning your car. Which would also risk me not finishing my work."

He took another swig of coffee. "I'm only thinking of our safety."

She shrugged. "I told you. Randall Kern is the one who poisoned Sarah, is the man who had the most to gain by killing those two execs who ruined his reputation. If we avoid him, we should be fine."

Jake gripped his coffee mug tighter. She had delusions of seeing dead people, but she was lecturing him on logic and motivation by suggesting they stay away from his hero in engineering?

"I disagree," he said.

"I know you do, because you worship the guy."

"Not worship, but respect, yes. The man accomplished things ahead of his time. You're blaming him for something when there's no proof."

She finished her coffee and stood up. "Fine. Let me finish my work at the park. The minute I send in my report tomorrow, we'll return to Georgia."

He stood up to meet her impatient gaze. A million responses flashed through his mind, but what good would any of them do right now? Amanda was dead set on not leaving Abandon today.

The only solution was to let her finish her carousel analysis. Hope that she could complete the work early, maybe by tonight? Then the two of them could get the hell out of Abandon before anything worse happened.

CHAPTER FORTY

Once inside Zephyr Land, Amanda pulled her notebook from her purse and walked toward the carousel tent.

"Want some help?" Jake asked.

"I'm good."

Jake stood still, looking like he didn't know what to do with himself.

"Don't you need to take more photos of the wheels and bolts?" Amanda asked. *So you can leave me alone?*

"I'm done with the research and photos." Jake followed her into the tent. "Want me to pin up these flaps so you get better air flow?"

She did her best not to laugh. The man was trying to engineer air flow because he had no other task to focus on. No wonder he'd been so antsy to get them out of Abandon.

"Sure." She picked up her camera and removed the lens cap.

She stepped onto the carousel base and examined an emu piece. Horrible paint loss on the long neck and tail. The humidity had seeped into the wood and probably rotted most of the outer surface. This piece would need spackling to replace the nicks and holes, and sanded and primed before more paint could even begin to touch the surface.

Jotting down notes, she glanced toward Jake. He'd taken the tent flaps and knotted them with themselves, providing a cool breeze into the area. Now he sat down near the entrance and played on his phone.

Good thing for cell phones. In a way, he was like a little kid who needed to be entertained. Maybe she'd made a mistake by not getting her own work completed sooner.

"Amanda."

She turned at the male voice, which hadn't been Jake's.

Declan appeared, sitting on one of the flag horses. "Hello. Brought your boyfriend to help, I see."

"He's done with his research," she whispered. "Can you please get off the horse so I can examine it?"

"Whatever the lady wishes." Declan hopped off and weaved between the animals to reach her. "I needed to tell you that our time frame is short."

"*Our* time frame?"

"Yes. I need these souls moved in the next thirty-six hours—"

"Thirty-six hours?" she yelled. Loudly.

"Amanda?" Jake said. "What's going on?"

Great. Conversations with one living being and one dead. These never ended well.

"Talking to a ghost," she said.

Declan's eyes widened. "You told him?"

"Yep."

"I'm impressed."

"Be impressed all you want. He wants me to see a shrink when we return to Georgia."

Jake stood up and walked over. "What's going on?"

No need to hide crazy anymore. Like Pearl had said, her gift could help people.

"Jake, I'm talking to one of the primary ghosts now. His name is Declan."

Jake's eyes narrowed. "Declan."

"Yes. He helps souls cross over. And he's just told me"—she glared in Declan's direction—"that the people who died in the derailment have to cross over into their next realm within thirty-six hours."

"Next realm," Jake repeated.

Declan pointed. "He's a bright one."

"Shut up."

"Hey!" Jake said. "No need to be rude."

"I was talking to the ghost. He…well, he made a comment that wasn't nice."

"I'm going to regret this," Jake asked, "but what did he say?" His eyes returned to their normal expression, with perhaps a bit of pity reflected in those baby blues. Or maybe he was curious about having a dialogue with a ghost.

"He said you kept repeating his words and you didn't seem too bright," she said, casting another angry glare Declan's way. Declan just smiled, clearly enjoying himself in the midst of the conversation.

"What?" Jake said. "Tell the ghost he's a damn bastard!"

Declan cracked up laughing. "I miss human relationships. They're filled with great moments."

"Stop it," Amanda said.

"Stop what?" Jake asked.

Crap.

"Okay, enough playing ping-pong." Amanda looked at Declan. "You stay there. I will talk to you in a minute about the plan."

She turned to Jake. "I need to finish this brief conversation with Declan, then return to my work. Please go. Reexamine the coaster or guard the door or do something so I'm not trying to have three conversations at once."

"That would be two conversations," he corrected.

She cocked an eyebrow. "Really? You're going to do this now?"

"I'd back away if I were you, dude," Declan said.

"Stop!" Amanda shut her eyes, rubbing her hands to her temples before opening her eyes once more.

"What?" Jake and Declan asked in perfect unison.

"Jake, please go outside the tent. I need to work."

"Is your ghost going to stay?"

"You know, you haven't even believed me. Some ghost makes a remark about your ego, and now you're responding?"

"Face it. The man is a hopeless nonbeliever," Declan added.

Jake shrugged. "I'm trying to give you the benefit of the doubt, especially if you're hearing voices that say bad things about me."

Chuckling, Declan said, "He's not convinced yet. The man wants to have you committed."

Enough! Aunt Anzhela wanted Amanda to embrace her gift? Fine. She would, but on her terms. And those terms included ghosts and humans playing nice in the sandbox.

Turning her dagger-filled glare at Declan, she said in a sweet voice, "I'm not going to help you anymore if you don't stop taunting me. Be quiet."

Even in his semitransparent form and Irish pale skin, Declan's face lost its color. "Agreed."

"Good," Amanda said. "Now, Jake, let's walk outside a moment."

"But—"

"Now."

With a sheepish grin, he stepped out. She glanced back to Declan and mouthed, "Behave." Then she met Jake outside the tent.

"So?" he prompted.

"I'm not sure if you believe me or you were just having fun with me like Declan was, but I need you to remain out here while I finish my work."

"Does your hallucination really say bad things about me?" Jake asked.

Ordinarily, his sense of humor would've relieved the tension hanging between them. Not today. Not when her deadline had been moved up and she had a ghost putting more pressure on her.

"Jake, stop. I need to concentrate. I respected your time and space when you analyzed the roller coaster. It's time for you to return the favor."

He looked at his feet, the color rising from his neck to his face. When he met her gaze, he nodded. "You're right. I'm going to remain close by, ensure your safety. However, I'll do my best not to get in your way. You go ahead. I'm going to check out the mechanisms on the Monster machine."

Her irritation subsided a bit. If he could keep busy doing something that interested him, then she could finally finish her research.

"Thank you," she said and returned to the carousel.

Before she walked inside, she took a deep breath. Time to deal with Declan.

"I need to finish my analysis," she said as she entered the tent.

Declan leaned against one of the horses. "The deadline is approaching, Amanda."

"Exactly."

He gripped each rusted gold pole through every horse's back, marching toward her with a sense of urgency. "I meant our deadline. For you to call the cops on Randall Kern, and for me to finally get these souls crossed over."

"You don't understand, do you? Other than the word of ghosts, there's no proof that Randall did anything. I can't call the cops and use ghosts as an excuse."

"Can you and Jake maybe keep an eye on him, watch his movements?"

The dead must think that the living have absolutely nothing to do, because that was exactly what Declan seemed to assume.

"You want me to do a stakeout? Are you crazy?"

"Might reveal Randall's motives, don't you agree?"

She held her notebook, the collection of carousel restoration notes she'd documented, as if it were the most valuable treasure on Earth.

"Right now, my report is important—"

"But so far, Randall has gotten away with murder—"

"Stop!" She clutched her notebook tighter. "I appreciate your position, but these ghosts have waited ten years. In case you haven't noticed, I'm still among the living. Unless I finish my research, and get the images resized, and get the report written and sent by noon tomorrow, unless I get that done and win the apprenticeship, then I'm headed right back into a job I hate without any prospects of entering the career I went to school for. I'm done hating my life from nine to five. This comes first."

Declan's eyes widened at her sharp tone, and for a moment, he remained speechless.

Honestly, she'd surprised herself too.

"I didn't mean to sound so curt," she said, "but you need to understand how important this is to me. It's the reason I came here, along with getting to know Jake better."

"And how's that going?" Declan asked with a knowing glance.

"Complicated."

"How much time do you need for this report thing?"

Her gaze moved across the various animals on the carousel. If everyone left her alone, she could probably get all her notes done within three hours. Getting people—alive and dead—to leave her alone? Unlikely, therefore extending her research time until the end of the day.

"At least eight hours with peace and quiet," she said using an authoritative tone. She gave herself an extra hour for padding, since thus far, the dead spirits seemed impatient. She couldn't give in to these spirits again. Yes, she'd help them. On her terms.

Declan frowned. "I don't suppose you could knock it down to three hours—"

"Argh! You're impossible." She wanted to hurl something at him, but she wasn't about to endanger her precious notebook.

He held up his hands, apparently expecting a projectile from her. "Okay, okay. Eight hours, then I'll check back."

"Thanks. Go ask the other ghosts if they have a way to prove Randall caused the derailment. Unless we get a confession, which is unlikely, I can't just call the sheriff. This is a small town. The sheriff and Randall might be friends, meaning no one will believe my suspicions without proof."

"I'm on it. Maybe Chester and Andrew know something they haven't said yet."

"Good. Leave me be. Go help gather proof. Good-bye, Declan."

With a charming smile, he said, "See you soon, Amanda," and walked out.

* * *

Six hours later, Amanda reviewed her notes in the diminishing sunlight. Incredible how much she had been able to analyze and jot down with some peace and quiet. She'd become aware of something glaringly obvious that she'd missed in all the ghost mayhem.

She'd been so rushed for time, analyzing every piece of this carousel, she'd never stopped to focus on the whole entity. The carousel in front of her had one glaring fault: it wasn't cohesive. The themes were all over the place, something that should have jumped out at her earlier.

An emu, two flag horses, a carriage, and some jumper horses comprised the carousel that shut down before it barely had the chance to complete its first rotation. What had the original designers intended with this bizarre mix-and-match scheme?

Most carousels stuck to a particular theme. Flag horses and other patriotic colors were often used in towns of historical significance—Valley Forge, Jamestown, and Plymouth. Why stick an emu in the middle of a red-white-and-blue theme?

If the designer wanted an emu, there should be zebras, tigers, and other African plains animals to complement the design in its entirety.

The theme would be her first suggestion, the overall observation for restoring the carousel. Second, much of the paint had chipped. Someone hadn't put a high-quality topcoat on those surfaces when the paint had dried. While certain colors weren't typically durable for an extended time without maintenance, a durable topcoat would have helped slow the decay.

Third, the Gulf Coast's humidity hadn't been kind to any piece. Depending on the carousel's future location, major rework needed to be done in addition to an implementation plan to protect the surfaces from nature's elements.

From what Amanda could tell, the original paint had been acrylic, which had its uses but wasn't the most durable. However, acrylic was fast drying, and perhaps the company had been in a rush to complete the carousel on time.

Based on the cracks she'd found along several horse manes, the original pieces hadn't been primed correctly either. Maybe not even once. She'd read articles stating that three coats of primer should be the bare minimum.

Hmm. Maybe Zephyr Land was better off having been abandoned a few days after opening. Chipped and rotting wood horses could easily cause an accident where a child could be harmed on the carousel. In combination with the roller coaster, that could have been a second disaster waiting to happen.

The wind blew a breeze into the tent, cooling her face. Almost done. She made specific notes about the paint colors, recommending metallic paints to create unique effects in color. By mixing oils and enamels, new colors and patterns could emerge and create something indicative of this particular carousel. A way to make it stand out from the others.

No matter which paints were eventually used, the necessary tasks of sanding, priming, and dusting each and every surface was imperative. She didn't know why these precautionary steps had been missed when Zephyr Land was in its construction phase, but to function going forward, these were items she would recommend— along with yearly maintenance and touch-ups.

She took three steps back, studying the noncohesive mess that she'd just analyzed. Amazing how many ideas came spilling into her mind once she'd summoned her focus. For the first time in her life, she looked forward to composing a thirty-page paper. No one else had access to a carousel like this one. The apprenticeship opportunity seemed closer than ever before, a chance for a new career—just within her reach.

CHAPTER FORTY-ONE

Jake paced the boardwalk, bored out of his mind. Given the roller coaster's excellent design, the Monster ride was its opposite. Poor quality tracks, shoddy seats in cars without much room, and the potential for electrical outages on every glowing light on the machine's eight arms that raised people up in the air and twirled them around until nausea arrived.

He checked his phone. Five in the afternoon, and his stomach growled to back up the time. Reaching into his pocket, he pulled out a granola bar. He'd tried to get Amanda to take a lunch break earlier, but she'd refused and insisted she be left alone. Not that he blamed her, but maybe she would finish in time for dinner.

Slumping against the old soda counter, he sat down. Settled in and started to play games on his phone. He'd become immersed in a game of solitaire when Amanda tapped his foot with hers.

"Hey, stranger," she said.

"Hey, beautiful." He stood up and smiled at her. "You get everything you need, or is this you taking a break?"

She cradled the notebook in her arms. "I have everything I need to start typing. There's still the matter of the thirty-page paper."

He frowned, hoping they could have left before nightfall to return to Georgia. Guess that wasn't an option.

"C'mon, spending one more night in Abandon won't kill you," Amanda said. "I'll type and submit my paper tonight. Tomorrow morning, we'll have breakfast, plenty of coffee, tell Pearl good-bye, get your car, and head back to Georgia with plenty of daylight to spare."

"You're right." He leaned in and kissed her cheek. "You're going to ace that apprenticeship. I know it."

She released the grip on her notebook, pulled him closer, and planted a long kiss on his lips. Wow. Giving her the hours of time she needed certainly had paid off.

"Come on," he said. "Let's head back to the inn. I want you, and not in an abandoned park."

After relocking the Zephyr Land gate and starting the car, Jake glanced up through the windshield. Was the sky getting darker? The translucent white clouds turned dark blue in a matter of seconds. The sun had dipped behind a cluster of cypress trees, outmaneuvered by the impending storm.

"We'd better get back fast, or we'll get caught in a downpour," Jake said.

Amanda pressed the buttons to ensure their windows were up. Just then, the sky cracked open and torrential rains fell. "Good timing," she said. "Should we wait until the storm passes?"

He checked his phone's weather app. "Look at the squall line. A big band of yellow and red passing through lower Alabama. Waiting won't help. Let's just get back to the inn."

She glanced out her passenger window and then settled back in her seat. "Drive careful."

"I plan to."

Going slow, Jake eased the car out of the lot and onto the long, narrow exit road leading away from Zephyr Land. Even with the windshield wipers on the highest setting, he still couldn't see five feet in front of them, but no one else should be on this exit road.

After several minutes of creeping along, he approached the main state road that led back to the inn. Glancing both ways, he didn't see any headlights. Made sense. No one would be out in this mess unless they had to be. Thank goodness Amanda had finished her research. They were done with Zephyr Land.

He pulled the car right, staying in the center of his lane. The headlights on the rental Chevy Malibu illuminated the white dashed lane lines on the road, even though he could only see one at a time in this monsoon madness.

A few yards later, with the Abandon Inn's silhouette in sight, his pulse raced. Had he seen something in his rearview? He checked again. Darted his gaze from mirror to road. Nothing except pounding water. Maybe he'd spotted a possum in his peripheral vision?

Wham!

Metal crunched as something hit them from behind. "What the hell?"

Amanda's head flung forward, then jerked back with the seat belt's restraint. The car bobbed and weaved on the shoulder, shaken off the road.

"Jake!"

"Hold on!" In the corner of his eye, he noticed another vehicle. No headlights. Dark blue.

Pulse racing, Jake gripped the wheel. It bobbed to the right, lunged to the left. Deep breath. Stabilize the car before they crashed

into something. He slammed on the brakes. No good. The car
screeched off the asphalt road and into the mud. Right foot, stomp on
brakes again. With this storm turning the ground into instant mud,
the brakes offered little traction.

If he didn't stop the car soon, they'd hit a patch of trees up
ahead. Think. Quick. Maybe speeding up and steering left would put
them back on the road? Why had the car rental agency given them a
car without traction control? In Alabama, for crying out loud!

"Brace yourself!" Jake yelled.

Amanda gripped the passenger handle.

He yanked the steering wheel to the right. Immediately back to
the left, floored the gas. Clunky at first. Sputtered and scraped
against the ground, but the car moved.

"It's working," Amanda said. "Do it again."

"Ahead of you." Jake repeated the steps. Yanked the car away
from the mud and pressed down on the gas. After a little more
sputtering and coughing, the car inched its way back onto the road.

They both let out collective sighs of relief. Jake kept his foot on
the gas. He wasn't risking the car stalling out again or losing its
balance on the road.

"What the hell happened?" Amanda asked.

"I saw something strange in my rearview before it vanished.
Seconds later, something rammed into us."

"Another car?"

"I never saw headlights, but it looked like a blue station wagon."

"We should call the cops. Maybe the same person who slashed

the tires followed us?"

Amanda's words were exactly what he'd been thinking, but he hadn't wanted to say them out loud. This was the primary reason he'd wanted to leave Abandon for good and not stay another minute.

"I'll call the police when we reach the inn. You work on your report so we can get the hell out of this town tomorrow morning."

"Just get us back to the inn," she said.

Her tone suggested she didn't seem as eager to leave Abandon as he was. No matter. He would convince her. He had to keep her safe.

"The trunk sounds like it's come loose," he said. "But I'm not about to get out of the car and check. We aren't stopping until we reach the Abandon Inn. No sense serving us up as sitting ducks."

He pressed on the gas, driving them into the dark, wet night. Who would be after them? And how did anyone know they would've been at the park today? Except that Abandon was a small town, and word got around in rural areas.

Jake shook his head, trying to make sense out of everything. Maybe whoever slashed the tires had followed them. What if some deranged psychopath was still after them? First the slashed tires and then being run off the road. No need to let "third time's a charm" come true for this maniac.

Only one thought permeated Jake's mind—he needed to get Amanda and himself the hell out of Abandon, Alabama. And never return.

CHAPTER FORTY-TWO

Amanda never thought she'd be so glad to see Pearl chasing Clive through the Abandon Inn lobby. He'd found his musket and sprinted around the large room while Pearl yelled obscenities and did her best to prevent any injuries.

Oddly, this was normal. Tires being slashed and being run off the road? Not normal. Not by a long shot.

"We need to call the police," she repeated to Jake.

"I'll do it." Jake ran his fingers through his hair. "I'll stay and wait for them. You go work on your report. I want us to leave at first light."

Jake's Civic had been returned and was in the parking lot when they arrived at the inn.

"You sure?"

"Yeah. Go get your stuff done." He pointed to Pearl, who'd managed to tackle Clive onto the sofa and retrieve his musket. "At least I'll be entertained until the cops arrive."

Amanda smiled and went upstairs to their room. After making herself a small cup of hot jasmine tea, she sat on the bed with her laptop on. Time to get this paper finished. She reached for her notes. Wait a second. Where was her notebook? It had been by her side only seconds earlier.

She lifted her feet. Looked under the bed. Got up, walked into the restroom, and glanced around to see if she'd left it on the counter when she'd made her tea. No notepad there either.

"Where the hell did it go?"

"You looking for this?" a voice near the window asked.

She spun around, her breath caught in her throat. Declan stood there, holding the spiral-bound book. "Declan. You scared me. Wait a second. What are you doing here?"

"Me? What are *you* doing here? We made a deal, remember? I leave you alone at the park for several hours to get your research done, then you help me."

Crap. She'd been so excited to finish the research. Then she and Jake had been rammed off the road, and she'd completely forgotten Declan had said he would return.

"I'm sorry. We wound up leaving the park sooner than I thought. Then someone tried to run us off the road—"

"What?" Declan's eyes widened. He immediately stopped leaning against the window. Sat down in a chair, facing her. "Are you both okay?"

"Fine." She cleared her throat. "I needed to finish my paper, so I'm here while Jake talks to the cops downstairs."

"I'm glad you're all right." Declan stood and paced the floor. "The more I talk to every soul at the park, the more they all blame Randall Kern. Have you and Jake been keeping an eye on him? Any strange behavior that might lead to his arrest?"

"No." Amanda sighed. "Sarah told me Randall poisoned her. I didn't trust the guy from the start, but Jake worships him."

"Nonbelievers are always the most gullible—"

"Stop with the anti-Jake comments," she said. "He may be stubborn, but he's a decent guy."

"Fair enough." Declan glanced out the window. "Why don't you go to Randall's house now? Search the premises? Maybe he has some trophies or reminders of that fateful day when the coaster derailed?"

Amanda turned away, taking a sip of her soothing tea as she racked her brain for an answer.

"Randall isn't stupid. The insurance investigators, the police, nobody could find any evidence that he caused the derailment. Truth be told, Jake's findings and his position paper might get the investigation reopened. That's probably the best chance you have to get these souls to cross over."

"I can't wait that long. I only have one day left!"

"Can't you go to your superiors, ask them to extend the deadline?" she asked.

Declan gave a sarcastic smile. "If you think the living are deadline oriented, just wait until you're dead."

"Okaay..."

"Think. There has to be something we can do," Declan said.

"I'm out of ideas. We've been to Randall's house twice. There's no evidence to link him to the derailment. All we have is the word of a five-year-old ghost who claims he poisoned her, along with my suspicions, which Jake refuses to acknowledge."

"If only Jake were gifted," Declan muttered.

"Would make my life easier too," she said. "But believing someone committed a crime and proving it are very different things. At the rate we're going trying to find evidence against Randall, an arrest isn't going to happen."

"I'll bet Randall is the one who ran y'all off the road earlier."

"Maybe," she said. "But he drives a 1978 Dodge pickup truck. It's pretty noticeable, and the car that swerved at us tonight was blue. Maybe a Honda, but we aren't sure."

Declan shook his head. "Maybe he borrowed someone's car. One thing is for certain. I'm never going to finish this job on time unless you and Jake help me every minute—"

"Wait. What else can I do, Declan? I embraced my gift. Told Jake the truth. Went with him to research the derailment. His position paper points to evidence never before considered. Granted, not enough for the police right now because the findings don't finger Randall as a suspect. The best we can hope for is when the paper is published, it could eventually get the case reopened. There's no statute of limitations on murder. Then you can help the souls cross over."

"My bosses are going to banish me to the worst possible location, make me wait for people to die while I suffer."

"I'm sorry. I'm not a cop, not part of some crime unit. What else should I do?"

Declan slumped into a chair. "I don't know. If only we could get Randall to confess, maybe you could record it? That's the way my little sister Brianna got Begley locked up in Savannah."

Amanda shook her head. "I don't know who Begley is, but hoping Randall will act like him is wishful thinking. Randall lives like a recluse. He didn't even want us in his house the two times we visited. I doubt he'd let us in if we went back."

The door creaked as Jake walked inside. She shot a glare at Declan, letting him know not to interrupt.

"Did you talk to the police?" she asked.

Jake nodded. "They're filling out a report so we can submit the claim with the rental car company."

"That's it? Do they know who ran us off the road? Any connection to the person who slashed our tires?"

"They don't have enough evidence to question anyone, and they didn't seem too enthused when I suggested they try."

She sighed, noticing the semitransparent Declan did the same. She'd hoped maybe Jake would've had more luck.

"They didn't think the car sounded familiar? A blue Honda?"

"The cops didn't, but Pearl pulled me aside after they left. Told me there are only two blue cars in town that aren't trucks. The closest one belongs to Mary Galden—"

"The woman who worked at Bello and Toale? The one we talked to about the lawsuit and the derailment?" Amanda asked.

"The same. I thought maybe I could go by her house, ask her a few questions."

"When?"

Jake shrugged. "You need to do your paper. I figured I'd give you some peace and quiet—"

"Be careful." In truth, she didn't want him going to Mary's without her, but she had to get the report finished. Delaying her dream wasn't an option.

"I will," he said. "So how's the paper coming?"

Amanda glanced toward the chair. Declan had vanished, leaving her notebook where he'd been sitting.

"Good," she said, swallowing hard. "I just need to finish it."

Jake nodded. "Why don't I give you some time, and I'll go talk to Mary?"

"Be cautious, okay? I mean, someone is obviously after us—"

"I'll be fine," Jake said. "But if I'm not back in a couple of hours, call the cops."

CHAPTER FORTY-THREE

After driving around in a maze pattern to avoid being followed, Jake finally parked his car at Mary Galden's house. Last time he and Amanda had stopped by, Mary kept her car in the driveway. Not tonight. Maybe she had it in the garage?

At least the monsoon rains had shifted to a slight drizzle. With a resolved breath, determined to stay focused and not dwell on the threatening events from earlier, he stepped out of the rental Malibu—which he'd driven so he could compare the damage to Mary Galden's vehicle—and walked around the car. Performed a general inspection. Looked for what he could under the glow of the street lamps. Maybe he could find some hints or scrapes of dark-blue paint on his fender.

The trunk had been mashed in and the rear taillight busted. Kneeling down, he spotted a few scrapes of blue paint. Bingo. He reached for his cell phone and took photos of the evidence. A shame Mary hadn't parked her car in the driveway or on the street, where he'd have easy access.

Still, he could talk to her and ask where she'd been all evening. Maybe she'd let him inspect her car… He sprinted up the steps and, with a firm hand, rammed the door knocker twice.

Long and loud sneezes echoed from inside, followed by several groans. "Hold on," Mary said, her voice barely recognizable being so congested.

"Hello? Mary?"

She unhooked the deadbolts and opened the door. Jake immediately took a step back. He didn't want to catch whatever terrible germs might be radiating off her person, for she looked awful. Clasping a light-blue robe around her, she pushed the worst case of bed-head hair he'd ever seen out of her eyes. Then she sniffled. Her nose turned a deep pink, probably from all the sneezing.

"Sorry," she mumbled. "I've been recouping from a cold. What's going on?"

"I don't mean to bother you at this late hour," he said. "But I just wondered if you were out earlier this evening on State Route 74?"

She gawked at him for a long minute and expelled the loudest sneeze he'd ever heard.

"Bless you," Jake said, doing his best to keep from breathing the same air.

"Thanks. And to answer your question, nope, I've been hunkered down on the couch all day with my jug of vitamin C." Mary gave a crooked smile. "Of course, I switched over to a hot toddy after five o'clock."

That would explain the bourbon scent Jake picked up in the air.

"So you've been home? All day?" he asked, just to confirm.

"Yes. Where the hell would I go in this condition?" She stepped back and sneezed three times in quick succession. "Sorry."

"No worries, ma'am." He glanced toward her garage door. Obviously she hadn't been driving earlier. Maybe someone had borrowed her car?

"I know it's none of my business, but Pearl at the inn mentioned you have a blue Honda? I thought I remembered seeing it when Amanda and I spoke to you a few days ago."

Mary's foggy eyes squinted. "Yes. Why?"

"Did anyone borrow your car tonight?"

She held up her hand as if she were going to sneeze, then didn't. Was she using a stalling tactic, a way to search for a lie? He couldn't tell, but her posture and tone seemed to suddenly shift when he'd asked her about her car.

"Ms. Galden? May I see your vehicle? Would you let me examine the front bumper?"

She pressed her hand against the doorframe, leaning on it for support. "I'm sorry. That hot toddy is just kicking in. What's all this about?"

"I'd like to take a quick look at your car's front bumper."

For a moment she stood still, the dull glaze in her sick eyes looking past him and into the distance. Why would she be so secretive? He hadn't told her the blue car had been involved in a hit and run. They were just chatting. No reason to hold back on friends borrowing her car. Though he did suppose asking to check out her bumper was odd...but why not show him if she had nothing to hide?

"I'm sorry. I'm not feeling well. You'll need to come back tomorrow," Mary said, pushing the door shut.

"Wait!"

"Young man, I'm sorry, but I'm feeling ill. Come back

tomorrow. Thank you."

"Ma'am, I need to find out—"

"Night." And with that, the door was shut and latched. Deadbolts clicked into place.

Jake stared at the door that she'd practically slammed in his face. Damn. He glanced toward the garage. There were a few small windows, but not enough for him to tell if there might be paint on the car's front bumper. Not even if he had a flashlight, which he didn't.

He supposed he could try to pick the lock of the side garage door, but breaking and entering... What now?

Amanda's unsubstantiated assumption rang loud in his mind: *I think Randall's guilty.*

Jake knew better, but why not get the proof? He had another forty minutes before he needed to return to the inn. Amanda likely needed the quiet time to continue her report.

Sure. Jake went to his car and drove the short distance to Randall's house.

When he knocked on Randall's door, a series of deep, guttural barks practically caused Jake to leap out of his skin. He kept forgetting Randall had a large shepherd. Every time, that adrenaline rush kicked in, despite knowing to expect it.

"Who's there?" the voice bellowed from inside.

"Sir, it's Jake Mercer. The engineer? We've talked before, and I had a few more quick questions for you."

A series of grumbling noises came from the other side of the door. Jake took a deep breath. He wouldn't stay long. Just enough to ask a few things about the roller coaster. Basic questions that would rule Randall out as a suspect. Prove to Amanda her assumptions had been incorrect.

Randall opened the door and turned toward the German shepherd. "Catfish, go to your bed!"

With a whine and a snuffle, Catfish sauntered over to his bed, turning around three times and clearly planning exactly where he would lie down in relation to his bushy tail.

"Good boy," Randall said, turning his gaze back to Jake. "What can I do for you?"

"I'm sorry to drop by unannounced."

"That's okay. I'm home now."

"Oh, you been out on the town?" Jake said with a hint of humor.

Randall walked over to his old-model fridge, pulled it open, and handed Jake a beer. "Mary and I went out to a movie. They just built that new movie-plex where you can eat dinner while you watch a movie. Ain't that something?"

A knot formed in the back of Jake's throat, and it slid down into his stomach. Randall had lied to him. Had Amanda been right? Jake knew Mary hadn't been anywhere tonight, but Randall didn't know Jake had just stopped by Mary's. Why would the man lie about his whereabouts?

Unless he was the one who'd borrowed Mary's car?

Jake bit his lip.

"Cat got your tongue?"

"What?" Jake racked his brain and tried to stay focused.

"I said them new movie-plexes are pretty amazing. You ever been to one with your gal?"

"Uh, sure. They have one where we live, plus dozens in Atlanta."

Randall took a swig of beer, staring at Jake for too long of a second. "I forget. You're from Georgia."

"Yes. We're actually headed back tomorrow." Jake glanced around the room. "I wanted to say good-bye. Thank you for your help with answering my questions the other day."

"You're welcome."

Jake swigged his beer. Telling Randall he'd come to say bye sounded logical, right? Jake thought so, although Randall's lie about stepping out on the town with Mary was a surprise. If the man would not be truthful on his whereabouts, what else would he lie about? Had Jake and Amanda stumbled onto something Randall didn't want either of them to know about?

The more Jake considered the possibility that Randall could've been the one to run them off the road, the more worried he became. Logic did point to Randall hiding something. And that didn't sit well with Jake at all.

"Say, that truck of yours—" Jake began.

"Yep?"

"What year is it? I've been aiming to get me a pickup truck at some point."

"Nineteen seventy-eight. Best year for music and trucks,"

Randall said. Catfish let out a bark, as if to agree.

"I love the style."

"It's one of a kind. My life was on top of the world that year. Before Bello and Toale became the greedy bastards who ruined me…" Randall shook his head, chugging the rest of his beer. "All in the past. I just hope Chester and Andrew rot in hell for what they did."

"As do I," Jake said. "Well, I'd better be getting back. I need to pack up."

"So y'all are heading back to Georgia, eh?"

"Yes." Jake hoped by mentioning that fact, Randall wouldn't see them as any kind of threat. If he had been the one to slash the tires and run them off the road, Jake needed to make sure Randall didn't feel threatened enough to do anything else.

"Y'all take care now," Randall quipped.

"I'll show myself out. Thanks again for the engineering Q&A from earlier. Night." And with that, Jake bolted to the car.

Tomorrow morning he needed to make sure he and Amanda left before anything else bad happened in Abandon.

CHAPTER FORTY-FOUR

Amanda placed her notebook on the small desk in their hotel room. Began to organize her thoughts for the apprenticeship submission.

A twinge of guilt nagged at her. If only she could do something more to help Declan and the other souls, but she'd done everything in her power. She couldn't change criminal procedure and have the cops arrest someone when there wasn't any evidence.

Stop. Focus. Time to get this paper done, once and for all. After making a brief outline, she began to type each module of her analysis. How the carousel needed a more cohesive design. How different types of paints should be used. How her proposed cost analysis would prevent weather damage and other time-related wounds in the future.

Her fingers flew across the keyboard. When she was in her element, thinking about what she loved and talking about it, time seemed to speed up. Not like her day job as an office manager, where the tiny secondhand on every clock dug in its heels and refused to move at a faster pace.

Color suggestions for the horse manes, primer necessities for the poles that centered in each horse's saddle, and gold leaf uses all came out in a slew of words, tiny black letters filling in—turning a blank page into a flurry of black lettering that could get her the career she yearned for.

When she glanced at the clock, ninety minutes had passed. Wow. She could've sworn only ten minutes had gone by. The power of passion.

Now to resize and rename each of the photos she'd taken with her camera. With any luck, she could get most of them done before Jake returned. Digging into her bag, she pulled out her camera. She pressed the button to open so she could connect the SD card to her laptop.

Oh shit. Where was her SD card? The piece that held all the photos she'd taken at Zephyr Land? She yanked open her bag again. Dug and scrambled through all its contents. No card.

The photos were a huge part of her presentation. She had to send them along with the paper. So where the hell had the SD card gone? Had Jake borrowed it when he'd taken photos of the roller coaster? Doubtful. She had used the camera after that to take additional snapshots of the individual pieces of the carousel.

The carousel…

Damn. Now she remembered. She'd removed the SD card when her camera hadn't functioned correctly. And placed the card on the base of the carousel by the emu. That's when Declan and Jake decided to have their little shouting match, and she'd forgotten to put the card back into the camera. She hadn't ended up taking more photos.

So the SD card remained at Zephyr Land. Crap. She and Jake would need to retrieve it at first light so she could modify the images and submit the paper.

Placing her head in her hands, she hoped nothing else would go wrong.

* * *

Twenty minutes later, Amanda heard a knock on the door. She peered through the peephole and saw Jake. Unlatching the door, she let him inside.

"Did you see Mary? What happened?"

He came in and slumped onto the bed. The tiny vein in his neck bulged.

"I talked to both Mary and Randall."

"Randall?" Amanda sat beside Jake and placed her hand on his knee. "Tell me what happened."

Jake's eyes held a sadness, a dark storminess behind those bright blues. "He lied to me."

"About what?"

"Where he'd been earlier tonight." Jake stared out the window and then met Amanda's gaze. "The guy claimed to have painted the town with Mary, only I'd just driven from Mary's place. She's the poster child for a flu epidemic. No way could she have gone anywhere."

"So she didn't use her car."

With a heavy sigh, Jake said, "No, she didn't. But she got real tripped up when I asked if anyone had borrowed it. She clammed up, told me she had to go, and practically threw me out of her house."

Amanda remembered how frightened Sarah had been of the man who'd poisoned her, the one who had seemed friendly and pretended to be a buddy of her dad's, but in reality, he had just wanted to kill her.

"Randall's had some practice with lying," Amanda whispered. "That's what the little girl's ghost told me in the lobby."

To his credit, Jake didn't scoff or dismiss her comment. He just sat there, staring at his feet. "Why would Randall lie to me? The only reason would be if he didn't want us to know where he really was—"

"Like borrowing Mary's car to run us off the road," Amanda said.

"Right." Jake stood up and paced the room. "I'm not even saying he's the one who tried to hurt us, but I got a weird vibe when I showed up at his house. I kept telling him you and I were leaving tomorrow morning at first light. I made sure he understood that we would no longer be in his way."

"You know the truth too," Amanda said. "I hate to say 'I told you so,' but in this case, I think Randall is the one trying to get rid of us."

"I won't say for certain," Jake said, but there was a doubt radiating from his eyes that hadn't been there earlier. "But we can't rule Randall out either."

Amanda reached for Jake's hand when he paced near her. Learning one's hero had flaws was never easy. Learning one's hero may have attempted to kill them earlier tonight was a whole other ball game.

Jake shrugged. "At least he knows we'll be out of here first thing in the morning."

She bit her lip. "Um, yeah. About that…"

"What?"

"I'm fairly certain I left my SD camera card on the carousel at Zephyr Land. I need it to submit my paper."

"Are you serious?" He dropped her hand. "I have some important photos on that card too! I didn't insert a separate card for my roller coaster pics."

"Afraid so. I looked everywhere. I even thought you might have put it in another spot, but then I remembered taking it out to check my camera earlier. I need us to return to Zephyr Land, just to get the SD card."

Jake sighed. "Fine. We'll go first thing in the morning. I would say let's go now, but with everything that's happened, I'm not putting us in more jeopardy at this hour."

"Agreed. We should go when the sun is up tomorrow."

"Will that give you time to finish your paper submission?" he asked.

"Yes. Everything is done. I've already submitted the paper piece online. All I need is to get that SD card, spend about half an hour formatting photo sizes, and then submit them as an appendix item."

"Do you have to do it here, or can we do it in an Internet café on our way back to Georgia?"

She thought for a moment. Technically, she could use her laptop anywhere with Wi-Fi and upload the photos. The design company knew she would be sending additional information before the noon deadline tomorrow.

"I can do it anywhere, but the photo appendix is due by noon."

Jake nodded. "Let's get up, check out, and grab the SD card first thing. No more back roads returning to Georgia. We'll go north to Mobile, then catch Interstate 65. Mobile is sure to have some Internet cafes. We'll have breakfast. You work on your photos and submit."

As much as she'd wanted to hang out and have breakfast and coffee with Pearl before leaving town, Amanda knew this was the better option.

"Sure. As long as we get to Mobile before ten thirty, we should be good," Amanda said.

Declan and the ghosts would remain stuck in the park, but what could she do? Aside from becoming a cop herself, she could only report her suspicions. She and Jake had already done that, only to fall on the sheriff's deaf ears.

Perhaps Jake's position paper focusing on the derailment could eventually bring justice to the victims of the tragedy at Zephyr Land ten years ago. She'd shared her findings with Declan, had done everything in her power to bring those souls a semblance of peace.

She hoped that would be enough.

"Great, then it's settled," Jake said. "We wake up at six, get your SD card, and get the hell out of Abandon."

Before anything else happens hung on the tip of her tongue, but she didn't say the words out loud. Jake probably thought the words too, and he'd be correct. They both needed to abandon the town of Abandon before someone succeeded in running them off the road—permanently.

CHAPTER FORTY-FIVE

The next morning, Amanda slipped out of bed and dressed in a comfy T-shirt and jeans. Outside, wisps of orange and pink appeared in the sky, signaling the early dawn.

"Jake." She shook his arm gently. "Jake, wake up."

"Hmm?" He moaned, pulling the covers up higher to his neck.

"Time to wake up." She flipped on the table lamp. "It's six thirty."

He moaned and tossed off the covers. "Give me a few minutes to get ready. Do you think Pearl will have coffee out this early?"

"I'm sure she will. I'll bring down a few of the paper cups so we can take our coffee to Zephyr Land."

"Good plan." Jake went into the bathroom to get ready.

Amanda finished packing and placed her laptop and notebook into her backpack. She'd be sad to leave this place. Seeing Pearl in the morning, watching Clive's antics, had become part of their normal routine this past week. Amanda's heart gave a tiny tug. She would miss this place. Not the danger, but the Abandon Inn. Even Declan…and the other ghosts. She wished again she could have done more.

Ten minutes later, she and Jake left the room and took the stairs down to the lobby. Pearl stood behind the desk and held a giant mug of hot coffee.

"Morning, y'all."

"Morning," they said in unison.

"Got any coffee to go?" Jake asked.

"Sure thing. Y'all getting on the road this early?"

"After we make one more stop at Zephyr Land," Amanda said.

Pearl cocked an eyebrow. "This early?"

"I forgot my camera storage card. It has all my photo analysis I need for my report."

"Well, be careful, sugar." Pearl turned and printed out a receipt. "I have y'alls' bill right here if you're ready to check out. I mean, we'd love to have you stay longer, but I assume with the luggage—"

"Thanks for everything, but yes, we'll check out so we don't need to make the stop on the way back," Jake said.

Pearl's warm brown eyes met Amanda's gaze, which Amanda clearly read—to hell with tradition. A hug was in order. Pearl came out from around the counter, and they hugged.

"You feel free to e-mail me anytime. You know our website," Pearl said. "And I'd love to hear how things go," she whispered.

"Thanks." Amanda unclasped the red pendant around her neck. "I want you to have this."

"What? No, honey, that's beautiful jewelry. I can't accept this."

"In case someone else…gifted…comes along. It could help them see," Amanda whispered. She hoped to not have to explain everything to Jake. He'd accepted her but likely still didn't understand much of it.

"Sweetie, thank you," Pearl said, pulling her in for one more bear hug. "Now, let's see to getting y'all some coffee for your road trip." She went and filled two large to-go mugs with coffee and brought out all the mixings to make it delicious.

"This is great!" Jake inched the sugar across the counter to let Amanda go first.

Amanda reached for a few sweeteners, poured some milk, and mixed up her elixir of caffeine. "Thanks again for everything, Pearl."

"My pleasure. Y'all be sure to recommend us to the big city folks in Georgia."

"We will!"

* * *

Amanda smiled wide when they approached the Zephyr Land entrance gate. This would be the last time they entered this haunted amusement park. As for the ghosts, well, if they tried to stop her from leaving, she would figure out something.

Jake parked the car and unlocked the main gate. "We go right to the carousel and get your camera card. Then we're out of here."

"Yes, provided you stop in Mobile for me to work on my photos."

"Deal."

Something seemed different about the boardwalk this morning. A warm breeze blew. An aura of peace seemed to fill the air. Not like the first time she'd seen this place and felt chills. Maybe she'd grown nostalgic because she would soon return home. Or maybe she was just thankful that more ghosts weren't standing in her way.

"Do you need anything else near the coaster?" Amanda asked.

"Nope. I'm good to go."

They strolled along toward the boardwalk just like they might have done had the amusement park remained open. Her holding cotton candy, him using a toy rifle to ping ducks on a straight line in order to win her a giant-assed panda.

Things that could have been...

When they reached the carousel tent, Jake's cell phone rang. He scrambled to look at the caller ID. "It's my department head. I need to take this."

"I'll get the camera card, no problem."

She moved around him and headed into the tent. Something whacked her on the head. Everything faded to black.

CHAPTER FORTY-SIX

Pain seared through Amanda's skull. Concentrated right between her eyes like the migraine headache from hell. Only worse.

She tried opening her eyes. May as well have tried lifting one-hundred-pound weights off the floor. What had...happened? She moved her right arm, wanting to pinch the top of her nose to ward off the stabbing pain.

That's when she realized her right arm was not doing what she wanted. Why didn't she have use of her arm? Take a breath. Start over. One. Two. Three.

She pushed her eyelids open. Strained her shoulder to see why her right hand wouldn't respond. Both her arms were pulled behind her back. What the hell? She pressed her feet to the ground and attempted to stand. No. She'd been strapped to a chair. Both feet zip-cuffed to a heavy chair. Her arms throbbed in pain from being yanked behind her, where metal cuffs kept her hands immobile.

"What...who...what's happening?"

Why couldn't she hear her own words? Each one sounded distant, unclear. She started to lick her lips but couldn't. Something was in her mouth. A gag? She blinked rapidly, doing her best to keep her eyes open while her head pounded. Trying to swallow, she found it difficult with a bandana-like gag messing with her tongue.

Who had gagged her? And why?

A breeze blew, rustling a few pine needles and specks of dirt across the floor. She reached deep in her vocal chords, straining to say, "Help?"

Her words sounded muffled. Could Jake hear her? Oh no. Jake. What if he wound up in here like her? She had to figure out a way to stop him before…

Randall charged toward her. Inspected the gag. Her pulse raced, her eyes widening in fear at seeing him.

"Need to keep quiet, or your boyfriend will hear," Randall whispered in a sickly sweet voice, the kind reserved for creeps telling bedtime stories.

She tried to scream, but only muffled noises came out.

"Let's see," Randall said. "You wanted to ask me what a nice guy like me is doing in a place like this."

Her head instinctively retreated several inches away from this psycho. When she dared to meet his gaze, she saw a maniacal ferocity brewing behind his light-blue eyes. He was truly insane—at least at the moment. He belonged in a mental hospital. Not her—or anyone else who saw ghosts.

Ghosts. Maybe she could signal one of them.

"Shh, your boyfriend should be joining us any minute," Randall whispered.

No. Warn Jake. Have to warn Jake to call police. She let out a guttural scream. The constrictive gag turned her desperate vocal pleas into a soft whimper.

Jake! Get help. Don't come in.

Randall banged a few pieces of metal together to hide the remnants of her soft whimper. He waited by the entry flaps, holding a shovel and ready to hit Jake on the head.

She screamed again. No use.

Jake pulled open the flaps. His eyes widened upon seeing her. "Amanda! What happ—"

Randall slammed the shovel's hard surface into the back of Jake's head. Jake crumpled to the floor and remained still.

"You stupid son of a bitch! What do you think you're doing?" It might have sounded garbled, but he'd get the gist.

Randall cocked a smile. "I can't quite understand you with that gag. What did you say?"

The sadistic psycho was enjoying his sense of power. Evil bastard.

Randall hauled Jake's limp body over to another chair. Chairs hadn't been there before today. The jerk had planned all of this, but how? When?

She watched as he handcuffed Jake's feet and hands. Inside her, a flicker of hope. Maybe Randall had been spying on them, wanted them to stop investigating the derailment. But he couldn't know Jake's hobby back in Georgia was magic and picking locks. She had to hold on, stay positive. Then Jake could somehow get free and take Randall down.

Was there a way to summon for Declan's help? Seriously, the damn ghost had been bugging her the entire week to help him. The one time she really needed assistance, he was nowhere to be found?

"Once I take care of you two," Randall spouted, "things will go back to normal round here."

She jutted out her chin to force her red amulet necklace forward and back. Maybe there was a way Declan or another ghost could get her signal? She'd never tried it from a distance before, but anything was worth trying at this point.

Nothing happened. Oh no. She'd given the amulet to Pearl at the Abandon Inn. Damn it! There was no way to signal for Declan now. Maybe she could try and negotiate with Randall?

"Let me talk," she tried to say.

Randall finished tying Jake and propped the shovel against one of the carousel horses. "What?"

She repeated her muffled words.

He sauntered over, put his hands on her gag. "If you scream, I put it back on. Then I hurt you. A lot."

She wanted to deck the guy with a right hook and watch him squirm on the ground. For now, she simply nodded.

Randall pulled the tie down. Amanda instantly gasped for more air.

"Why are you doing this? We were leaving town today."

"You aren't going anywhere, missy."

"Missy? Who the hell are you? What do you want with Jake and me?"

Randall adjusted his stained baseball cap. "You two kids meddle in everyone's affairs. Mary called me, told me your man here visited her last night. Jake knew I lied. Eventually he'd figure out why."

Anger flooded through Amanda's veins. "You sabotaged the roller coaster, didn't you? You killed all those people."

Jake moaned, struggled to move his head.

"Lookee who's awake!" Randall shot her a grin. "Now the fun can begin."

That didn't sound good. Not at all.

CHAPTER FORTY-SEVEN

Declan stormed away from the crowd of angry souls gathered at the House of Mirrors. He marched over to the kids' playground near the swings. This was where he'd begun his adventure at Zephyr Land, where he'd first encountered Becca and learned about their situation.

Now the thirty-plus souls had become an angry mob. And he'd been nominated to play the role of Dracula. Didn't end well for the count, and it definitely wouldn't end well for him.

"Why did you go away?" a tiny voice asked.

Startled, he turned. Saw Becca's sweet face staring up at him. Apparently she'd followed him when he'd left the rest of the souls.

He knelt down and stroked her shoulder. "Everyone is mad at me right now. They want to leave, but I can't help them cross over."

"Why not?"

"I need Amanda's help. The bad guy has to be brought to justice for what he did to all of you."

Becca shrugged. "So go get the bad guy. My sister says the bad guy is here now."

Declan's eyebrows arched. "What?"

"Promise not to tell anyone?"

"I do."

"Sometimes I can hear Sarah talking to me. And I can talk back."

He didn't know whether Becca spoke the truth or if her imagination was in overdrive. She was just a young child. Even imaginary friends could seem real at her age. Then again, he'd read about twins being able to feel and understand more between each other than regular siblings. Maybe after death too.

"Sarah told you that the bad guy is here, in Zephyr Land?"

Becca nodded, her ponytails emphatically bouncing up and down. "She said Amanda gave Mama the amulet, and Sarah is touching it now."

Declan looked into Becca's dark-blue eyes and knew she spoke the truth. "Okay. You go back to your Aunt Opal. I'm going to get the bad guy."

"Sarah said to be careful. He's got Jake and Amanda."

"What?"

"I don't know—that's what she said."

"Okay. You return to the others. Tell them to go to the carousel. I might need their assistance. If they help out, maybe that can free everyone."

"Where are you going?"

"To catch Randall Kern once and for all so I can help y'all cross over." Declan smiled wide. "And avoid whatever Liam and Connell have planned for me."

CHAPTER FORTY-EIGHT

Jake forced his eyes open. Damn, his head hurt! What the hell happened?

"Wake-ee, wake-ee!" Randall sneered.

"What the hell are you doing?"

Randall moved in close, so close Jake could smell the liquor on his breath. Randall tilted his head, grinned wide. "We're going to have some fun. Payback for you and your girl invading my business."

Jake darted his gaze around. Whoa. Moved too fast. His vision blurred. He closed his eyes. Focused. Then reopened them.

"Amanda?"

She was tied to a chair across from him. A gag prevented her from yelling, but those wide eyes contained their own silent scream.

"You let her go right now! Why are you doing this?"

Randall puttered away and began to organize a bunch of gas cans.

Gas cans? What did this guy intend to do?

Jake jutted his chin toward Amanda. "How come you didn't gag me? Let her speak at least!"

"And listen to her high-pitched yelling? No thanks."

"Let her go. I'll stay."

Randall turned, honest surprise flickering in his evil glance. "Ah, true love at its best."

"What happened to you? I know Bello and Toale ruined your reputation, but why are you acting like a psychopath? You're the father of roller coaster engineering, for heaven's sake!"

"Doesn't much matter what I did in the past, once those bastards got their jaws into me." Randall shook his head. "You and your girl shouldn't have stuck your noses into a case that got closed a decade ago. Such a nuisance. Mary's freaked out, and I can't let you submit your paper, or the cops might reopen the investigation."

"It's an academic paper," Jake said. "In another state. You don't have anything to worry about. Let us go. We'll leave this place and leave you alone."

"Maybe you don't understand," Randall said. "You *are* going to leave."

"Great, let us go."

"No, not leave Abandon. But trust me. You'll be gone."

What the hell did that mean? The man—this intelligent man who'd given so much to the engineering world—had lost his mind. Turned into a psycho. No way would Randall listen to reason. The best Jake could hope for was to find a way to get him and Amanda out of there.

Amanda coughed, and he noticed her glance pointing down her arms, then meeting his gaze once more. She wriggled her wrists, wanting him to take notice.

Message received. He could do his best to get out of these cuffs, especially since the ones on his hands were metal and not the zip kind. Good thing picking locks had been a hobby all these years. Jake moved his legs, trying to feel if his cell remained in his pocket. Nope. Randall must have taken it, but it couldn't have gone far.

They were inside a carousel tent.

Jake scanned the floor, the carousel base, for the phone. Aha! There it sat, on top of a gas can. If he could get his hands loose, he could stand and prod into Randall at just the right moment to knock him over. Reach for the cell and call the cops?

It might work. Jake just needed to keep his attempts to get out of the cuffs unnoticed. Then he could save himself and Amanda.

When Randall's back was turned, Jake mouthed silently, "Keep him occupied."

She nodded and proceeded to give the best performance of a coughing fit he'd ever heard.

As predicted, Randall focused on Amanda, giving Jake a few seconds to finagle the cuffs. Leverage and pressure worked best. That and having double-jointed wrists.

"Can't you stop that awful racket?" Randall asked Amanda.

"She needs to breathe," Jake said. "Maybe if you remove the gag, she'll quiet down."

Randall spun around and gave an angry glare. "And maybe she'll scream to high heaven and bring the cops."

"We're in an abandoned amusement park, remember?" Jake asked. "No one will hear her, but I guarantee she'll stay quiet. Just let her breathe. Please."

He continued to manipulate the cuffs. Almost free.

Amanda yelped "Please?" through the sweaty-looking gag.

Randall shot Amanda a knowing glare. "You make a ruckus, I'll kill you and make him watch. Got it?"

Eyes widened, Amanda nodded. Randall bent over slightly and removed the gag.

Jake took a quick breath. This was his chance. Slipping his hands out of the cuffs, he leapt up. Charging forward, the chair stuck to his ass, his legs still constrained. With his free hands and velocity of his body weight, Jake shoved Randall away from Amanda and onto the ground.

CHAPTER FORTY-NINE

Amanda gasped at Jake's sudden escape plan. Good thing the man had bad-ass skills when it came to locks and cuffs. She strained against the cuffs on her own wrists, to no avail.

Scrambling across the floor, Jake and Randall hurled punches. Fists, arms, kicks. With the chair still attached to Jake, he didn't have the quick movements Randall did. Still, Jake bent his body over, managed to whap Randall in the neck with one of the chair legs.

He punched Randall in the nose. Apparently broke it, based on all the blood. As Randall screamed, Jake manipulated the cuffs around his feet. Got loose so he could fight without a chair attached to him.

Jake crashed forward, slamming Randall against a wall. Randall returned with a right hook to Jake's kidney, making him scream in agony. Amanda's heart raced. She knew how much that had to have hurt.

"You can take him!" she yelled. Neither one listened. They were too busy writhing on the floor, throwing fists at each other.

Something touched her hands. What the hell? She turned and saw Declan standing beside her. "What are you doing here?"

"Helping save your ass, as well as mine," he said with a grin. "Let me get you out of these things."

She held still, not sure how a ghost could unlock handcuffs, but she wasn't going to argue. The cool air from his presence blew across her fingers.

"Can you get it?" she asked.

"Trying my best. Ropes are made of more Earthen materials. Would've been easier. There's only so much control the dead have over objects."

If she couldn't get free, she needed another plan. Keeping her voice low, she said, "Forget the handcuffs. My cell phone, over there at the base of the carousel. Need to call 9-1-1 and turn on the recording app."

"Doubt I can press three digits on your phone, even if I summon every ounce of energy in my semitransparent form. Might be able to press one digit though."

"Then press the record app," Amanda said. "Jake can call the cops once he subdues Randall."

"I'll do my best," Declan said, maneuvering his way through the fighting pair. He managed to reach her cell. Now the punching pair took up most of the ground. No straight shot or safe way to kick the phone over to her.

Declan nodded, bent down, and used a gust of air to press a button on her cell. She didn't know how ghosts had the power to touch real objects, but she wasn't going to object.

Jake's scream turned her attention. Randall threw a gut punch and then another. Jake lunged toward him. Randall gripped Jake's wrist and used the force to smash Jake into the wall. With Jake debilitated, Randall trapped him in a neck grip.

"Stop!" she yelled. "Let him be!"

In seconds, Randall's forearms turned bright red from

squeezing. Jake's eyes shut, and Amanda watched in terror as he blacked out.

Wiping his bloody nose with his hand, Randall glared at her. "He started it. Both of you did, by coming here. Snooping around."

She glanced back to Declan, who nodded. Good. He'd hit the record button. Now to get Randall to incriminate himself.

"We weren't snooping. We had permission to be in the park," she said. "What do you have to hide, Randall?"

"Don't play stupid with me," he said. "You two went to the library. Been talking to people in town about the derailment. Only a matter of time."

"Matter of time until what?"

Randall heaved Jake onto the chair. This time he used ropes to tie Jake's hands and feet. He pulled a cigarette from his shirt pocket, lit it, and took a long puff. "I only meant to kill Chester and Andrew. Not everyone else."

"The two execs from Bello and Toale?"

"Yes. Those two asses bragged about the all-important debut ride, just the two of them. Narcissistic jerks. Their roller coaster, the design I made but they stole. The bolts I threatened to expose them on, then they shifted the blame to me."

"And?"

"And they were supposed to be the only passengers in that rail car."

Amanda kept her breathing steady, trying to remember everything and say the right words so the right amount of information could be recorded.

"But other people decided to ride the coaster too?"

Randall nodded, letting out a smoky exhale. "Yep. Women. Children. I didn't want them to suffer. I only wanted those two monsters to go down for what they did."

"How did you do it?"

She knew the answer. Jake had talked about the safety wire being tampered with, but anything she could get out of Randall for the recording would be beneficial to their side.

"What do you care?" Randall stood up, pointed to the gas cans. "I need to get these prepped."

"For what?" Her voice cracked at the question.

Randall stared at her and gave a wicked smile. "I'm going to set a little fire, right inside this crappy tent. With the old wood and paint of the carousel, I might not need my forty gas cans. Since you and your boyfriend will be trapped inside, better to use too much accelerant than too little. Call it another Zephyr Land tragedy."

Amanda's throat tightened. Sweat beads dripped from her brow. "No...please..."

"What did you think, missy? I was going to release you? Let you and your academic boyfriend here make a bigger fool out of me?"

"We didn't think you were a fool. Jake respected your engineering work. He called you his mentor for years—"

"Yeah, well I used to be that guy. Before those assholes decided to frame me for something I didn't do. They wanted to use subpar equipment. I cared about the public's safety. Not them. What did I get for it? Fired and disgraced."

Amanda looked around, noticing Declan doing his best to untie the ropes that bound Jake's hands. She needed to stall, keep Randall talking. Incriminating himself until he had no way out.

She swallowed hard, looking at the forty-plus gas cans. And hopefully they could call the police before the psycho burned them alive.

CHAPTER FIFTY

Declan stared at the endless strands of the thick rope that kept Jake immobilized. Being dead had its quirks, one of which was the ability to still remain in contact with human objects.

It could be done…with concentration. And not for long periods of time.

He'd managed to press one button on Amanda's phone, but with all his might, he couldn't have dialed 9-1-1. Or talked with the emergency tech on the other end.

On to the problem at hand—Jake's entrapment. Declan could probably tug on a rope strand for a second or two at a time. Then he'd need to recoup his energy to tug more.

Jake didn't have that kind of time.

Wait a second. There were thirty other ghosts across the park. Things might get a bit crowded, but if everyone helped out, it could be done.

He raced outside the tent and yelled for everyone to come help. Opal came running first, followed by Chester, Andrew, Becca, the whole slew of Randall's victim pool.

Amanda's eyes widened when she saw everyone arrive. Declan gave her an assured wave and said, "Keep Randall busy talking. We're going to get Jake free."

She nodded slightly and began to ask Randall how he skillfully changed out the roller coaster's safety wire without anyone noticing. Randall took the bait, just like an egomaniac would. He started to brag, retelling his wisdom and expertise.

"We don't have much time," Declan told the ghosts. "So let's do this. I need each of you to pull deep inside. Take every ounce of emotion and anger you have over being left in Zephyr Land for a decade. Remember every tear you cried, every person who betrayed you."

Becca glanced around. "Huh?"

Declan smiled. Even in this tense moment, she was such an adorable kid. Of course no one had betrayed her, or at least not enough to make this little girl bitter.

"Except Becca," he said. "Becca, you wish with all your might that we will get Jake free."

"Okay." She closed her eyes tight.

"Good." Declan gestured toward the others. "Once you feel ready, take that push of emotion and press against the ropes. It's an acquired skill, but I'm giving you all the crash course."

"We're up for the task," Chester said. "Especially if it means getting justice for that Randall son of a bitch."

"It does," Declan said. "Okay. I'll go first so you can see how this is done."

Deep breath. He dug deep, searched his soul for the most painful memory. Brianna, his little sister. Held down by leather constraints on white sheets. Asylum beds. Long needles.

Once the memory raced to the surface, Declan reached out and yanked a handful of rope. It moved about an inch.

"Wow," Opal said, her eyes wide and staring. "Knowing about this would've been a good thing while we were left to rot."

"Keep that memory. Give it a try."

Opal closed her eyes. Breathed. Then pushed against the rope. It moved two inches.

"Great!" Declan said. "Everyone else, keep going. We need to get these loosened enough so Jake can get loose."

Declan glanced back to Amanda, who'd managed to engage Randall in a conversation about safety inspectors and Zephyr Land. She provided the missing puzzle piece to keep Randall from moving ahead with his burn-them-alive plan. She had given him the chance to tell his side of the story. Randall now had an audience, at least for a brief time.

Opal and Chester did well at loosening the ropes. Declan had a flicker of hope. Maybe he wouldn't get shipped off to some awful place. Maybe Connell and Liam would be impressed at his show of teamwork with the ghosts. Then again, maybe his bosses would be so pissed off at the delays that he'd never see Savannah or his sister, Brianna, again.

CHAPTER FIFTY-ONE

Jake blinked. Felt a stabbing sensation in his lower back. Fleeting memories rushed in. Randall hitting him in the kidney. Damn, it hurt.

He wiggled his hands. Wait. No cuffs, but ropes? And he'd been confined to the chair once more? For several seconds, he analyzed the situation. Figured out the best means of getting himself and Amanda out of there.

Randall babbled away about how clever he'd been to switch out the safety wire. Amanda kept asking questions. Great job on the stall tactic. Jake smiled wide. *That's my girl.*

He gave three concentrated tugs on his hands. The ropes loosened. Amazing. Randall must not have realized he did a crappy job tying Jake up.

Now to determine the best strategy. Randall hadn't noticed he'd freed his hands. Amanda kept him occupied. Jake scanned the room, looked for options to help them take Randall down. Then, as Randall was in midbrag about his tactics, Jake quickly loosened his legs from the chair.

Based on where everyone was situated, Jake's best bet was to take Randall by surprise. Knock him down, subdue him. Then he could grasp Amanda's cell phone and call for help.

Yes. Breathe. Time to act.

With all his strength, he harnessed his body weight and leapt from the chair. Slammed into Randall. Pinned him down. The bastard put up a fight, flailing his arms and trying to poke Jake in the eye to get him off.

Jake cracked a grin. He'd been in the military and had training to subdue such efforts. He managed to avoid Randall's nipple-crippling attempts.

"You selfish no good son of a bitch!" Jake punched Randall repeatedly while the bastard screamed in pain. "How could you kill all those people? How could you think about killing us?"

Amanda fought to get free but couldn't. "Because he's a loser. Deep down, he knows that's what he became."

Randall glared at her through a bloody eye. "Stupid nosy bitch."

"Hey!" Jake hurled another punch at Randall's face, broke his jaw. "That's my girl you're talking about!"

Amanda grinned wide at Randall. "And that's my guy kicking your ass."

Jake laughed, reached for the cuffs he'd escaped earlier. Dragging Randall's bleeding body over to the carousel, he lifted him onto the base and snapped one cuff around a horse's foot and the other to Randall's hand.

"I ought to kick you until you beg for mercy," Jake said.

Randall coughed, spit up blood.

"He's not worth it," Amanda said. "My cell is over there. It's been on record this whole time. Call the cops. They'll know Randall killed everyone. Tried to kill us."

"You got it," he said with a wink. He called 9-1-1 and told the operator their location. Then Jake unhooked Amanda with his magic skills.

"Someday you need to teach me how to get out of handcuffs," she said.

He leaned in and kissed her. "Okay, but we'll require lots of practice."

Her cheeks turned pink at his innuendo, which had been the goal. "You look beautiful when you're blushing."

"Why don't you two get a room?" Randall grumbled, clearly grumpy at his defeat.

"As a matter of fact, we might," Jake said. "But for now, I believe justice is served."

* * *

Amanda let out a relaxed breath at the thought. She'd done it. The cops arrived fifteen minutes later and arrested Randall. The man who'd killed all the roller coaster riders was on his way to jail. Now the ghosts could be free. So could Declan.

"Wait a minute," she said.

The taller cop with a buzz cut turned and looked at her. "Is there something else you need, ma'am?"

"Randall Kern has a dog, a German shepherd. What's going to happen when Randall goes to jail?"

The cop frowned. "Standard policy is we take any pets to the animal shelter. Unless a relative or co-owner claims the animal."

"Don't you dare let my dog be put down!" Randall shouted, doing his best to break free of the cuffs.

The cop tightened his hold on Randall. "Quiet, sir! They don't allow dogs where you're going!"

Randall kept still, sent a pleading glance to Jake and Amanda.

Jake arched his eyebrows. "I'd love to adopt Catfish, but both our apartments don't allow pets."

"I wasn't thinking about us," Amanda said. "But someone else."

"Who?"

Amanda smiled. "Pearl. She mentioned that Clive does well around animals. Dogs and cats keep him grounded to reality. Provide a daily routine. Give him something to care for."

Jake smiled wide. "That's certainly a better deal for Catfish than the pound."

The cop nodded. "We'll be required to admit the animal into the shelter. It's procedure. But you call your friend, tell her to go to the Abandon shelter tomorrow. Tell her Officer Gayne sent his okay. That way the dog gets to have a home."

Randall hung his head. "I sure would appreciate it."

Officer Gayne walked Randall out of the tent, smiling wide at his collar for this cold case.

Amanda reached for her cell and called Pearl to give her the information.

"Sweetheart," Pearl said, "you are wonderful. I was just saying that we need to get ourselves a watchdog. To watch Clive more than intruders, but Catfish is a good dog. I'll go first thing in the morning to adopt him."

"Thanks," Amanda said. "Just because Randall deserves to go to jail doesn't mean Catfish should suffer. I'm sure he'll be happy with you both."

"Keep in touch, hon. And y'all are welcome back here anytime."

"Thanks." Amanda smiled, tapped End on her phone. "Done."

Jake pointed to the exit. "Officer Gayne wants us to stop by the station and give our report. They'll probably need a copy of your recording on your cell."

She nodded. "Before we get there, let's stop at a Wi-Fi café. Let me send in my images for my apprenticeship. It's only ten thirty. I still have time to submit it, and why let Randall ruin my chances of a great career?"

"Why indeed," Jake said, his voice warm and affectionate. Amanda smiled at his rather battered face. "One thing puzzles me though."

"What's that?"

"How'd you get the record button to start if you were tied up?"

Amanda glanced to the thirty ghosts gathered together near where Jake had been captive. They looked like a bunch of smiling clowns packed into a Volkswagen.

"I get by with a little help from my friends," she said.

Jake cocked an eyebrow. "What friends?"

"Well, to be honest, the ghosts. The souls of the people who died helped. Along with Declan."

Biting his lip, Jake said, "I see."

"I swear. I know you may not believe in all the supernatural—"

"I don't, but I promise you one thing. I'm going to try to be more open minded going forward."

She beamed ear to ear. "What changed your mind?"

Jake's smile faded as he looked off in the direction where the cops had left. "Randall. I had such a strong belief that he wasn't guilty. How could such a great man be capable of murder?"

"I guess he hit his breaking point."

"Well, I was obviously wrong—believing he didn't have anything to do with the derailment. If I'd been more objective, less stubborn, maybe I wouldn't have put you in danger."

Warmth fluttered through her. "You're such a Southern gentleman, worried about me."

His deep-blue eyes gazed into hers. He traced her cheeks with his fingers. "I am, Amanda Moss. 'Cause you're my girl."

CHAPTER FIFTY-TWO

A half hour later at an Internet café, Amanda hit the Submit button. Her photos for the apprenticeship had been sent. Officially. She let out a thankful breath. Their lives were no longer in danger. She'd made her deadline. Things were looking up.

Jake took the two coffees from the barista and brought them to their table. "Here we go."

"Thanks!" She stirred in the milk and sweetener and took a few sips. "My proposal is officially submitted."

"Good job." Jake skipped the milk but added some sweetener to his cup before taking a long sip. "I'm glad this trip worked out for both of us."

"I'm glad we're still alive, in one piece."

Jake grinned. "You can say that again. Say, since we need to spend some time at the police station getting your phone recording into evidence, I'm thinking we won't make it back to Georgia tonight—"

"We could still head back, swap drivers if you want. I know you've been eager to get home."

"Nah, just hold on a minute." Jake beamed at her, mischief in that handsome glance. "How about we take a side trip to Fairhope and spend the night? I hear the town has its own little French Quarter, and there's a state park that's supposed to be a fantastic spot for stargazing."

I know.

"Sounds like fun."

"Good. We'll finish whatever business we have at the police station, then head on."

Nodding, she drank the rest of her coffee. She would've hooked it up intravenously if she could have.

Jake's idea sounded good. No need to remind him she had been to the exact spot for stargazing that he mentioned. It was where she and her aunt went the night Jake was angry. But this time would be different. Alone, under the stars, with Jake. Sounded like a great way to spend an evening.

* * *

Amanda glanced at the clock. They'd been at the police station an hour now. Randall had been arrested, along with Mary for being an accessory after the fact. The detective used Amanda's cell and copied Randall's confession to a computer.

She and Jake had given their statements, and the detective was reviewing the evidence before releasing them. Meanwhile, they sat in a room. Waiting.

Jake sighed. "We'll eventually get out of here, right?"

"Yep." She reached for his hand. "Listen, when we return to Georgia...about that time when I said I would get psychiatric help..."

"Yeah?"

"My parents took me to see tons of shrinks when I was younger. It's not going to help."

Jake shrugged. "At the time, I thought you were crazy."

"And now?"

With a wink, he said, "You're still crazy, but I'm beginning to be okay with it."

"I know it's hard to accept the paranormal," she began. "So what if there was a way to prove it to you?"

"You already said the ghosts helped to push the record button," Jake said. "I can't say I believe that in its entirety, but I was unconscious, and there's no way you could've hit the button from where you were. Maybe some things are best unexplained."

"Maybe I can summon Declan somehow. Get him to answer some questions. I don't know...perhaps he can arrange a meet with your mom?"

Jake's pupils grew huge. "I don't know about that."

"Do you want me to try?"

Amanda realized she didn't even know how to get in touch with Declan anymore. When she and Jake left after the police, Declan was last seen leading the ghosts away. Meaning their souls would have crossed over by now. But where would that leave Declan?

Jake pinched the top of his nose as if warding off a headache. "I'm not good at any of this."

"Tell you what. If I can do something to help you talk to your mom, I will. If not, no worries."

"Sure."

The detective returned, told them to sign their statements, and handed her the cell phone. "You're free to go. We'll be in touch if we need you again. With the confession, they'll probably plea out. I doubt you'd have to return to a trial."

"But if so, we'd be happy to do so," Amanda said. Anger flared within her for everything Randall had put her and Jake through.

"Thanks, folks. Y'all have a good day now."

Standing up to stretch, Amanda said, "So, off to Fairhope we go?"

CHAPTER FIFTY-THREE

Jake drove the Civic north along Alternate Route 98, taking in the scenic view of Mobile Bay on their way to Fairhope. The sun was high in the sky, reflecting on Mobile Bay, making the water look like shimmering diamonds.

Amanda's eyes had closed as she leaned against the passenger window to sleep. He didn't blame her. After getting up so early, then the scare with Randall at Zephyr Land, he was ready for a nap too.

Yet another reason to not try to go all the way back to Georgia tonight. Besides, it was only Friday. They didn't have to return to work until Monday. May as well enjoy some of the local culture.

He rolled down his window and let the salt-smelling breeze blow through his hair and keep him awake.

How had that record button on Amanda's cell been pushed?

She claimed ghosts. Now she claimed he might be able to talk to his mother? All his life, he'd presumed death was final. But to Amanda, it was just a crossing over to another place. A place where communication might still be possible.

Shaking his head, he kept driving. Amanda defied all logic, for certain. But as he glanced over at her beautiful face, those long locks draped across her shoulders, he had to face facts. It didn't matter if she was crazy as ever. She was his. They'd survived this together. Could work well together.

He reached the Fairhope town limits. Immediately the scenery shifted to dark-red barns, bright-green tractors, and large fields of cotton. The way of the land.

Amanda adjusted her position. "Where are we?" she mumbled.

"Fairhope. You hungry?"

"Starved."

"Good. I've got a place picked out for us."

* * *

Panini Pete's looked more like an elegant greenhouse than a place that would wind up on the Food Network's *Diners, Drive-Ins, and Dives*. It wasn't a dive at all. Sage-green French doors were between each room. Giant ferns hung from the ceiling rails, with some geraniums added in for color.

Jake dug into his order of beignets. Scrumptious. "Yours good?"

Amanda nodded, her eyes gleaming as she looked around at the nature décor. "Best panini ever."

His cell beeped. He wiped the powdered sugar off his hands and then checked the screen. A message from the head of his department, saying the notes he'd sent in on his position paper were great. That he could meet with the department head on Monday to discuss the upcoming promotion.

Jake smiled, sharing the news with Amanda.

"Congratulations!"

"I know you'll get your apprenticeship too," he said. "You're just as stubborn as me when it comes to following your dream."

She blushed again. "Let's hope so."

CHAPTER FIFTY-FOUR

After the fabulous lunch, Amanda and Jake walked around the mini–French Quarter awhile and then returned to the car.

Once she slipped inside and put on her seat belt, a voice from the backseat said, "I hear you want to ask me something?"

She spun around, her pulse racing. Whew. "Declan, yes. You scared me."

He shrugged. "I do that to the living sometimes."

Jake opened the door and got into the driver's seat.

"Hon, wait just a minute before starting the car."

"What's up?"

"Remember when I said I wanted to ask Declan something?"

"Yeah…"

How could she say this? Oh, to hell with it. He already knew her ability, whether he believed or not. He wasn't dumping her. May as well come out with it.

"Declan's in the backseat of the car."

Slowly, Jake turned around. "I don't see anyone."

Declan shook his head. "Nonbelievers, I tell ya."

"Whether you see him or not doesn't matter," Amanda explained. "Let me just try to do this for you."

"Okay." Jake plopped the keys up on the dash and rolled down his window to enjoy the air.

Amanda leaned toward the backseat. "Did you get everyone crossed over?"

"I did. Thanks to you, and thanks for asking."

"Were your bosses angry?"

"You could say that."

Amanda felt a pang of guilt. If she had helped or done something else sooner, could things have been better for everyone?

"What happened?" she asked, unsure whether she wanted the answer.

"Nothing as terrible as what might have occurred had I failed completely," Declan said. "But the powers that be have mandated I have to work with a partner from now on. Everyone does. No more solo jobs. Guess they figure having a partner will make the job get done twice as fast."

"I hope it works out for you," she said.

"Thanks." Declan leaned forward, placing his arms over the top of the seat in front of him. "I know you didn't need to talk to me just to ask me about the Zephyr Land ghosts. What's really on your mind?"

She looked at Jake. At the man she loved, cared for. She wanted to heal those wounds he had from his mother's death. But how to say that to Declan? How to phrase it?

"Oh, I think I understand," Declan said, to her complete surprise. "You want Jake to talk to his mother or someone else who's crossed over."

"Yes. Can you do that?"

"No."

Amanda waited a long moment as she looked into Declan's

green-eyed stare. "No?"

"What's he saying?" Jake asked.

"Just give me a few minutes," she said. Returning her attention to the backseat, she asked, "Why not?"

"Family contact is complicated. For one, his mother has already crossed over. Finding her if she isn't an afterdeath consultant like me will prove almost impossible. Second, there are rules about humans and deceased family. Rules I barely squeaked by for my own sake in Savannah so I could see my sister. I doubt my boss will look too fondly on another favor request."

She frowned. "Is there anything you can do? Tell me where she is? How she's doing?"

"I can assure you she's in a good place. Safe, healthy—the dead lose all the mental issues they have on Earth once they've crossed— so his mother is truly in a better place. Ministers all over the world aren't lying when they say that."

"Good to know."

"I wish I could be more help—"

"No, I completely understand." Amanda gave him a kind smile. "Just a few days ago, we were having this exact conversation, only reversed."

Declan laughed. "That's true."

"Anything else I can tell him before you go?"

He thought a long moment. "I can't speak for his mother specifically, but having been in my position for decades and helping souls cross from their lives into the next realm, I can say that most souls just want the humans they left behind to be happy. They don't want their children, parents, friends, worrying about them. So if you can convince Jake that his mom is in a good place, not to worry about her, I think that would make her happy."

"I like that explanation," Amanda whispered.

"What did he say?" Jake asked.

Amanda retold the things Declan had mentioned.

"Thought-provoking points," Jake said.

"Yep." She turned to thank Declan, but when she looked in the backseat, he'd already disappeared.

* * *

Later that evening, after a long nap in a local Fairhope hotel, Amanda woke up to her cell phone chirping. Who would be calling her now? She scrambled to reach it, but the call went to voicemail.

Seconds later, she dialed the two digits to access her messages.

"Hi, this message is for Amanda Moss. This is Lena Cole with the carousel restoration project. I wanted to say congratulations. We received your submission, and your talent is exactly what we've been seeking. Give me a call back when you can, but we hope you can start on Monday. Thank you."

Amanda grinned wide, shaking her hands in a happy dance as best she could without waking Jake up. This career opportunity was her chance to pursue the artistic work she yearned to do. Not only could she and Jake have a fresh start upon returning to Georgia, but her career would get a new beginning too.

Ten minutes passed. She couldn't hold in the news any longer.

Shaking Jake's arm, she woke him up and told him the news.

"That's fantastic, hon! Congratulations."

"I know! So we definitely need to return to Georgia tomorrow, but as far as tonight—"

"Tonight, you're mine," he said with a wink. "Come on. I want to take you out to that stargazing place. Fairhope is supposed to have one of the best views of the night sky in the South."

"Sounds wonderful, as long as I'm with you."

"Aww, how romantic," he said with a smile.

Thirty minutes later, Jake spread out a blanket in the open meadow. The air had cooled down and cicadas chirped a symphony in the trees surrounding this patch of flat land.

She and Jake lay on their backs, looking up at what had to be the most beautiful night she'd ever seen. Too many city lights back in Georgia drowned out the stars. Even out in the woods, only a few stars bothered to show up in the night sky.

But here in this pocket of Fairhope woods? Every cluster of stars in the galaxy and beyond had travelled to this very spot. Picked this meadow to shine down upon, to send twinkling lights and a smile to her and Jake. A blessing for them starting their life together—with full acceptance.

"I love you, Jake Mercer."

He rolled onto his side, leaned in, and kissed her. "I love you more, Amanda Moss. Here's to a great future together."

THE END

Dear Reader,

Thanks so much for reading TICKET TO DIE, Book Two in the Southern Ghosts Series. I hope you enjoyed Amanda and Jake's story.

Book Three of the Southern Ghosts Series, KREWE OF SOULS, will take place in Louisiana and will release in late 2015. This one will have a carnival/parade theme and is sure to delight!

To learn when additional books will be released and to receive coupons, go to my website and sign up for my newsletter.

I appreciate all reviews and love to hear from readers. Connect with me online at http://www.elainecalloway.com. There are freebie short stories and prequels to my other series on my website.

Additional Books by Elaine Calloway:

No Grits No Glory (Southern Ghosts Series #1)

Water's Blood (Elemental Clans, #1)
Raging Fire (Elemental Clans #2)
Earthbound (Elemental Clans #3)
Windstorm (Elemental Clans #4)

Go to www.elainecalloway.com to learn more about books, ordering, and connecting on social media.

About the Author

Amazon bestselling author Elaine Calloway writes paranormal fantasy romance books for eBook and paperback. Whether the subject matter is Elementals fighting against evil or ghost stories in the Deep South, all books are set in iconic cities such as New Orleans.

She is currently working on two series of books:

- The Southern Ghosts Series: about those humans who have the gift to communicate with the dead, and are often requested to bring justice to the deceased. There will be at least 8 books in this series, then possibly some offshoots.
- The Elemental Clan Series: about nature's four elements— water, fire, earth, and wind—and their battle to save innocent souls from the evil Fallen Angel packs. The four main books have been released and several offshoots of this series are planned.

Originally from New Orleans (she can still do a decent Cajun accent upon request), Elaine Calloway grew up with a love of all things supernatural and gets back to the Crescent City as often as she can. She loves taking ghost tours on her vacations, and when not writing she enjoys photography and spending time with her family and friends (and very spoiled dog).

Made in the USA
Charleston, SC
18 July 2015